MODEL BEHAVIOR

Randi D. Rigby

Cover designed by Cover Creator

Printed in the United States of America

First Printing: Dec 2018
Independently Published

ISBN-97 817-9-03587-9-3

For Alice, Isla, and Claire

Who walk like beauty in the night,
But also do a bang up job rocking it through the day.

1

"I get knocked down, but I get up again"

Chumbawamba

Someone famous, or maybe it was just my middle school choir director, Mr. Moss, who had an abundance of red curls and bounced around more than any highly caffeinated person I know and was fond of throwing his arms heavenward to shout at us with his booming voice to SING TO THE BACK OF THE ROOM, in a moment of somewhat quieter introspection once said, "The answers to all of life's questions can be found in the lyrics of country music."

Mom laughed her throaty laugh when I told her that, tucking her feet delicately beneath her on the gray striped couch in her art studio we seemed to have all our heart to hearts on, looking every inch the southern belle while I was still gathering my sprawling limbs. "Baby, that only holds true if you drink beer and drive a pickup truck."

Her religion was classic movies. She believed all a girl needed to take on the world was a quick wit, a sense of style, and perfect posture.

Which is why the moment I was born and the nurse dried me off and handed me over, wide-eyed, blinking, a fuzzy tuft of blonde hair emoting in a pink blanket, my mom turned to my father and cursed me. "Grace Kelly. Lucas, we're calling her Grace Kelly."

I'm basically a 6′2″ giraffe who took ballet for ten years and still trips over her own feet. But Mom only ever saw Grace in me.

"Kel? You okay?" Dad steps inside Mom's art studio, looking as wrung out as it's humanly possible to look and still remain upright. He clears his throat. "We need to leave for the church, sweetheart."

Swiping at my eyes I untuck my legs, carefully smoothing the wrinkles out of my little black dress as I rise from the gray striped couch and slip back into my heels.

It's the dress's first outing; it hasn't been in my closet two weeks. Mom and I found it – or as Mom would say, it found us – on one of our unhurried weekend jaunts through one of her favorite vintage shops on her never ending quest for artistic inspiration. We'd sorted through a plethora of odd and enchanting china patterns, silky scarves, perky pill hats – some with bits of netting attached, one even had a pearl hatpin still clinging to the underside –and a stack of fur stoles that smelled mostly musty and were moth eaten when she first spotted it, hanging half hidden and winking at her from the rack. There was audible intake of breath as she reached reverently for it, shaking it out slightly to free the folds of the swishy skirt.

"Look Grace, this was *meant* for you."

I raised an arched eyebrow. "For when I finally decide to go all Stepford Wife: Queen of the Night?"

"Come on now, every girl needs a little black dress in her arsenal. This should be yours. Why this cut is just darling. And it appears to be in pristine shape. Try it on?"

She was right, of course. It fit like a glove and felt like a dream. "Where am I going to wear it?" Together we stared at my pale reflection draped in uncharacteristic sophistication in the three-way mirror of the shop.

"Who knows?" She smiled smugly. "Just so long as I'm there to say I told you so."

Dad stops suddenly, looking distracted. "Is that country music I'm hearing?"

I turn off the sound system that normally piped in the classical music Mom liked to listen to while she painted. "Never mind, it didn't work."

My beautiful, elegant, gifted, vivacious, irreplaceable mother is lying cold and lifeless in a coffin and I still have absolutely no idea how to make any sense of it.

That was early February, Groundhog Day to be exact, which seems fitting. Dad and I can't seem to be able to get past it and we're now deep into April.

"I want to talk to you about something." He puts his spoon down by his bowl of granola, dark brows drawn and pinched, there are lines furrowing his forehead. I hand him his vitamins and protein shake and slide into the stool next to him at the kitchen island. We never eat at the table anymore. We sort of exist in a tight little triangle of kitchen, bathroom, bedroom – and Dad has been sleeping on the couch. "What would you think about us moving to Austin?"

Dad is from Austin. His family, with the exception of Uncle Chris, is still all there. He met Mom when they were both students at the University of North Carolina: he played basketball on scholarship for the Tar Heels until he was sidelined by a rapid succession of injuries, giving him plenty of time to nail a degree in chemistry on his way to pre-med and then dental school; she was an art major from Georgia running late for class who literally knocked him sideways – which is hard to do. He's 6′10″ and built like a tank. Dad always said she swept him right off his feet. He asked her to marry him after they'd only dated a couple of months. I don't think they ever stopped honeymooning.

They moved to Chicago when I was three and Dad opened a flourishing practice as an oral surgeon. We've been here ever since. We have roots. We have ties. We have way too many memories of her here.

"Really?" For the first time in ages I hear myself sounding excited. "Can we?"

He looks surprised. Probably because he's been so lost in his own fog that he hadn't noticed how deeply lost I was in mine. "We'd have to wait until school is out," he says slowly. "That would give me time to sell my practice here and find something in Austin."

"Okay."

"We'd have to put the house on the market."

"I'll help."

"I want you to really think about this, Kel. You'd be starting your senior year in a completely new school. You won't know anyone."

"None of that matters, Dad. Not anymore. I just need a change."

He runs a hand wearily through his rapidly graying hair, suddenly relieved and grateful. "So do I kid, so do I."

We divide and conquer: I take the house sale, Dad, his practice. There are an unbelievable number of YouTube videos that offer advice on selling a house. *Find a reputable agen*t is a breeze, I've been good friends with Ben Porter since kindergarten – I never lost to him in Four Square, he brutally and consistently picked me off in dodgeball, unfair really, given I was already practically a foot taller than everyone else and an easy target. I even set him up with the girlfriend he's had since sophomore year, dragging Carrie to Froyo Chicago after ballet and then lingering over the scrapings of my Mango Sunrise sorbet for ages because Ben was late. Anyway, his mom Nancy is like the Meryl Streep of Chicago real estate; her office is lined with trophies. She is delighted to be our agent. Nancy is delighted about pretty much everything.

Remove personal items to make it easier for potential buyers to see themselves in the space takes longer. I haul several trips worth of boxes and bubble wrap home in the back of the Mini and invest in an industrial tape gun. Mom always took pictures of things she wanted to paint so she was also a skilled photographer and her favorite subjects to shoot were her family. I strip the rooms bare of our faces and pack them all away with the exception of one: it's a picture of Mom, me, and Charlie - our toffee and cream colored mostly Airedale with bits of poodle and spaniel thrown in just to keep it interesting. She took it with a timer the day school let out for the summer last year. Mom and I are wearing faded blue jeans and white linen shirts with the sleeves pushed up, lying on our stomachs barefooted in the grass, elbows bent, our pointy chins in our hands; our long, ash blonde hair lifted in the breeze, Mom's perfectly styled, mine – per usual – a bit of a bush; identical winged eyebrows, toothy grins, wide-set blue eyes, and tip turned up noses stamp us undeniably and forever as mother-daughter. We're laughing because Charlie was trying surreptitiously to lick my face. In the split second the shot was taken he succeeded; there's so much happiness captured in that one moment that it never fails to make me grin. And then, now, irrepressibly heart sad. But I can't bring myself to pack it away. Instead, I stash it under my bed.

Streamline – get rid of anything you no longer want or need means tackling a project I've been dreading. While

Dad's gone on a trip to Austin to look at a practice, I briskly sort through Mom's stuff, deciding what to keep and what to donate to her favorite charities. It's the unexpected notes in a sweater pocket: *Don't forget to pick Grace up from Lexi's,* the razor sharp memory of how she looked the last time she wore something, or the sudden catch of her scent I'm terrified I'll never smell again that hurt the most. I'm ugly crying the whole time I'm packing her away into cardboard boxes. And then, blotchy and red-faced, my eyes puffy and swollen, I change into shorts and lace up my running shoes and hurl myself faster and further than I've ever gone before, until my lungs are burning and my heart and muscles feel ready to explode.

Charlie runs with me. He patiently sits and waits without any judgment, head cocked, tongue panting, his little sides still heaving from our punishing pace as I throw up repeatedly in the park bushes.

Then I go home and shower and make some calls. By the time Dad returns looking thinner and more hollow than when he left, the boxes have all been picked up and taken away. *I spared him that.* I suddenly feel very grown up and capable. The next day at school I wear a classic red lipstick and sandals with a three-inch heel, which basically means I'm taller than most of the basketball team, but I hold my head high. Maybe Mom was right. It feels incredible.

The house and Dad's practice sell within a week of each other and close just as my junior year does. Mrs. Porter – Nancy – is delighted for us.

"We should celebrate," I tell Dad as we walk out of the title office together.

"Celebrate?"

"Celebrate. You know? Do a little victory dance in the parking lot? Charlie has mastered most of the Macarena – you haven't seen that yet. He's getting pretty good. *Or* we could just go out to dinner. It's my night to cook if you need a reason."

Dad grins. It's more of a slight upward lifting of the edges of his mouth but it's closer to a real smile than anything I've seen from him in ages. My heart soars. "Okay, Kel," Dad says, opening my door for me. "Where do you want to eat?"

I pick a restaurant we've never been to with Mom. The desolation Dad has been wearing like a second skin almost disappears as he relaxes into dinner. Any misgivings I might've had earlier when I was exchanging yearbooks for signing and saying good-bye to all my friends are completely gone.

We will be fine in Austin. We. Will. Be. Fine.

Should you ever need to drive from Chicago to Austin you should know it takes roughly nineteen hours – probably less if you're a machine and can drive straight through, but I'm driving Mom's Mini and have a bladder. We have to make pit stops. Even then, by the time we hit

Memphis my long legs are seriously whining. By the time we reach Dallas they're screaming profanities.

"You drove here in that?" My cousin Jake whistles, heading straight for me, barefooted and incredulous. Uncle Nick and Aunt Jill are hugging Dad in their driveway while Charlie tears around their lawn like a lunatic freed. "Brave girl."

Jake is the handsomest of my cousins and the least aware of it, which is strange given how crazy smart he is – he's home from M.I.T. for the summer and even for them he's brilliant. But he lives in rumpled, nerdy slogan shirts (he's currently sporting a white T-shirt with some formula scrawled across his chest, underneath it says: Get a half-life) and he tends to hang out a lot in research labs so that incredible face goes largely unappreciated.

"Give me a hand? Please, Jake?" I am not above shamelessly begging.

"How about a can opener?" He bends way over, ducks under my arm, and bodily hauls me out. With one arm still around my waist he's keeping me upright. "We good? Because you still seem a little wobbly to me."

"You *poor* thing." Aunt Jill reaches to hug me around Jake's assorted limbs. She always looks like she just stepped off a golf course, probably because most of the time she has. Trim and tanned, she has straight, swingy dark hair that she tosses when she laughs and amazingly expressive eyebrows that she can move independent of each other, a trick that used to entertain me for hours when I was little. "Well at least you made it, Kel. I'm *so* glad you're here."

"Me too. Thanks for having us."

"There's my girl." Uncle Nick crushes me in a bear hug, lifting me right off the ground and making me squeal. He's solid, beaming, and pretty gray for someone only in his mid-fifties, although Dad is rapidly catching up to him. "Okay Squirt, let's get you to bed; you two look dead on your feet. We'll talk in the morning." He's carrying my suitcase. Even at this late hour of the night it's stifling hot outside. *Welcome to Texas.* "It's nice to have you home again, Lucas." He snakes a long arm out around his little brother's shoulder and gives it a squeeze. And by "little" I mean "younger." Dad might be the baby in the family but he's the tallest, though not by much. The McCoys only come in XXT.

When we come down for breakfast, Pops; Gran; Dad's oldest brother, Bryce and his wife, Shae, are sitting at the kitchen table waiting for us. We're only missing Uncle Chris and Aunt Liv, who are currently stationed in Egypt. Chris is just older than Dad and a Lieutenant Colonel in the Marines. They made it back for Mom's funeral though. All the McCoy brothers were there, dignified and serious as they proceeded through the church carrying the casket, a solemn wall of solidarity with Dad and I at the gravesite in their dark suits. They stayed to help fill the space in our gapingly empty house with their big bodies and rumbling voices for as long as they could. Because when the unthinkable happens and a drunk driver crosses the median into oncoming traffic suddenly upending the world of those you love, if you're a McCoy, you show up and remind them you've got their back.

They all spring to their feet when we wander into the kitchen. Dad is freshly showered. I'm yawning, still in my PJs, wearing my glasses because I just couldn't bring myself to put my contacts in yet and I'm practically blind otherwise, my hair thrown up into a sloppy bun – not quite ready for the onslaught, although I did brush my teeth.

The McCoys are big huggers. Frequently, we look like bumper cars whenever we first get together. But given we missed out on the earlier hugfest, we begin dutifully making our way through the receiving line.

There is a moment, fleeting and infinitely tender, when Gran pauses before embracing Dad: she, searching, her brilliant blue eyes working as a mother's truth serum on her youngest son; he, allowing her a brief glimpse into his private pain. It is filled with profound grief and loss and self-doubt, so honest and raw it makes me catch my breath. The love and confidence emanating from Gran is palpable and encircles him just before her arms do. I'm not the only one in the room swiping at tears but I've never missed my mom more.

"Let's eat!" Uncle Nick says, his voice a little thick.

"Has everyone seen the house but us?" Dad asks as he pours Gran some orange juice and then sinks down into the open seat next to me.

"Why do you think we're all here?" Uncle Bryce says with a grin. "We want to see your face when Nick opens that front door."

"Hey, you said you wanted a project." Uncle Nick is piling eggs on his plate and reaching for toast.

Dad shoots a look at me. "Bryce has got your back, Kel. He's making me let him take over all the major renovations."

"I have to sleep at night. So does my favorite niece," Uncle Bryce winks.

As all my cousins are boys, I'm his *only* niece. Still, it's been awhile since we've been a part of anything breezy and light; I'd forgotten what it feels like. "Thanks Uncle Bryce," I smile sweetly at him as I pass the strawberries to Aunt Jill.

After breakfast and after I manage to pull myself together, we all pile into two cars and head to the "new" house. "So, the good news, as I told you, is it's on Lake Austin," Uncle Nick says, looking at us through his rear view mirror. He's a real estate developer. When the property came open the end of May, he snatched it up and he and Uncle Bryce, who runs McCoy Construction now that Pops has retired, mulled over their options. When Dad said he wanted to build instead of buy they suddenly found themselves with one more. "You can't beat the location."

"What's the bad news?" I ask.

"I hope you like camping."

The house is boxy and musty and dark and depressing. It smells old. The ceilings have water stains and are sagging in places. Even Charlie looks nervous as we traipse through halls and up and down stairs. Gran takes my hand and pats it consolingly. "The boys will have it fixed up in no time, you'll see."

"Ta-dah! This is it." Uncle Bryce waves his hands wide as we crowd into a little alcove off the kitchen.

"This is it," Dad repeats quietly as he looks around.

"It is? What is it?" Gran asks.

"It's the only corner we're keeping. Everything else goes," Uncle Bryce says cheerily.

He retrieves a sledgehammer he obviously stashed away earlier from a nearby closet and hands it to me. "You want to have the honor of the ceremonial first strike, Squirt?"

Uncertain, I hold it like a baseball bat; it's heavier than it looks. "Are you sure?"

"Absolutely. Aim here." He points to a section in the living room wall. "I don't want you to hit a post. With that arm you just might bring the house down."

"To new beginnings!" Aunt Shae shouts just before I swing and break a terrific hole through the drywall. Charlie barks. The family cheers. I feel a bit breathless and oddly invigorated destroying something. *To new beginnings.*

Outside, parked on the lawn facing the lake, is a motorhome. Pops and Gran are foregoing discovering what parts of America aren't on fire this summer so we have some place to live while construction is going on. Dad lets me and Charlie have the little bedroom in the back of the trailer. Even though Pops had the motorhome custom made to fit his tall frame, important particularly for the shower, it's still going to be a bit of squeeze.

"Come hang out with me anytime you want," Aunt Shae whispers leaning into me with a flash of her dazzling smile, smelling deliciously expensive, tucking a silky strand of her platinum blonde bob back behind her ear with French-tipped nails. Mom always said Aunt Shae was high maintenance on a constant simmer.

Between setting up his practice and picking up a hammer with Uncle Bryce, who is overseeing the demolition and framing, Dad's days and most evenings are full. He still isn't sleeping well at night but if he's not quite back to happy he at least looks a little less lost.

Charlie and I, on the other hand, have serious cabin fever. Austin in June is unthinkable without air conditioning. We've started getting up at 5:30 a.m. to run. Dad took pity on us and gave me a job at his office at the front desk checking patients in, answering phones, filing, and scheduling appointments. Charlie does PR on demand. I'm volunteering at pet shelters on Saturdays. It's still not enough.

"I want to learn how to play the guitar," I tell Dad one night after work as we squeeze into the little kitchen table in the trailer over his grilled salmon and my chipotle sweet potato strips, a hastily thrown together green salad and plenty of sweet, fat blueberries.

"Okay."

"And learn how to knit."

"While playing the guitar?"

I roll my eyes. "Gran said she'd teach me. I could make you a sweater."

"We live in Texas. I'd love one."

I ignore that. "Also, I found a place not too far from here that offers rock climbing classes in the evenings. I did some research; they seem pretty reasonable. And they come highly reviewed. Very safe. What do you think?"

He studies me silently for a moment. "I think it sounds like you're taking up rock climbing." He puts down his fork and helps himself to another scoop of blueberries. "Just promise me you won't fall, Kel. Or break anything. Crutches would be a nightmare in here."

The next day after work Charlie runs errands with Dad while I walk to Strings, a music shop a few blocks away from our office. The doorway tinkles as I step inside. Hanging on the walls like dazzling tiles in a brightly colored mosaic are a myriad of guitars. I blink, a little overwhelmed at the immediate vast and varied selection as I look around.

"Hey there, can I help you with something?"

I'm suddenly and strangely very aware of my heartbeat. And grateful my favorite flippy skirt was clean this morning and that Aunt Shae insisted I get my hair highlighted and reshaped when she took me to her stylist last week, even if it's currently up in a high ponytail making me look like I'm twelve years old because of the stupid heat. "Um, I'm looking for a guitar," I stammer. Because I am. Was.

In a pivotal scene ripe for back lighting, an instrumental score, and a snappy opening line I've already royally muffed my entrance.

Possibly the best-looking guy I've ever seen in real life, with the kind of chiseled perfection usually reserved for male models on runways or in broody ads for GQ has left his spot behind the counter and is walking unhurried and half-smiling toward me.

You've seen National Lampoon's *Christmas Vacation*? The Griswold family wades through bitter cold and snow up to their knees in search of the perfect Christmas tree out of a forest filled with trees. Suddenly they step into a clearing and there, bathed in a pool of celestial light, a heavenly choir proclaiming its divinity, stands *their* tree, enchanting and sparkly.

Seeing him standing there in a patch of late afternoon Austin sunshine, candescent and otherworldly in that white T-shirt and faded blue jeans, I feel taut and tingly and pin-pricked alert: *This boy.*

He is tall – taller than me, by more than a couple of inches, which feels significant, miraculous even, given how rarely it happens. In the Venn diagram defining "Kel McCoy's Dream Man" there is no data set for too tall. He is lean and muscled; the white V-neck he's wearing isn't necessarily tight fitting but he's broad shouldered and narrow waisted so it pulls tight across his chest, with a slight looseness where it brushes against his beltline. His dark hair is longer on top and thick – bits of his overgrown bangs refuse to lay flat and you just *know* it's cowlick induced and not product. He has olive skin, high cheekbones, a strong angular jawline, generous Cupid's bow lips and a perfectly proportioned nose; his light blue eyes are wide-set and heavily lashed.

"Well, you've come to the right place." His smile broadens along with his Texas drawl, which is rich and deliciously lazy. "What's your name?"

I find my smile. "Kel, Kel McCoy."

"Nice to meet you Kel McCoy, I'm Drew Jarrod. First time buying a guitar?"

Focus, Kel. When you come face to face with the physical embodiment of all your dandelion and shooting star wishes, you want to be on top of your game. "What gave me away?"

He grins. I'm rapidly becoming obsessed with the pronounced dip just above his upper lip; it's just big enough that I could settle the tip of my forefinger there, something I find I'm itching to do. "That deer in the headlights look on your face when you first walked in." I force myself to drag my gaze back up into his eyes, which let's be honest, are just as distracting. "Don't worry," Drew says. "You're not the only one. Do you know if you want acoustic or electric?"

I finally find my footing. "Definitely acoustic. We live in a very small trailer." With a toss of my ponytail I pull my phone out of my handbag and show him a picture. It's a Seagull S6 Original; my research said it was the best acoustic guitar for beginners. *Worth every penny*, reviewers promised. And they didn't even know about Drew.

He nods approvingly. "Seagull. Very nice. And you're in luck, we even have some in stock." He hands me back my phone, our long fingers bumping in the transition, making my skin tingle and sing at every point of contact. "This way, come on."

Strings is a maze of displays and shelving that Drew somehow manages to navigate while still looking back at me. This boy is big on eye contact. *Please, on all that's holy, don't let me be the one who trips.*

"So Kel, you from around here?"

"Just moved here actually, from Chicago." I nimbly sidestep a circular upright rack holding sheet music on my side of the aisle and mentally high-five myself.

"Chicago? What brings you to Austin?"

His question, innocent and ordinary, hits me hard. I haven't actually said the words out loud yet and I don't now on the off chance that it'll make me cry. I knew at some point, probably when school started, I'd have to have something prepared, something I'd practiced. But that's a couple of months from now.

"We were ready for a change," I temporize, forcing myself to look him squarely in the eye as I settle on something that is mostly true. "My dad is originally from Austin. I think he wanted to be closer to his family."

Drew smiles at me. "I hear that's a thing. Do you like it here? We treating you well?"

This time I don't hesitate. I respond openly, effusively, urgently. "I love it here."

And by *here* I mean this music shop, which has suddenly become my favorite place on the planet. Austin contains it, and Drew, so I love Austin too. In fact, my enthusiasm for Texas in general just skyrocketed.

"Good. I'm glad." He returns my smile, maybe just as earnestly as he lingers in the moment a beat. Outside cars might be passing by, people hurrying to get home and start dinner or meet friends after work. But right here, right now, time has sealed us off in a very tall, pearlescent bubble. Then Drew blinks. "Your Seagull." *My Seagull.* He leans over to take a guitar off a rack. "Here you go."

Not sure what else to do, I take it from him, holding it awkwardly by the neck like a croquet mallet. "Er, thanks."

His lips twitch. "You're probably gonna want a strap with that. Let me show you what we've got here in the store. If you don't see anything you like we can always order one for you." His eyes are dancing. "Want me to hold that for you while you look?"

He tucks it under his arm. Of course he does.

I don't dither picking out a strap. I select a black leather one with a discreet white edge pattern that is repeated on the circle around the sound hole on the guitar. It's classic and clean and will coordinate with practically everything in my wardrobe. I plan on playing this guitar a lot.

Drew looks surprised when I hand it to him. I can't shake the feeling that he's been studying me like I'm something smeared on a slide. "I actually have this same strap on my Gibson – I really like it."

"Great minds I guess." I shrug, smiling. Obviously we're meant for each other.

He's helping me adjust the strap for my height, which involves glorious close proximity. As you knew he would, he smells amazing but it's more freshly scrubbed and woodsy than the result of any kind of cologne or aftershave. "You're kinda short." His voice rumbles in my ear, making me shiver. "Let me loosen this a bit, you'll be more comfortable. What are you out of those heels? 6′1″?"

"Maybe freshman year. Try 6′2″."

Drew grins. "I think that was *my* freshman year."

Pushing his bangs out of those beautiful eyes, he steps back to survey his handiwork. "That looks good." Which isn't exactly the same thing as saying *I* look good but I still blush. "Hang on a bit, Kel. I'll be right back." He disappears into the back room and emerges moments later with a black case, which he lays on the floor at my feet, demonstrating how to put the guitar securely away and where all the storage pockets are.

"You'll need them to hold these." He's plucking items off nearby shelves like low hanging fruit off a branch and displaying them one by one in his large hands. "Picks. An extra set of strings for when they break. And a tuner – we have others, but this one is the best bang for your buck."

"Wow. Audrey Hepburn made this look so easy."

"Audrey Hepburn?"

"*Breakfast at Tiffany's*? Strumming *Moon River* on the windowsill? Really?"

"Sorry, haven't seen it."

"You should. I mean, Mickey Rooney will absolutely make you want to plunge a fork in your eye but everything else about it? Essential viewing."

Drew is writing something on the tuner package with a pen he's just pulled out of his back pocket. "Say you'll watch it with me Kel and I just might."

I'm staring at Drew Jarrod's phone number.

That half smile of his is devastating. He stands my guitar in its case next to me at the register. "I also give private lessons. Just give me a call or text me if you're interested and we can set something up."

I hand him my debit card. I've never wanted anything more.

Behind me the door tinkles; it's my father. He's pushed up the sleeves of his dress shirt and loosened his tie since I saw him last – definite signs he's ready to go home. Pocketing his sunglasses, in just a few long strides he joins us at the counter. "Hey sweetheart, did you find what you were looking for?"

"I did." I smile at Drew whose glance is flickering from Dad to me: Freakishly tall. The McCoy lips. Hair like a Kabuki doll. *Must* be related. "Thanks for helping me to get set up, Drew," I say, sliding the little sack holding all my extras off the countertop. "I'll be in touch."

Dad raises his eyebrows as he takes the guitar case for me but thankfully says nothing until we're safely outside. "Why exactly are we getting in touch with McDreamy back there?"

"He teaches guitar lessons." I shrug and nonchalantly slip on my sunglasses as I scoop Charlie up off my seat, slide in, and buckle up.

"Are these guitar lessons supervised?" Dad asks, putting the car into reverse.

"I sure hope not." I grin and playfully scratch Charlie behind his ears.

The moment my father heads over to the construction site after dinner, I dive for my laptop, fingers flying. You don't want to overdo the cyber stalking – it's too easy to slip up and reveal something you shouldn't know, basics only. I start with Google.

Drew Jarrod played wide receiver and power forward for the MacArthur High Knights as a 6′6″ junior last year – we're the same age. He was one of their top scorers in both sports but they failed to advance in district playoffs, abruptly ending their seasons.

Drew's Twitter is filled with mostly music related tweets– his musical tastes are all over the map. But there are also a few pictures, which I linger over. Unsurprisingly, given that face, he's *very* photogenic. His Instagram confirms this; the camera loves Drew. Most are taken with friends, a lot of them in the water or on a boat. But he's always surrounded by beautiful girls, many happily hanging off his neck or with arms wrapped around his waist; just never, it seems, the same ones.

I pick up my phone and pull up his number. And yes, I've already entered him into my contacts. Defying my family's strict rule about cell phone use when another breathing and awake human being is close by and deserving of personal attention, I plugged it in on the drive home from Strings so I wouldn't lose it.

"This is Drew."

"Hi Drew, this is Kel McCoy, I was in your shop earlier today buying a Seagull?"

"Kel McCoy. The girl who's going to make me watch *Breakfast at Tiffany's* with her?"

"Hey, Audrey Hepburn is a revelation in that – there should be no arm twisting involved. I'm calling about lessons. Do you have anything available in the evenings? I work until 5:00 Monday through Friday."

"Really? What do you do?"

I blink in surprise at his unexpected question. "My dad is an oral surgeon. I work in his office, we're just down the street from you, actually."

"Austin Oral?"

"That's the one."

"*Don't* put ketchup on him. Now you're just being wasteful. Hang on a sec, Kel?"

"Sure." There's a lot of laughing in the background. A dog is barking. I can hear Drew telling someone to clean the mess up.

"Sorry, I'm back. I'm babysitting. Do you have any little brothers or sisters?"

"No, I'm an only child."

"Want some?"

"How many are we talking?"

"You can have all three. And the dog. Although he smells like condiments at the moment."

I smile and hug my knees. "Sorry, we live in a really small trailer, remember?"

"Oh yeah, why is that? I mean, it's none of my business but isn't your dad a doctor/dentist?"

"It's kind of a long story but he's building our house."

"Building it himself or having it built?"

"Building it himself. Mostly. Yes."

"Okay, that does sound like a long story. And sometime when I can hear myself think I'm going to get it out of you. Give me a sec to look at my calendar? I'm putting you on speaker. Guys, come on, I'm on speakerphone, keep it down." They don't keep it down. They get noticeably louder. "Ryan, I swear, put that in Will's pants and you're getting swirlied. I am NOT kidding. Sorry Kel, I'm a crazy person right now. I'd go in the other room and shut the door but I'm afraid they'd kill each other if I left them unsupervised. I've got Monday open right after you're done with work. Can you make it to Strings by 5:15?"

"I can."

"Great, see you Monday at 5:15 then."

"I'll be there."

There seems to be some sort of fighting going on in the background. He's almost shouting now in order to be heard. "I'm sorry, what?!"

"I'll be there!" Now I'm yelling. Charlie looks alarmed.

"DON'T FORGET YOUR GUITAR."

I immediately begin practicing with some Australian guy with his own YouTube channel who seems legit and emphasizes the importance of technique. I'd planned on impressing Drew by appearing to be a fast learner but quickly realize I'm not going to get away with it. By Sunday night my fingertips are so sore I want to layer them in bubble wrap. Rock climbing class was excruciating. Knitting with Gran, also a bust. Obviously, timing-wise, I didn't think my goal setting choices through very well.

It takes me extra long to get ready for work Monday morning, and not just because I'm being girly. I mean, yes, I change my entire outfit three times and my shoes twice but it's hard to straighten your hair and apply makeup in a trailer bathroom the size of a shoebox when your fingers are all blistered.

I force myself to stay busy all day so I'll stop watching the clock. Finally, at 4:55 I step into the office restroom to check my teeth for anything weird and touch up my lipstick. *What are you doing, Kel?* I shake my head. *That boy is going to break your heart.*

It's no good telling my reflection it's just a guitar lesson. We both know better.

A busty brunette with pouty lips and wearing Daisy Dukes and high-heeled wedges is leaning over the counter talking to Drew when I walk into Strings carrying my guitar case.

"Hey Kel," Drew's smile is immediate and just for me, which does strange things to my insides. "Jason, my 5:15 is here. Can you help Stacy? She's thinking about buying a karaoke machine. Catalog is on the counter. Jason here will take good care of you," he tells Stacy, excusing himself as he steps out to meet me.

I'm his 5:15. That feels important to remember.

"How was work?" Drew asks, steering me briefly with a hand on the small of my back. "We're just over here."

"Work was good."

"Yeah? What makes a day good for you?"

He looks sincerely interested and curious, surface answers never seem to be enough for him. I take a deep breath, "Everyone showed up on time. We stayed on schedule. No one cried or threw up. All the office equipment worked. I found the last piece of Dove's Dark Chocolate in our secret office stash. There you go. Day made. How was yours?"

Drew pulls out a chair for me and closes the studio door. "I like Mondays. I didn't used to but I sure do now." He winks at me as he picks up his guitar and sits down, folding his long legs underneath his chair. "But now that I know how you feel about punctuality, I'm thinking we should probably get started. Got to stay on your good side."

I wipe my suddenly sweaty palms on my carefully chosen skirt. I went with it because while still office appropriate, it showcases my long runner's legs and looks fabulous matched with the ruffled, bell sleeved pink blouse I'm wearing. I hadn't taken into consideration its possible need for moisture absorption, but I can't think about sweat stains now. I lick my lips and find my voice. It's tremulous. "First, I have a confession to make."

Drew slowly leans forward in his chair, peering at me through piecey bangs and resting sinewy forearms along the edge of his guitar. "You're actually nervous. Come on, Kel. It can't be that bad. What happened?"

"I'm so Type A. You should probably know that about me up front. Like I should seriously come with a warning label. I've never played an instrument before, I wasn't sure if I would be any good at it. I couldn't wait to find out, here, in front of you. I've been practicing guitar all week with an Australian guy on YouTube. I guess I was hoping I'd be able to master enough chords that you'd think I was a natural. Stop laughing, it's not funny. Look at my fingers."

"Sorry. I wish you could see your face right now."

He takes my hands gently in his and examines each fingertip. "Yeah, looks painful. You just got to play through it. But look," he's rubbing his thumb slowly over my scabs. "You're already starting to develop callouses. It won't hurt like this for much longer."

I let out the breath I didn't realize I was holding. "Well, that's good."

Drew releases my hands and shakes his head, still grinning. "You must've practiced a lot."

"Let's just say my dad is happy I didn't take up the trombone."

"Alright Chicago, let's see what the Australian gave you."

I pick out my E minor, C, G, D, A minor, E and A chords for him. We work on moving fluidly from one chord to the next while keeping rhythm strumming, which is much harder to do than it sounds. My fingers and my brain seem to be at odds with one another. It doesn't help that Drew keeps leaning in to adjust my fingering position. "A little more arch, I know it hurts more right now to do it that way but we're in this for the long haul, right?"

I raise my pointy chin at him and nod. The longest.

Drew downloads a metronome app onto my phone for me and hands me some sheet music for Lady Antebellum's *I Need You Now.* "You ready to make some music together?"

I look at him in surprise. "I don't know, am I?"

"Yeah. You are." He shows me how to secure my capo to my 4th fret and explains how to read the music for chord changes. "Don't worry if you can't keep up Kel, just jump back in as soon as you can. I'm gonna play it all the way through at tempo so you get a feel for what it should sound like."

Drew not only plays it, he sings. I can carry a tune; I've been in choirs since grade school so I definitely know my way around a register, but he's got an *incredible* voice. "Wow," I say when the last chord I've clunked through ends and it's suddenly very quiet in the room. "That was amazing, Drew. You're really talented."

"Thanks. You weren't so bad yourself." His grin is wicked. "I think you might be a natural."

I sheepishly return his smile. "Fine. I deserve that."

"Hey, I was being serious. Don't roll those pretty blue eyes at me. Are we good now or do I still need to be worried about the Australian? Yeah? Okay, homework this week: let's just spend some more time on perfecting these chords and maybe this song. Work on smoothing out your transitions."

"Would you do something for me, Drew?" I pull out my phone and open it up to voice memo. "Would you play it again for me, please? I want to record it this time so I can practice with it."

He does. Being able to experience the intimate beauty of Drew performing is the single best moment I've clocked this miserable year. I listen to the recording on a loop and not always with my guitar in hand, although I'm practicing every chance I get. His voice lulls me to sleep at night and fills my dreams – not all of them pleasant. That song has become the anthem for the howling emptiness that in my darkest moments finds me inescapably without my mother and completely alone with my grief.

Well, not completely alone. Charlie is always there to lick away my tears. He inches his furry body from his preferred spot curled into my hip, up to my pillow, and lays his wet nose next to mine. His warm body is reassuringly comforting.

"Don't *you* ever leave me," I whisper somewhere between sorrow and heartbreak and I hold him tight.

The trouble is, I know now there's always a real possibility that he might.

2

"This is what you came for"
NOT Calvin Harris...nicely played T. Swift

"How did I let you talk me into this?" Jake asks as he fastens his harness.

"Moan all you want, I saw you watching Mateo climb. You've probably already calculated the most efficient route to take given your height differential."

He has the grace to blush. "Shut up. I don't have your freakishly wiry legs."

"All those years of ballet were good for something," I grin. "Last one to the top buys ice cream."

Jake surprises me; I beat him up but just barely. I hadn't noticed because all my attention was on the task at hand but a small crowd has gathered to watch us. A cute redhead with freckles and a tablet is smiling at us as we return to ground.

"You guys looked really good up there." She's shaking our hands. "Hi, my name is Rachel Williams, I'm working on a marketing campaign for Austin Climbing Center's relaunch when we open up our expansion this fall. I've had my eye on the two of you since you came in this morning. I was wondering if you might be interested in being highlighted in some of our publicity materials? Of course we'd compensate you for your time. We'd just rather feature actual customers in our photo shoots where we can, especially if we can say that you are."

"You want to take pictures of us climbing?" Jake is struggling with finding any kind of logic in this. "Today was my first time."

"Really? I'm sorry, I didn't get your names." We introduce ourselves; it's not my imagination. She practically purrs when she discovers Jake and I are cousins and not boyfriend and girlfriend. "Well, you must be a fast learner, Jake. You certainly looked like you knew what you were doing up there."

I'm mentally rolling my eyes. *It's your face, Jake.* But to be fair, for a nerd he's deceptively athletic. "May we get back to you on that?" I ask. I need time to wear him down.

"Sure. Here's my business card; all my contact info's on there. I hope you'll take me up on this."

"Thanks Rachel, I promise we'll be in touch. Lovely meeting you." I'm tugging at Jake's *Still in Beta* T-shirt. "You owe me ice cream."

"You can't seriously be thinking about doing this," Jake says as we climb into his Jeep.

"Why not? I think it would be kind of cool. Don't you?"

"No."

I switch gears. Not literally, Jake is definitely driving. "Rachel sure is pretty. Don't you think she's pretty?"

He looks at me. "So?"

"So, when was the last time you had a date?"

"What are you Kel, my mother?"

"Just saying. You think she's hot, she thinks you're hot. You should do something about it."

"How do you know she thinks I'm hot?"

"She wants you to be a model in her campaign, Jake. Trust me, it wasn't because you looked like you knew what you were doing. Because you so didn't."

"Remind me again why I hang out with you?" He knows I'm right.

"I'll let you call her."

Our photo shoot is scheduled for two weeks from Saturday. Jake insists on dragging me to the ACC every night after work between now and then – with the exception of my Monday guitar lessons with Drew, which he knows are off limits. It doesn't hurt that Rachel is there most evenings watching him in action. The Tuesday before the shoot Jake finally summons up the courage to ask Rachel out for dinner Friday night while I pretend to look incredibly interested in the upcoming class schedule posted on the wall.

"She said yes." I might be gloating as I punch his arm on our way out to his Jeep.

Jake smiles sheepishly. "She said yes."

Which is good, because I've invested so much time and energy trying to push the two of them together my guitar practicing has definitely suffered. And I'd finally been making some serious progress on my rendition of Jason Mraz's *I'm Yours* but there are only so many hours in a day.

Dad's still at the construction site when Jake drops me off at the motorhome. Hugging Charlie, I flop onto my bed, kick off my sandals, toss my bag of climbing gear onto the floor, pull out my phone, and euphorically text Drew: It's been a REALLY good day. Sorry. Just had to tell someone.

Drew: Glad you picked me. Do I get details? You know I love it when you talk punctuality.

Me: I played Cupid and it worked! Just basking in my victory.

Drew: Congrats. I think they make an SPF for that. Anyone I know?

Me: My cousin Jake and Rachel, this woman we met rock climbing.

Drew: Sounds romantic. No. Wait. It really doesn't.

Me: Right?! Thank you. It was a LOT of work.

Drew: Guess it paid off. Hey, what are you doing Saturday?

I immediately sit up straight on the bed, heart pounding, my fingers trembling as I text him back: Rock climbing with Jake.

Drew: All day?

Me: Probably. Why?

Drew: My friend Matt is taking his dad's boat out. Thought you might want to come.

"I hate my life," I tell Charlie just before I plow my face into my pillow. Figures. The *one* time a boy I like might actually like me back and I'm on wingman duty.

Me (still groaning): Wish I could. Sounds fun.

Drew: Tell Jake to take Rachel rock climbing by himself. He's a big boy.

Me: I don't actually know if Rachel climbs.

Drew: ?

Me: Rachel is doing an advertising campaign for the Austin Climbing Center. She asked Jake and me if we'd be part of it. The photo shoot is this Saturday.

Drew: Seriously? Wow. A professional model! I might need your autograph.

Me: Sure. Have your people talk to mine.

Drew: Will I see you Monday?

Me: Of course. I'm your 5:15.

Saturday morning Jake is whistling – whistling – when he picks me up. "I'm guessing your date with Rachel went well?" I say, fastening my seatbelt.

"I'm taking her out again tonight after the shoot."

"Nicely done, Jakester! I'm impressed. And grateful. Today might've been kind of awkward if things totally tanked for you last night."

"Rachel's a professional. She told me she normally doesn't date the talent but she just had to make an exception for me." A streak of pink is creeping up Jake's face. It's kind of adorable.

"Aww, Jake. I'm so happy for you I'm not even going to mock the fact that she calls you 'the talent.'"

When we arrive at the Austin Climbing Center we're ushered into a side room where they've set up a rack with clothes from their shop for us. A lady named Espe is there, waiting to do our hair and make-up. Jake is surprisingly agreeable about having his face done for something that is meant to look natural and athletic.

Rachel has a series of shots mapped out on her ever-present tablet that she wants captured. We start with me being slightly ahead of Jake on the middle of the wall and then reverse that. They take angles from below and angles from above. Jake and I get short breaks to rest our arms and legs while they set up the equipment and crew for the next shot.

Jake uses his breaks mostly to flirt with Rachel. I've never seen Jake flirt before. He's so shy I couldn't even imagine what that would look like. But Rachel has a way of drawing him out and making him relax. They're cute together.

Happy in their bliss, I pull out my phone. I've got a text from Drew: Good luck today. Smile pretty for the camera.

Thanks! Have fun skiing. Without me. I text back.

At my next break he's sent me a shirtless picture of him looking swoonworthy in jammers, sunglasses, and a backwards baseball cap; he's sunning his washboard abs and grinning with a couple of his friends in the back of a boat that is obviously zipping through the water at a pretty quick clip given the visible wake behind them: Wish you were here.

I send him a mirror selfie of Espe touching up my foundation, which I've mostly sweated off: Sorry #modellife.

Drew: You're rocking it, Chicago. Text me when you're done being glamorous? We'll pick you up at your place. You have a dock, right?

Me (squealing – definitely startling, possibly alarming Espe): We do and I will. FYI: I'm never NOT glamorous.

I remind myself of that when Rachel asks to wrap our shoot using equipment from some of the other classes they offer – but she doesn't just want posing; she wants us to have worked up a real sweat. By the time we're done planking on Bosu balls and kickboxing, jumping rope, and doing multiple sets with kettlebells and resistance bands after already putting in hours of climbing, I'm wiped.

"Thanks guys!" Rachel finally claps her hands. "Good work, everyone. I think we've captured something special here. Can't wait to see the final product. Jake, Kel, you were amazing."

"I think I've sweated my eyebrows off," I tell Jake as he extends a hand and hauls me up off the floor. "You so owe me," I mutter under what's left of my breath.

He swipes at his forehead with the bottom of his already damp T-shirt, flashing a fine set of abs that Rachel will no doubt get to appreciate at some point. Who knew Mr. Research Lab had all that going on? "May I remind you that this was your idea, Kel?"

"Of course it was, but I was just trying to help you get the girl. You know, the one you're taking to dinner tonight?"

Jake wraps a sweaty arm around my sweaty neck and squeezes. "Fine, I owe you, Squirt."

I text Drew while Jake is saying a lingering good-bye to Rachel: On my way home.

Drew: We drove by your place earlier. I could see your car parked by a motorhome in back of the construction. Matt's on the wakeboard. Be there in 20?

Me: Make it 30? I still need to shower and change.

He sends me the thumbs up emoji.

"Dad?" I'm hollering over the sound of the whine of the saw. He's in the kitchen with Uncle Bryce and Justin, my married cousin with a nine-month old son. Justin works at McCoy Construction with his dad.

"Hey Kel. How did the shoot go?" Dad asks, quieting the saw and pulling off his safety goggles.

"Long. I shouldn't have run this morning. Turns out modeling is surprisingly hard work."

"Still can't believe you talked Jake into doing that." Justin grins, shaking his head as he hands Uncle Bryce a board. "So when do we get to see the two of you blown up in high def and on the sides of buses and billboards?"

"I don't know. I don't think he cares – he's taking Rachel out again, tonight." Outside, I can hear the sound of a motorboat approaching our dock. *Deep breath.* "Hey, is it okay if I go boating with some friends?"

For the first time Dad realizes I'm wearing a swimsuit under my tank top and shorts and carrying a towel in my tote bag. He, Uncle Bryce, and Justin all turn in unison and stare out the framed kitchen window as Drew hops onto our deck and ties off Matt's boat. "McDreamy?"

"His name is Drew, Dad."

"You *know* this guy?" Uncle Bryce says. Drew is making his way toward the motorhome looking like a Greek god, blissfully unaware he's being scrutinized. Thank heavens he put a shirt on.

"He's her guitar teacher."

"Seriously? What were you thinking, little brother?"

"Dad?"

"Give me a minute," Dad says, ignoring Justin's snickering. "Bring him over, Kel. I want to talk to him first."

"Are you going to embarrass me?"

"Possibly."

"Don't. Please?" Drew is knocking on the motorhome door. "Be right back." I dash out of the house. "Hey, Drew. Over here."

"Hey Kel. You ready to go?"

"I am." I can hear my dad clearing his throat behind us. They've all followed me outside. "Drew, you remember my father, Lucas McCoy? Dad, Drew Jarrod. And this is my Uncle Bryce and my cousin Justin."

"Hi. Nice to see you again, sir." Drew extends his hand. I'm nervously chewing at my bottom lip and looking imploring at my father. He shakes Drew's hand and then stands with his legs apart, arms crossed, his head cocked, doing his best and succeeding at looking very imposing.

"Kel says you're taking her boating?"

Drew nods. "Yes, sir."

"There will be no alcohol consumed while my daughter is with you. Do I make myself clear?"

"Yes, sir."

"I'm taking you at your word, son. And that's not something I do lightly. You're operating a vehicle with her in it – I want you sober. Do we have an understanding? Okay. Have fun. Don't stay out too late. Kel, you've got your phone and some emergency money?"

"I do. Thanks Dad. Bye guys." I grab Drew before my father thinks of anything else mortifying he feels he should add in the line of fatherly duty. "Sorry about that," I say when I'm sure we can't be overheard.

"It's fine, Kel. I get it," he shrugs, our flip flops clacking in time against the pavers leading to the water. "Is everyone in your family ginormous? Because I suddenly feel short."

"Kind of. It's a McCoy thing."

"Yeah?" Drew suddenly stops, catching me by the arm, halting our progress.

I turn in surprise. He simply says "Hi." And he slowly grins, taking me in. I've known Drew for less than three weeks and already I find myself cataloguing his smiles. Engaging, encouraging, encompassing and flirty – all of them intimate in their own way; every single one of them has found a way into my heart.

"Hi." I'm suddenly feeling a little shy under the warmth of his stare.

"I'm glad you could come."

"Me too."

"Tell me about your day?" And just like that our long legs fall back into their easy rhythm again.

"It was mostly a lot of holding very awkward positions for long periods of time and then being told to act natural. Which apparently means 'happy' but I think they eventually had to settle for 'intensely focused without looking constipated or like a serial killer.' And I'm not even sure I managed that."

"Did you stick your tongue out like you sometimes do when you're changing chords?" Drew playfully bumps me.

"I don't know what you're talking about."

"Hey everyone, this is Kel," Drew says as we reach the dock. "The guy behind the wheel there is Matt. That's Travon, Mandy, Striker, and that's Chris."

"Hi," I say as Drew releases the mooring line and we step into the boat with everyone watching. For the record, I don't trip or fall. "Thanks for stopping by to pick me up."

"No problem," Matt shouts back over his shoulder, an orange Longhorn ball cap pulled down over the top of his overgrown, sun-bleached sandy colored hair as he reverses out and heads for deeper water. "You ready to ski?"

My body is still aching from my day with Rachel but there's no way I'm going to wimp out in front of Drew and his friends. "Okay. Sure." I quickly shed my shirt and shorts, grateful I braided my hair and put on waterproof mascara when I got out of the shower earlier as I fasten the buckles of the life vest Drew gives me.

Travon is holding up my options. "What'll it be, little girl: board or skis?" He's built like a tank and about my height, his hair is cut so short there's no visible curl, and he has a deep, rumbly voice with a sweet southern accent.

"Skis, please. I'm still kind of new at this."

Matt idles while I jump into the water and get my feet in the skis. After a few wipe outs trying to negotiate the wake I finally manage to stay up. The sun feels glorious on my shoulders and there's very little wind; it's a perfect day for skiing. Chris takes my place in the water with the wakeboard when I'm done. Drew wraps my towel around my shoulders and scoots to open a spot for me next to him.

"Thanks." I blot the worst bits dry and sit down. There's not a lot of room on the bench. With the exception of Mandy, Drew's friends are all broad shouldered and bulky; I'm practically sitting on his lap. "Sorry, I think I'm squishing you."

"You say that like it's a bad thing." He throws his arm around the back of my shoulders to open up a little more space and pulls my long legs over his. "There. Better?"

Not if anyone expects me to be coherent.

"My man Drew says you're from Chicago," Striker says and in his mouth *Chicago* sounds like a bad word. He's got wavy brown hair and very hairy legs that are splayed out in front of him. Mandy, a petite blonde who obviously didn't get in the water today – her hair and make-up are still perfect – must be his girlfriend. They're pretty free with the PDA.

"I am." I'm squeezing the excess water out my braid and feeling a little self-conscious. "We just moved here the end of June. How do you all know each other?"

"Football, mostly," Travon says. And suddenly all the muscle mass makes sense. "Except for him." He indicates Striker with a nod in his direction and a roll of his eyes. "He's too big a wuss."

"Just protecting my asset." Striker pats his right arm lovingly.

Travon snorts. "Is that what we're calling it now?"

"That or 'Full-Ride,' take your pick."

"Yo, Chris is down," Drew shouts to Matt, who begins to circle back.

"Drew says he's teaching y'all how to play the guitar." Travon leans forward, his elbows on his knees. "He any good?"

Our close proximity is making me brave and possibly a little flirty. "I don't know Drew, are you? I hear you're only as good as your students."

He grins and winks at me. "Then I'm a natural."

Striker stops sticking his tongue down Mandy's throat for a moment. "Hey, we going to eat anytime soon? I'm starving."

Travon sighs, shaking his head as he hops up in a swift, graceful movement that belies his heft and leans over the back of the boat to shout at Chris. "Y'all done? Bring it back in then. Princess here is hungry."

Chris nods and pulls out of the boots, swimming for the boat with the board in tow.

"You okay to hang a little longer?" Drew asks, his voice soft in my ear. His thumb occasionally trails across my knee, sending shivers up my spine even though it's still blazing hot out.

"I can stay."

We drop the boat off at Matt's and pile back into his family's suburban to find some pizza. At some point, while we're waiting for Chris – who is the skinniest guy in the group but absolutely *pounding* it down, slice after slice – to finish eating, Drew threads his fingers through mine under the table. We're holding hands and grinning goofily at each other while everyone else is bemoaning the fact that there's only a month of summer vacation left.

"So what school will you go to, Kel?" Mandy asks.

Because I'm a little bit giddy with what Drew's dreamy blue eyes are telegraphing it takes a moment to realize everyone's waiting for me to respond.

"Won't be MacArthur, I'll tell you that much." Travon flicks his discarded straw wrapper into an open pizza box lid. "Her zip code's too steep."

I blush. "I'm at Barton."

I've gone to private schools since kindergarten; Dad didn't think there was any reason to change that my senior year. But the table has suddenly grown very quiet.

Striker whistles, darting a quick glance at Drew. "And you call *me* Princess."

"You are," Travon glowers.

"I don't think we have a football team though. I'm hoping I can come cheer on yours," I say, wanting to change the subject. "When's your first game?"

"First Friday back," Matt jumps in, saving me. "You should come, Kel. We're pretty good. And by that I mean we *look* pretty good."

"Or if you're Jarrod, you just look pretty." Striker makes a face.

"Football envy," Drew coughs.

"Why would I want to play football? You guys suck."

"Yeah? I don't remember the last time the baseball team made it past playoffs. Anyone want that last piece?" Chris asks, reaching for it.

At the end of the night, Drew drives me home in an ancient black Ram truck he calls *Betty*. "Thanks for coming, Kel," he says as he places Betty in park next to Uncle Bryce's truck. I can hear Dad still hammering at the house; the glow from the series of portable lights he's set up so he can work at night is visible from the car. Charlie's left him and is already bounding out to meet us. "I think my friends might like you better than they like me."

"Really? I'm pretty sure Striker hates me."

"He hates everyone."

Good point. "You want to come in for a bit?"

"Yeah? Okay."

"Hey Charlie," I scoop him up and dust him off; he's got a fine layer of sawdust on his fur. "You've got to stop hanging out with Dad, buddy. This is Drew. Say hello."

Drew scratches Charlie behind the ears in his sweet spot, earning him an automatic lifetime of love and devotion, which Charlie immediately starts to dispense by enthusiastically washing Drew's entire hand with his quick, pink tongue. "Sorry about the slobber." I open the motorhome door and start to step inside before stopping cold, causing Drew to bump right into me. "Promise you'll close your eyes for a second?"

"Seriously? What if I trip?"

"I won't let you." I put Charlie down and turn to face him. "Give me your hands."

He does. I take them in mine. "And I'm doing this because?"

"What? Do you have trust issues? Because I tore out of here earlier. And I have under— er, embarrassing articles of clothing thrown around. No peeking."

He laughs. "I'm not."

"One more step up. Okay, I've got you. Turning you around. Sit here. There's a chair just behind you." I let go of his hands once I'm sure he's backed up enough to feel it hitting the back of his legs. "Eyes still closed?"

"Still closed."

I dash around tidying. It doesn't take long; one of the great things, possibly the ONLY great thing about living in a small space is you're forced to live virtually clutter free. "Okay."

"Okay, it's safe to open my eyes?"

"Yes. Open away."

Drew blinks up at me and grins. "Hi. Again."

"Hi."

He gets to his feet and looks around. "So this is Home Temporary Home?"

"Cozy, right?" I open the fridge and survey our options, even though I just did the shopping. "I'm sorry we don't have any soda. Would you like some lemonade? Juice? Ice water?"

"Water's fine, thanks. Are the glasses in here?" He takes two down out of the cupboard. "Hey, looks like your mom's home."

I freeze.

Strangely, I keep pouring. Even though it feels like all the air has left my lungs and there's a dangerous buzz growing weirdly in my brain, I continue to pour. *Steady.* I slowly look up, through the window over the sink. It's Aunt Shae. She's painstakingly picking her way through uneven ground in high heel sandals from the construction site to Uncle Bryce's truck.

"That's not my mom." It comes out so quiet I'm not even sure I said it out loud. *Just rip the Band-Aid off, Grace.* "My mother. She...she was...killed. She was killed in a car accident...in January. She was hit by a drunk driver. She's dead."

"Oh, Kel. I'm *so* sorry."

I can see in his stricken face that he is. He's mentally putting together my dad out there alone in the dark, driving himself to assemble a house that's more about consuming long, empty, evening hours than a need to actually live in it, and desperately wishing he could rewind back to moments ago when everything was light and breezy and unsaid. But it's not his fault. I hand him his glass, suddenly exhausted. "Me too."

He puts the glass down on the counter and takes me in his arms. For the longest time we just stand there, as if clinging to each other can ward off everything bad in this world. At some point he starts humming a song I don't recognize and rubbing soothing circles along my back. That's when the tears begin to fall in earnest. And Drew just holds onto me as tightly as he knows how.

"Mom would say I'm milking this. 'Enough already with the damsel in distress, Grace,'" I sniff with a watery laugh, lifting my head off his very solid and reassuring, now very moist chest to swipe at my eyes. "I really miss her, Drew. Sometimes so much it hurts to breathe." Clearing my throat I disentangle myself from him, mopping up my face and blowing my nose with several tissues. "Sorry. I didn't mean for any of that to happen. I must be really tired. It's been a long day. Aren't you glad you took me up on my invitation to come in?"

"I am, actually." He rubs his thumb tenderly along my jawline, his eyes taking in every inch of my face. I'm pretty sure I'm a horrible, blotchy mess but I hold his gaze. "But I should go; you look like you're ready to drop. You going to be okay?"

"Yes. I'm fine." Well, not *really* fine. But good enough. Sometimes good enough is all you get for a while; it's a placeholder, not a final destination. "Thank you, Drew."

He kisses my forehead. "Get some rest, Kel."

I don't brush my teeth or wash my face or take my contacts out. I don't change out of my clothes or get under the covers. I lay down on my bed and am fast asleep before Drew even backs out of the drive.

3

"We're walking the wire, love"
Imagine Dragons

"How are you feeling, Rob?" I ask, his post-surgery care instructions that Dad just went over with Rob's mother printed out, along with a little brochure I made that has a few humorous dos and don'ts, in my hand.

Rob is grinning goofily and drooling slightly after just having his wisdom teeth extracted. He isn't feeling any pain. "You're pretty."

"You know, I get that a lot from guys who are on drugs, but thank you." I hand the printed materials to Rob's mother. "Let me get the door for you."

"That's very nice of you," Rob slurs. "I'd kiss you but your lips are WAY too far away." He's cackling as his mother drags him out.

"Kel, your cell phone is buzzing," Maggie, Dad's office manager says, handing it to me from behind the front desk. In her other hand she has a stack of brightly colored folders – her new filing system, and she's very proud of it.

"Thanks." I don't recognize the number. "Hello? This is Kel."

Have you ever gotten an unexpected call – so unexpected you're suspicious you might be the victim of a prank? You hear them talking but you can't quite believe what they're saying. I start taking notes so I can keep everything clear. "May I get back to you shortly with an answer? I work, so I need to make sure I can get Friday off first."

Disconcerted, I find my father looking at x-rays in his office. "I just got a call from a friend of Rachel's – Jake's Rachel." I don't know why I feel the need to clarify this. He only knows one Rachel that I'm aware of and she's all anyone in the family talked about – when they weren't giving him a hard time about Drew – at dinner yesterday. Maybe it's because it IS Rachel and that makes the rest of this somehow more believable.

Dad nods and leans back in his chair.

"Her friend Ashley is in charge of putting together a back to school fashion show for the mall. One of her models broke her leg over the weekend. Ashley wanted to know if I'd be willing to step in last minute and be her replacement. I guess Rachel recommended me." I glance down at my notepad. "There's a mandatory meeting Friday morning from 9:00 to 1:00 so they can assign everyone their outfits and do a run through before the real thing Saturday afternoon. Crazy, right? What do you think?"

"About you taking time off or this modeling thing?"

"Either. Both."

"Check with Maggie but I'm pretty sure Cheryl can cover the front for you. Is this something you want to do, Kel?"

"I guess. I mean, it's flattering to have been asked. And it sounds like Ashley's scrambling. Obviously - she's calling me."

"Okay then. Work it out with Cheryl."

If you're a McCoy, Sunday is family day. Gran has a big wicker basket sitting on a lace doily on the table of her front entry that we all have to drop our cell phones into when we first walk in the door: house rules.

Because we're the only ones currently living in a trailer and in desperate need of large amounts of air-conditioned space to roam freely around in, Dad, Charlie, and I are usually the first ones there and the last ones to leave. Every Sunday we go to church with Pops and Gran. I help Gran in the kitchen. And after dinner, after everyone else has gone home, we work on the sweater I'm knitting for Dad, originally for his birthday in September but at the rate I'm going he'll be lucky if he gets it for Christmas.

So, besides responding to an early morning text to make sure I was okay, I haven't really had a chance to talk to Drew since my emotional meltdown Saturday night.

"Hey," Drew's face lights up when I step into Strings with my guitar case in hand for my 5:15 lesson. He dusts off his hands and then wipes them assiduously on his jeans. "Sorry, Jesse wanted this promo display reset. We should clean more."

"It looks good."

"Yeah? So do you. Come on." He takes my free hand in his and I follow him back to the studio.

I wait until we're seated across from each other, our guitars tuned and ready to go before launching into the little speech I've been mentally composing for most of the day. "So, I just wanted to clear the air about Saturday night first, if that's okay?" I'm rubbing nervously at the slick surface of my pick. *Deep breath, Kel.* "Sorry again for the waterworks. You're just the first person I've actually told about my mother's death. Back in Chicago everyone who knew us already knew. I think my father might've told Maggie, his office manager, when he was opening his practice here and she spread the word because the staff kind of tiptoe around conversations that have anything to do with mothers. Or drunk drivers. Or funerals. Anyway. It's not something we ever really talk about. Like ever. I don't want you to feel bad, Drew. It had to happen at some point. I'm glad it was with you."

"Me too, Kel."

"Really?"

"Really."

I tuck a fallen bit of hair back behind my ear and smile shyly at him as I position my fingers for playing. "Did your shirt eventually dry out?"

He grins. "Almost."

"Well, I guess the good news is I'm officially now all out of secrets."

"I hope not." Drew picks through a quick series of chords that starts out flamboyant and charged and ends up flickering away into nothing. "I kind of like these confessional sessions of ours, *Grace*."

My eyes fly to his.

He shrugs. "It slipped out the other night when you were giving me an impression of something your mom would say. And I have a confession of my own to make. I pulled up her obituary online when I got home. 'Grace Kelly McCoy' was listed under *survived by her daughter*."

"Right. Well, I was terribly uncoordinated as a little girl. At some point I even think my parents had me checked for an inner ear imbalance. *Grace* just left the door wide open for much mocking."

"Private school kids can be so mean."

"What? Did you Google me too?" As if I hadn't done the very same thing to him.

"Yeah. I did. Am I in trouble?"

"That depends. What did you find out?"

"You don't have a boyfriend."

I blush. "That you know of."

Drew is staring at me intently. "Do you?"

I can't hold his gaze. "I went to a fairly small high school. There were only three boys there taller than me. And they all had really short girlfriends. Why is that? Short girls can date *anyone*. It's so unfair."

"I agree. Tall people should only date other tall people – much less neck strain." He tugs on my knee looking particularly winsome. "We're tall people."

I haven't had a lot of practice with flirting but I summon my very best *To Catch a Thief* Grace Kelly, shimmering and coy in diamonds. "I know."

Aunt Shae stops by the office Wednesday morning, whirling in on a cloud of Chanel and a click of kitten heels, a frown the only thing marring her immaculately made up face. "Kel McCoy, tell me your father inadvertently hit you on the head with a 2 x 4, rendering you concussed or with amnesia."

I blink. "I'm sorry?"

"You've known since *Monday* that you were going to be in the back to school fashion show and I only found out about it twenty minutes ago. From your uncle, of all people. What were you thinking? You weren't. You've absolutely left us no time."

"For what?"

In her younger years Shae competed in a series of beauty pageants; she was runner-up to Miss Texas and still looks like she's being judged whenever she walks around in a swimsuit. She's deftly pulling business cards out of her purse and spreading them out in front of me like tarot cards. "Call Kirstie Adderson. Immediately. She's the CEO of Adderson Modeling Management and a dear friend. I spoke to her on the drive over and told her all about you and she agreed - as a personal favor to me - to help get you ready."

"I don't think it's really a big deal, Aunt Shae. We're just basically wearing outfits supplied by different stores in the mall so you'll want to buy them and maybe have some idea of what's in for fall."

"It's an opportunity Kel, and one you need to make the most of. I've always thought with a little training you'd make an incredible model. You look more and more like your mother every day. The underpinnings were always there; you just needed time to grow into all those McCoy inches and get comfortable in your own skin. Kirstie can help, honey. Just promise me you'll give it everything you've got so the option is there for you if you decide you want it. That's all I'm saying."

By the time Shae leaves I've not only got an appointment with Kirstie, I have another to get my highlights "touched up" (is there such a thing as too blonde in this state?) and I am making time around my lunch hours to get waxed, a manicure and pedicure, and to have my "flawless skin" detoxified. She also leaves me with a large, pink (her signature color) water bottle and strict instructions: "Hydrate. You need to drink at LEAST three of these a day. Five would be better."

After work that night I drive to the Adderson's home and change into the swimsuit and heels Kirstie asked me to bring. She's sitting straight-backed and perched in a chair in a dance studio in the back of her house, her glossy dark hair up in an elegant chignon, and even though she's wearing capris and a sleeveless shirt and wedge sandals, she's looks like royalty. "Just walk toward me, Kel."

I do. Apparently, wrong. In my defense, gliding around in a swimsuit and heels is not something I've ever done before. She has me do it again and again, her head cocked, lips pursed, her Windex blue eyes laser focused in on dissecting my every movement.

"Okay." Kirstie joins me at the barre where she delivers her verdict. "The good news is you haven't picked up too many bad habits. You have amazing posture for someone your age and height, and a high level of fitness – both are incredibly helpful and put us miles ahead of the game. Shae said you've done ballet for several years. It shows; there's a fluidity to your movement most girls are missing, but that also means we're going to be battling a tendency to walk with your feet turned out. You also look at the ground when you walk. A lot. The bad news? We don't have much time to fix things. We'll need to stay focused if we're going to pull this off."

She puts on music. "Ready? Watch me first and then we'll go together, side by side, in front of the mirror. Look ahead and fix on a point. Now let me see some confidence. Sell me on this." She shakes her head as I start over. "Your body is moving with confidence Kel, but if I don't see it in your eyes I don't believe it. Tell me you're someone worth looking at."

I try again. And again. We work at walking and stopping and turning and stairs for almost two hours.

"Yes. Much better. Tilt your chin down just a bit. Perfect. Remember Kel, confidence is key. And for you that means practicing as much as you can for as long as you can stand it. We're cramming muscle memory here so it will kick in when your nerves do."

Given I only have two days left and my lunch hours have all been filled up with appointments, on top of practicing walking confidently any time I'm already on my feet, I sacrifice part of my early morning running time – the one thing that keeps me sane. Instead of staring at the ground I force myself to look straight ahead, which only results in a couple of stumbles. One involves a small dog I don't even see until it's too late. To be fair, the dog was off his leash, which is against park rules, but I still feel bad.

"Hey Wonder Dog," I reprimand Charlie, after apologizing profusely to the owner. "You're supposed to save me from this sort of thing."

Charlie lifts his little leg and dampens a nearby patch of grass he's been sniffing. Obviously, he feels terrible.

Drew: How goes the supermodeling?

Me: How much water do you drink in a day?

Drew: I don't know. Some. Enough. Why?

Me: Triple it and then we'll talk.

Drew: Poor baby. Can I come see you tonight?

Me: I don't know. I'm walking. And I should probably practice my guitar at some point. I'm trying to impress my teacher with how good I'm getting.

Drew: You don't need to – trust me. You're a natural. And he's easily impressed. I have something I want to show you.

Me: Do you want to come to dinner? I'm making fish tacos.

Neither of those things deter him. He texts me back that he can be over as early as 6:00.

We can't fit three long-legged people at our little kitchen table so we eat outside at the picnic table set up by our grill. Because Mom always insisted on having a bouquet of fresh cut flowers out whenever we had company over, I stop and pick some up on my way home from work. Dad says nothing when I arrange them in a vase and place them at the end of the table but he softens considerably and is on his best behavior when Drew arrives.

"Kel tells me you play football?" Dad says politely, passing Drew the cantaloupe.

"Wide receiver. Yes, sir." He takes a spoonful and hands the bowl to me.

"We're hoping to catch a few of your games once your season gets underway."

"Thanks, I'd like that. This should be a pretty good year for us. Our O-line is finally coming together; our quarterback might actually get to stay on his feet for a change."

"The green salsa is pretty mild; the mango, muy caliente. Pick your poison." I offer both. Drew takes the mango.

Uncle Bryce and Justin drive up unexpectedly as we start eating. I look over at Dad suspiciously with a raised eyebrow. He just shrugs.

"Oh good, looks like we're just in time for dinner." Uncle Bryce hops out of his truck with his perennial grin. "Nice to see you again, McDreamy. Bunch up, Blondie. I almost didn't recognize you. You might want to steer clear of Shae for a while. You're starting to look Nordic." He scoots himself in next to me. Drew and I move over; Justin drops in next to Dad. "What's this?" Uncle Bryce is pointing at my food. "I didn't think supermodels ate?"

"I'm *not* a supermodel. Were you serious about wanting dinner? I can grab a couple more plates."

"We just ate. Your windows came in, Lucas. Justin and I loaded them in the back of the truck because it was empty – and who knows when that will happen again. Do you want us to just put them up in the rooms for you?"

"Give me ten minutes and I'll come help," Dad says, tucking into his taco.

"No rush. You coming to watch our girl on the catwalk Saturday?" Uncle Bryce asks, leaning forward so he can see Drew better.

"Wouldn't miss it."

"See? Did you hear that? *He wouldn't miss it.* I don't know what you're talking about, little brother. I think this young man's just fine. He is too, good enough for Kel." He winks at me and pops a piece of cantaloupe off my plate into his mouth.

"Do you want us to save you a seat with the family, Drew?" Justin asks. "Gran will be there the minute they start putting out front row chairs. She's already roped a few of us into stretching out and covering until everyone arrives."

"Think carefully before you commit," I warn him. "The McCoys are without mercy. And you're fresh meat."

"Our friend Chris wanted to come too; we'll help you save," Drew says.

I'm suddenly getting nervous. I better forego running entirely tomorrow morning so I can practice walking confidently some more.

"Hey, the more the merrier." Uncle Bryce gets to his feet. "Come on Justin, let's leave these fine folks to finish up their dinner in peace. See you later Squirt, McDreamy. Lucas, we'll start upstairs."

Drew helps Dad while I clean up from dinner. I answer his knock at the motorhome door with Charlie, furiously wagging his tail, tucked under my arm. "Consider this a blanket apology for my family." I make a face and place a hand over my heart. "I'm so sorry for everything they've put you through – and will put you through."

"I like them," Drew grins, stepping inside the motorhome and scratching Charlie's ears. "Your family seems pretty tight."

"We are. That's not the problem." I put Charlie down. "Would you like something to drink? Options haven't changed much since the last time you were here. They just might be served with less drama."

"I'm good, thanks." He's pulled his phone out of his back pocket and is scrolling through his messages. "Got something I want to show you."

"What is it?" He hands me his phone and I can tell he's battling to contain his excitement.

The Dotted T is sponsoring an amateur musician night the last Saturday of summer vacation. He's been given a performance slot. "What?! Drew, that's amazing!" Impulsively, I throw my arms around him and give him a big hug – the full McCoy. He smells *really* good. It's hard to let go, but I don't want to be weird so I do. After a bit. "I didn't even know this was something you were chasing. Why didn't you say something earlier?"

He shakes his head. "It's still all kind of new. I wasn't sure if it would go anywhere when I auditioned. You're the first person I've told."

"I am? Aw, thanks. I feel special." I'm teasing him but I really do. "What'll you sing?"

"It's a five song set, so maybe a few covers. But I've also been working on a couple of things of my own that I might want to try out."

"This is so wild. We need to pack the place. What kind of promotion will you get?"

"For me? None. I think they just promote the event in general."

"Well, Drew Jarrod," I sidle up to him. "*This* is your lucky day."

"Yeah?" He places his arms loosely around my waist, drawing me in with that killer smile of his, his eyes half-lidded and liquid – the boy can smolder. "It kinda feels like that."

It's my turn to blush, but I won't be deterred. "I just happen to be a whiz at graphic art. It's my thing. Don't laugh; it's true. I was president of the yearbook committee at my old school. I can make promos for you. We can use them to light up our socials – really get the word out."

His hands are slowly making their way up my back and into my hair. "You'd do that for me?"

"Of course. What are friends for?"

"Friends?" His voice has deepened; his lazy Texas drawl seems to be slowing time down so that I'm hanging on his every word. "Is that what we are, Kel?" The air between us has grown electric and heavy. He's looking at my lips and slowly bringing his closer to mine, waiting, asking. And it's too late to worry if I have any residual cilantro stuck in my teeth from dinner or if my breath smells like fish. I meet him in the middle and we kiss. And it's everything I dreamed a first kiss would be.

"I think," he whispers against my skin as he brushes his lips once more against mine and nudges my nose. "I'm going to *really* like being your friend." He exhales softly and leans his forehead against mine. I'm grateful he's still holding me in his arms because I'm feeling a bit weak-kneed and melty inside.

Suddenly, there's a sharp rap at the door, startling us both. We spring apart. "Five second warning and then I'm coming in!" Uncle Bryce yells from outside. He throws open the door and leaps up the stairs. Behind him Justin is grinning and shaking his head. "Just wanted to say good-bye. Also, your dad asked me to check on you. You know, in case there was any making out going on." He looks at my reddening face with some interest. "Thank heavens that's not the case." He rolls his eyes. "Do me a favor, will you McDreamy? Just be careful with her. Kel's our little girl – a lot of really big McCoy men will be seriously up in your grill if you hurt her. Come here." Uncle Bryce grabs Drew and hugs him, pounding him on the back like he does everyone in the family. "I have a feeling we're going to be seeing a lot of each other. Good thing you're so ugly."

"See *you* Saturday, Squirt." He squeezes me tight and tousles my hair as if I was still six. "You kids should probably call it a night. Supermodels need their beauty sleep. And I think your dad wanted to put in another good hour of work on the house, worry free."

"Okay, we will." I hug Justin good-bye. And just like a tornado touching down and whirling off, they're gone.

"You sure you still want to be my friend?" I say as we watch them drive away.

Drew snugs in close behind me and wraps his arms around my shoulders; I relax into him. "More than ever."

Friday morning I show up ten minutes early to the makeshift runway they've assembled in one of the conference rooms of a hotel in close proximity to the mall. I sign in and am given a name badge. A lot of tall (but sadly, still not as tall as me), long-legged girls are walking confidently around carrying their phones, wearing earbuds, and sipping from their water bottles - apparently Aunt Shae knows what she's talking about. I'm having 6th grade Nutcracker flashbacks.

Ashley, who already looks slightly harassed and like she might have the beginnings of a tension headache, gets on the microphone and asks us all to please be seated so we can get started. She'd asked for some fairly detailed measurements over the phone – I had to get Maggie to help me with some of them – when I accepted the job. I now know why; she's already assigned us all outfits. I have twelve. A guy named Dustin takes a picture of me in each one. Marta checks them for fit and makes sure there's nothing that needs to be repaired or altered. She's bagged all the accompanying accessories and placed them on the same hanger as the clothes they go with. She hangs everything on a rack with my name on it, in the order that they'll be worn and the shoes are placed underneath them. Aliyah will be doing my hair and there are three different style changes she's creating that correspond with the three different segments we're showing: Back to School, Game Night, and Homecoming. Stefan is doing my make-up in close quarters with Aliyah.

Preliminaries are brief. Ashley wants to run through the entire show twice in the time we have remaining today and we only stop to fix things in the first run-through. The second time she wants it to be as close to the show the audience will see tomorrow as she can get it.

I've never dressed and undressed so fast in my entire life nor have I had any help with either past the age of three, but you quickly lose any sense of shyness because everyone's all business. My final outfit of the first two segments is planned to be the quickest switch because there has to be a hair and make-up change as well. I can't tell if I'm nervous or just filled with adrenaline trying to make sure I'm where I need to be when I'm supposed to be there but I don't think my heart stops racing through either run.

Don't outwalk the music. Pick a point and fix on it. Chin slightly down, I try to calmly remind myself as I step out onto the stage and head down the runway. Backstage, chaos reigns. And then, finally, it's over.

"I want you here at 11:00 tomorrow – we'll feed you lunch. If you have any food allergies, let Bev know on your way out." Ashley sighs and then wearily hands her headset to her assistant.

"Because we're all going to want to eat right before we have to walk," A doe-eyed, olive skinned girl with unnaturally white teeth says, shaking her glossy curtain of silky dark hair. Her cheekbones are so pronounced they look like they could cut glass.

"Right?" I reply, mostly because I don't know what else to say. She probably *is* right. If tomorrow is anything like today my stomach will be in knots. "I'm Kel, by the way. You looked incredible in that silver strapless number. I really liked the shoes they paired it with."

"Thanks. I'm Cara. They're pretty but they pinch. Isn't that the way it always goes?"

I grin, gathering my purse. "Sadly, yes. Guess I'll see you tomorrow." I'm dashing to make my skin detoxification. Also, after the constant hydrating, I really have to go to the bathroom.

"Hey, there's my girl – all detoxed and glowing," Drew says with a smile that starts in his eyes. His hair is still wet from a recent shower and his bangs are sticking up more than usual. Pulling my earbuds out and pushing my sunglasses back onto the top of my head, I give him a big hug and a shy kiss. We arranged to meet after my work and his football practice at a park close to his house so we'd only have one car for the night. I changed out of my work clothes and into some shorts and running shoes earlier so I could practice walking for an hour before he arrived. He kisses the tip of my nose. "Hungry?"

"Starving. I sort of skipped lunch - no time to eat. But do you mind if we do drive-through? Gran just texted me. She's come through for me big time. I need to stop by her house for a minute to pick something up. It shouldn't take long."

Gran is always excited to see me but she's practically fawning all over Drew as I make introductions. "Please, come in, come in. Isn't this a lovely surprise?" Gran says, ushering us inside. "I've heard so much about you, Drew."

Drew shoots a look at me. "Should I be worried?"

"Absolutely. It was Uncle Bryce."

"Is that Kel I hear?" Pops asks, walking into the front hall where we're all standing.

"Kel *and her young man*, Drew Jarrod," Gran beams. I cringe. Drew catches my hand in his and breaks out his half-smile just for me.

"Nice to meet you, Drew. Bryce McCoy – but we've got a few of them around here so everyone just calls me B. Or Pops. That works too." Pops extends his hand, He's wearing shorts and tennis shoes but I can tell he just got back from golfing because the front pocket of his shirt still has a couple of tees in it. Even having shrunk with age he's still taller than Drew.

"Sir," Drew says, shaking his hand.

"Do you kids have time to come in and sit for a bit?" Gran asks.

I shake my head. "Sorry Gran, but we're in a bit of a rush at the moment. We're taking pictures of Drew tonight for some promotional materials I'm helping him with. Drew's a musician – he's performing at the Dotted T in a couple of weeks."

"A musician?" Gran smiles at him and then looks at me with a twinkle in her eye. "You must be very talented. I hope you'll come back and play something for us sometime soon."

"I will," Drew promises.

"We'll hold you to that, young man. Well, let me get those cookies for you then so you two can be on your way. I've already got them packaged up," Gran says, disappearing into the kitchen.

"You know you're the greatest, right?" I tell her when she emerges carrying a large plastic container filled with heaven. I kiss her wrinkled cheek. "I can't thank you enough, Gran. I promise I'll help you make more for the hordes Sunday."

"These smell *incredible*," Drew says, the container settled on his lap. We're folded into the Mini on our way back into the city. "What are they?"

"Gran's famous chocolate chip oatmeal cookies – they're life changing. She made them for me so I could give them out to my team tomorrow as kind of a thank-you. When Gran says she wants to help she doesn't mean maybe. Want one?"

"Seriously?" He's got the lid off, his teeth solidly into one, and is making some sort of contented chewing noise bordering on ecstasy. By the time we get to Strings he's already wheedled three more out of me.

We decided to stage his photo shoot in the studio where Drew gives lessons. I can Photoshop in a more exciting background later but it's a quiet space where we won't be interrupted and we've got access to as many musical props as we want, making it ideal.

Drew brought in a few different shirts so we could experiment with some different looks. I've got Mom's camera and one of the two lenses I actually know how to use. I put him on a stool in the center of the room.

"Okay. Sing...something." I've got him in focus and made a few adjustments for the lighting. "And try to just ignore me."

Drew grins and begins crooning the opening lines to *Row, Row, Row Your Boat*, which he then transitions into Kane Brown's *There Goes My Everything*, his eyes flirting audaciously with me as he sings and plays along on his acoustic guitar. I circle him, snapping pictures as rapidly as I can at as many different angles as I can manage given that he keeps making me laugh.

"Stop looking at me, dork."

"I can't, baby – you're the best looking thing in the room. *She's everything I wanna need. And then she's even more.*"

We scroll through the first series of shots we've captured, Drew's chin over my shoulder, his arm around my waist as we look at them together. The boy can't take a bad picture – even with me working the camera. A couple are stand outs. "What do you think?" I ask. "Change into the black shirt just so we have some options?"

He does.

Saturday morning I quietly dress in my running gear so as not to wake Dad. I don't know what time he finally called it a night but it was much later than usual. I woke up briefly at 2:17 and his bed was still empty. He doesn't even stir as Charlie and I slip out of the motorhome.

Running is something I started doing shortly after Mom died as a way to deal with the crushing reality that I was suddenly motherless; I figure I can always turn to drugs and alcohol or intensive therapy later. There's something soothing about your body kicking into a rhythm just above discomfort and fatigue. Your lungs expand and your mind clears and for a short while your body and brain work in harmony toward one simple and straightforward goal: keeping one foot in front of the other. It's highly addictive. Because I'm a junkie I try to get a fix of 5-7 miles/day. I need it. I do.

When I can't: Sundays (my recovery day), I had the flu once for a week back in April, when I have to practice *walking* – something some people can do in their sleep; it throws me off my schedule, leaving me a bit jittery and unsettled. With the fashion show looming over my head I'm a full blown bundle of nerves.

I stop after our expanded loop has turned into 11 miles, not because I've finally managed to sort myself out, but because I feel guilty for dragging Charlie along to deal with my issues in this scorching heat. I can't wait for Dad to wake up so I can take a shower and cool down. Peeling off my shoes and socks and leaving them in a little pile with my electronics, Charlie and I dive off our dock and into the shockingly cold but refreshing depths of the lake.

"Guess what, buddy?" We're lying stretched out on the wooden slats of the dock in the hot Texas sun, already mostly dry. "I'm going to be wearing heels today. Walking and wearing heels. In front of a lot of people. Me. Grace Kelly McCoy." In response to my obvious distress, Charlie's eyes shift ever so slightly under his furry brows. I don't think he has the energy for anything more. "Yeah, I know. What was I thinking? I'm so going to fall."

"I'm so going to fall," I tell Jake miserably from between my knees. He pushed my head down there seconds earlier because he was worried I was going to pass out. It's a good thing my first hairstyle is basically my every day hair or Aliyah would have both our scalps – even with Gran's cookies to smooth my way.

"You're not going to fall, Kel." Drew is rubbing my back. He and Jake slipped unnoticed into the staging area in stealth mode in response to my desperate text for help.

Jake is watching the line-up closely. I'm last to go on in the rotation, four more until I need to be out there. "So what?" He calmly kneels down beside me and gently pushes my chin up, forcing me to look him squarely in the eye. "You fall all the time, Kel. Who has more experience with falling than you? No one. You know how to recover, that's all that matters. Plus, the McCoys have the entire front section. You stumble, no one will be able to see it over the top of us. We got you covered."

"Yeah?"

Jake's steadfast blue eyes are filled with a quiet confidence. "Yeah. Come on, Squirt." He pulls me to my feet and tosses my hair back behind my shoulders. "You got this. Now get out there and make us proud." And he gives me a little push toward the direction of the stage.

I got this. Okay. Don't outwalk the music. Pick a point and fix on it. Chin slightly down. I take a deep breath and throw my shoulders back and step out onto the runway. *And don't throw up.*

I do stumble – once – but it's at the very end when all the models have joined me on stage wearing their prom finery for the finale and it's more because the girl to my left tripped on the train of her gown in 4" heels. Righting her throws me slightly off balance but Jake's right. I do have mad recovery skills. And an embarrassingly loud rooting section.

"Was that your family sitting in the front?" Cara asks as we hand off our gowns for hanging on their racks.

"Sorry. I think this might've been the first fashion show for some of them. We tend to do more sporting event kind of things."

"That would explain the posters."

"And the cheering," Stefan says, shuddering as he gathers his tools. "I thought we might be in real danger of them trying to start the wave."

But not even Stefan could resist Gran's cookies.

"For me?" He raises a perfectly groomed eyebrow at me in surprise as I hand him the little package tied with a bow.

"I know: Carbs. But they're gluten-free. And absolutely divine. " I kiss him carefully on the cheek so as not to leave a lipstick mark. "Thanks for making me look pretty, Stefan."

He rolls his eyes. "Not a chore, darling. Your skin is practically porcelain." Deftly extracting an angled brush from his apron, he offers it to me. "Perfect cat eye flick. Every. Time. But dry it carefully, upside down like I showed you. And *no* harsh cleansers."

"Really?! Thank you!" I throw my long arms around him, sincerely moved. "You're the sweetest. I'll take good care of it, I promise."

"There's our girl!" Pops says with Gran and Dad at his side as I step out of the staging area and into the large space that is rapidly being cleared of chairs and the portable runway. My cousin Landry, a part-time assistant coach for the Longhorns' swim team lets rip his distinctively piercing whistle – not for the first time this afternoon – and there is more cheering, followed by a lot of laughing and hugging.

"You two looked like you were having a pretty good time," I say to Drew and Chris, who appear to have already become BFFs with all my cousins.

"Your Uncle Nick invited us to the family BBQ tonight at his place. Cade and Landry are taking the boat out," Drew says.

My cousin Sam drapes an arm over my shoulder. "Try and talk Jake into coming, Kel. He thinks he needs some 'alone time' with Rachel."

"And *that's* why he has a girlfriend and you don't," Trey says, thwacking Sam on the chest. Trey is Uncle Bryce's firstborn son and following the McCoy tradition of passing down the name "Bryce" through the oldest son of the oldest son, is *also* named Bryce. To avoid any confusion we call him Trey. Trey's firstborn son, Bryce IV, is Q. You have to feel for Claire; I'm not sure she realized what she was getting into when she married Trey.

"We got to split, Kel; Q and Noah have a birthday party at 4:00," Trey says, hugging me again. "Good job up there today, Squirt. I was seriously impressed." He scoops up his youngest, Brody, and throws him onto his shoulders. Behind Drew's back Trey's eyes grow wide as he looks at Drew and gives me the big thumbs up.

"Meet you back at the motorhome?" Dad says to me, handing Justin back his sleeping baby.

"Oh, okay. That makes sense. How about if I just meet you at Uncle Nick and Aunt Jill's?" I say to Drew. "I need to get this make-up off my face and take these pins out of my hair and grab a swimsuit anyway. I'm sure the guys will take care of you until I get there. You've got the address?"

Uncle Bryce wraps a consoling arm around Drew. "Don't worry McDreamy. At the end of the night I bet she goes home with you."

4

"Be True to Your School"

Beach Boys

Two things happen as a direct result of the fashion show: I can no longer show up at a McCoy family function without Drew in tow or a rock solid reason for why he's not by my side. Apparently: *he has his own family*, doesn't count. The second: Kirstie Adderson wants to sign me to her agency. She calls and asks if she can meet with me sometime soon to "discuss my future" so I drive over to Adderson Modeling Management Tuesday during my lunch hour. She's sitting behind her desk in a very posh office with a view of the city behind her.

"You're taller than most. That may limit us option wise, especially if a client wants side by sides – finding a male model to balance you out won't be easy – but you're absolutely magnetic, Kel. I watched you own that runway; I couldn't take my eyes off you." Kirstie places demurely folded hands in front of her while I look in surprise at the contract she's just offered me. "That's not something you can teach. Either you have it or you don't. You do. I'd like to see where that could take you."

Dad isn't so sure. I drive straight from her office back to his. He has a break in his schedule and is using it to pour over house blueprints and call vendors, but when I softly knock on his office door he wraps up his call. I hand him the contract. I'm a minor; it requires his signature. "Modeling?" He's leafing through the pages in confusion. "I don't know, Kel. This just all seems a little sudden. You've never even talked about wanting this until a couple of weeks ago."

"I didn't. I mean I didn't even know it was an option. Let's be honest – it wasn't. I've been awkward and all knees and elbows most of my life; I tower over practically everyone. And I don't think I actually settled into my face until last year. But Kirstie thinks I have something."

Dad rubs his temples. "You do, sweetheart. I just don't know if *this* is the best use of your time and energy. From what I've seen and heard, the modeling industry can be brutal. I'm not sure I want that for you."

"I get that Dad, I do. I can't really explain why I want this – it terrifies me. Jake and Drew had to talk me down from a ledge Saturday to get me to go on. But then I did. And I felt...alive." This feels important to get right. "I don't want to play it safe anymore. I want to take chances and put myself out there. Even if I fall. That's what Mom did. Every day. She really *lived* her life."

Dad smiles but it's sad and distant. "Yeah, she did."

The first official job I book under Adderson Modeling Management is catalogue work for a medical supplies company – I'm wearing scrubs and lab coats. Because summer vacation is winding down, Cheryl has pretty much taken over my responsibilities at Dad's office and that's a good thing because the shoot eats up most of my day. It's almost 5:00 before I'm able to check my phone and see how Drew's promo launch is going.

Me: 1,927 retweets?!! What?!

Drew: I know. Crazy, right? My Instagram is blowing up.

Me: It IS crazy. You ready for this?

Drew: Think so. Been rehearsing pretty hard. Row, Row, Row Your Boat's starting to sound pdg.

I manage to book one more job the last Friday before school starts. It's for a local designer with a Pilates clothing line. The photographer gives me the creeps. He's handsy and has a bad habit of staring at my chest whenever he's talking to me – and I'm not *that* much taller than him.

You wanted this, I remind myself.

Saturday night, Cade and Jake bring their girlfriends, Sarah – whom I've never met – and Rachel, to Drew's gig at the Dotted T. Landry and Sam are flying solo. "But the night is still young," Sam says, waggling his eyebrows and crowding in next to me with a drink in hand as he checks out the lay of the land. A few tables over Matt, Travon, and Chris are sitting with a bunch of their friends. Striker has his tongue down the throat of a different girl. The place is packed.

Some of the performers are quite good. A couple of them could probably stand a little more practice time under their belts but I'm just impressed they had the courage to get up there in the first place. I couldn't do it.

"Wish me luck," Drew says when it's finally his turn. He pushes long fingers through his hair, looking impossibly handsome and slightly nervous as he starts to get to his feet.

I reach for his neck and kiss his cheek. "Good luck."

"Rock it dude," Landry grins, fist bumping him.

"He *can* sing. Right?" Cade says as Drew makes his way to the stage.

"I dunno." Sam shrugs as a lot of girls start screaming their approval when they get a good look at Drew. "I don't think it's gonna matter. We're not gonna be able to hear him one way or the other."

"How y'all doing?" Drew is at the mic, looking out over the raucous crowd as he tunes his guitar. "Thanks for coming out tonight. Wow. You guys are loud. Thank you. I'm gonna play a few of my favorites for you – hope they're some of yours too." He opens with Snow Patrol's "Chasing Cars" and then transitions into The Script's "Breakeven." When he plays the first few notes of Shawn Mendes' "Mercy" the girls in the crowd go wild and start to sing along.

He's squinting into the bright lights as he strums through the last notes and then he grins. "Hey everybody, my mom just walked in. I wasn't sure if she'd be able to make it tonight because she's working a double shift at the hospital. Would you help me make her feel welcome? Put your hands together for hard working moms and nurses everywhere!" The crowd cheers and whistles their loud support. "In her honor I'm going to switch things up a little if that's okay. She likes to dance. Mostly in our kitchen when she thinks no one else is watching. And she really likes to dance to this. So, Mom, this is for you."

Drew plucks through a beautifully intricate intro and then sings in perfect Spanish, Luis Fonsi's "Despacito."

"Did you know he could do that?" Sam asks, hitting me on the shoulder. I'm still trying to find his mom in the crowd but there are too many people in the way. "Dude totally needs to come with us on our next surfing trip to Mexico."

"Thank you. Te amo, Mama." He adjusts his mic and pulls a stool over, a huge smile on his face. It's obvious he's having a blast up there and that this is what he was born to do. "I'd like to close my set out tonight with a little something of my own." He starts to slow things down with the beginnings of a sweet and tripping melody. "It's about...a girl." His eyes find mine. "Hope you like it."

I'm all tangled in her smile,
Moon River in her eyes.

She floored me when she walked right in
She just don't realize
My head is filled with her perfume.
All I can see is her.
She moves, she breathes; I feel that heat.
It all changed for me
In the space of a heartbeat

So now it's you and me girl,
Taking on the world.
And we stand tall when we're side by side,
And I think we're going to make it.
You reach for me and I take your hand;
And we play our song on repeat.
Baby, I was already yours
In the space of a heartbeat.

Girl, you had me at hello.
Yeah. In the space of a heartbeat.

Drew holds the last few notes and then quietly strums them away, his dark head bent over his guitar as the crowd erupts in applause. Landry lets rip his piercing whistle.

He wrote a song for me.

"The really sad thing is, he's gonna come back to our table and all these women are gonna follow him over."

Sam rolls his eyes as he leans back in his chair. "I'm getting a high school kid's leftovers."

"What makes you think they're going to want you?" Cade smirks as he empties his glass and stretches an arm around Sarah.

He wrote a song. *For me.*

Jake tugs at my elbow. "Kel."

Drew is threading his way through the crowd, making his way toward us, his arm around a woman I'm guessing is his mother. I quickly get to my feet.

"Mom, *this* is Kel. Kel, my mom, Gabriela Davis." She's almost painfully thin but her edges are unexpectedly softened by her radiant beauty. She has Drew's olive skin and the same thick, dark hair, which she's wound up in a tidy bun. She obviously came straight from the hospital; she's still wearing her uniform.

"It's so nice to meet you, Mrs. Davis." I give her the compulsory McCoy hug. She's not short but I've got at least six inches on her.

"For me too. I've wanted to put a face to the name so frequently on my son's lips," Mrs. Davis says in her soft lilting Spanish accent. Behind her, Sam is grinning like an idiot.

Drew, who is surprisingly cagey about his father, finally opened up about him late one night when we were sitting at the end of our dock with Charlie, staring out at the reflection of the full moon on the water. His parents met when his dad was assigned to Morón Air Base straight out of the academy and his mom was working as a nurse. They soon married and he brought his new bride, who spoke little English at the time, and young son back with him from Spain when he was ordered to Randolph Air Force Base in San Antonio. Their marriage fell apart shortly after that. Armed with her newly minted citizenship and a license to practice nursing in Texas, Gabriela packed up her broken heart, her belongings and Drew, and moved them all to Austin where she'd found a job. They've been here ever since. His father, not so much.

"We're about to grab something to eat. Can you stay?" Drew asks her.

Gabriela shakes her head. "It took me forever to find parking – that's why I was so late. I'm sorry mi hijo, but my break is over and it was busy tonight. I need to get back to the hospital."

Drew and I walk her back to her car. "You must come very soon to our home for dinner. Drew, you will arrange for this?" Gabriela says, kissing both of my cheeks.

"On it, Mom."

She whispers something in Spanish to him and then slides behind the wheel of her Ford Focus and drives away. "She likes you." Drew grins by way of an explanation, catching my hand in his as we start to make our way back to the Dotted T.

"Well, I *really* like her son." I turn into the crook of his arm, stopping us on the street, and I might've placed my forefinger in the pronounced dip just above his flawless upper lip – because I could – right before bestowing a kiss there and thinking to myself: *In this moment, I am perfectly happy.*

Important to recognize those moments when they happen, I think, because they never seem to last.

I've had first days at new schools before, transitioning from grade school to middle and then finally to high school. But those were mostly building changes with the same classmates I'd grown up with year after year and an occasional new face thrown in here and there. At Barton I'm the new face. And I wake up knowing that my mom – who always made the first day of school epic: we'd go shopping together for the perfect, elevate the school uniform outfit; hunt down the most ridiculous, funkiest school supplies to throw in with what was blandly unavoidable; and choose a theme song for the new year, which she would then blast at high volume when I came down for breakfast that morning and whenever she felt I needed a pick-me-up throughout the rest of the school year – is gone. The void seems overwhelmingly huge and unbreachable.

So I already feel a bit wobbly and unsure when I try to slide into English lit relatively unnoticed, not easy when you're a 6′2″ girl, and discover with dismay an alphabetical order seating chart projected onto the white board. *Grace Kelly McCoy* has been assigned the second seat of the third row.

Dad and I met with the Head of School briefly at registration and Dad made it perfectly clear that while Grace Kelly was indeed my given name, we would be enrolling me under *Kel.* Apparently someone didn't get the message. Strike one.

Putting someone of my height in front of three other students who are inevitably shorter and therefore unable to see without hanging over the side of their desks is mortifying and precisely why I always try to get to class early so I can get the back row. Strike two.

With a start I realize everyone is whispering and staring at me so I quickly take my assigned seat; head held high, back straight, a growing knot in my stomach and a tight lump in my throat as the whispering grows: *She's* Grace Kelly?

I've never exactly been part of the popular crowd but they're always easy to spot. I glance at the seating chart as I open my copy of Forster's *Howard's End* and pretend to start reading it while waiting for class to start: Whitney Halloway, a short, perky blonde to my left – and given the way she constantly tosses her hair, I'd bet money she's a cheerleader – is definitely in that upper echelon. She appears to be holding court at her desk; several girls are pressing her breathlessly for details about her recent trip to Europe but she already sounds slightly bored and her smile has developed a pasted-on quality. "The French," she says airily. "They're impossible."

I wait, curious for her to expound on what it is, exactly, that makes an entire nationality impossible but she does not. Instead she gushes, "Blake!" And although I haven't known Whitney long enough to know if she's being sincere, she does seem genuinely excited. "I wasn't sure if you'd be back in time for first day."

Blake *Michaels* - he slides into the open desk behind me - is obviously also part of the in crowd. Everyone seems to be calling for his attention. His long legs stretch out on either side of my seat, white pants rolled up a couple of times at the bottom to reveal tanned legs and no socks with his deck shoes as he fist bumps a few guys, tells someone their new boat is sweet, and then settles in. "Grace Kelly? Well, well," he says and I realize he must be leaning forward in his desk because his voice is suddenly very close to my left ear. "Hey, new girl."

I turn around in my seat. "It's Kel, actually."

Blake's smile broadens, flashing a row of even, white teeth that seem even whiter against his summer tan. He has light gray eyes and dirty blonde hair, artfully styled to look casually messy, and is saved from being almost too pretty by a bit of scruff. "Nice to meet you, *Grace Kelly*." He winks.

"How was St. Thomas?" Whitney asks Blake, trying to coax him into an intimate circle of shared favorite exotic spots they've both actually been to. I return to my book.

"Warm." But Blake isn't about to be sidetracked. His voice is back in my ear. "Let me know if you need someone to show you around. Because I'm *very* available."

Mr. Oliveria walks in just as the second bell rings and stands for a moment at the front straightening his collar and surveying his class. "Welcome back everyone, I'm sure you're just as eager to get started today as I am but it looks like we're going to have to do a little reshuffling first so people can see. May we please have Mr. Michaels and Ms. McCoy move to the back of their row and everyone else move up?"

We stand. Hair product not included, Blake is still slightly taller than me. That surprises me. "After you, Grace Kelly," he says with a grand sweep of his hand.

"It's Kel," I mutter under my breath and take the second to last seat in.

"Get a good look at your neighbors," Mr. Oliveria says, reaching for his copy of *Howard's End*. "You're going to be seeing them there the entire semester."

Strike three. And the day just officially got started.

"It was HORRIBLE," I tell Jake. He's leaving for Cambridge in two days and very sweetly wanted to go rock climbing with me one more time before heading back to school. "I have three classes with Blake and two with Whitney and between them they seem determined to make my life a living hell."

Jake waits for me to move up to the next foothold before adjusting his position.

"I couldn't get my name sorted out until lunch and by that time it was too late. I'm Grace Kelly. Both barrels, not just *Grace*. Only my teachers call me Kel and even they sometimes forget."

He nods sympathetically, his hands reaching upward.

"And I already have so much homework; it's crazy. It's like the teachers are all trying to make up for a summer of having nothing to grade," I sigh. "But actually, I got a good start on it over lunch – it's amazing what you can accomplish when you eat alone."

"Nice try, Squirt. Something good must've happened today. Dig deep."

I stretch out and push off with my right leg. "Both the girls volleyball AND basketball coaches tracked me down."

"Kel McCoy and team sports?" Jake grins.

"Yeah. I'm a real disappointment."

"You and me both. And you didn't have to follow Cade and Landry. I'm the McCoy who can't."

I've reached the top. "Psh. I'll remind you of that when you're accepting your Nobel Prize for curing cancer or building better hair plugs. What about Rachel?" I say, a bit breathless. "You two still a thing?"

He shrugs as we start to make our way back down. "We're trying out the merits of the long distance relationship. I've been told there are a few. We'll see. She might meet someone better dropping me off at the airport."

"Now who's the Debby Downer?"

"Yeah, I know. Got time to drown our sorrows in a banana split? I'll treat."

"Ooh! May I have three scoops *and* extra sprinkles?"

Jake rolls his eyes. "If you ever get out of that harness. You've got homework and I've got a hot woman waiting on me. I hope you can shovel all that down fast. And we're doing drive through."

"Geez Jake, love sure has made you pushy."

The next day in chemistry I'm *assigned* a lab partner. No one else volunteers so Mr. Frantz puts me with the only other friendless person in the class: Becca Bryson. Becca has charcoal rimmed eyes, a nose ring, and aggressively purple hair that is even more shocking against her abnormally pale skin. Her nails are painted black and she has a recent tattoo of a spike driven into her left wrist with blood spurting out of it – her skin is still red and irritated around the ink.

"Back to school gift to myself," Becca says, shrugging when she notices me noticing it.

I pull out my troll pencil topper. Not at all practical with a mechanical pencil but I just needed *something* to remind me of my mom. Becca stares at me for a moment and then reluctantly grins. "You're weird, McCoy."

"Thank you."

"So, you just move here?"

"I did. From Chicago."

"Why Austin?"

"My mom passed away in January. I think my dad just wanted to be close to his family. Austin is home for him." It comes out smoothly with no audible catch in my voice, just as rehearsed.

Real compassion stirs amongst all that eyeliner. "That sucks. Sorry."

"Thanks. How about you? Have you always lived here?"

"Born and raised. Probably will die here," Becca says, flipping her chem textbook open. "And if so, please God let it happen before lunch."

"What happens at lunch?"

She looks at me like I'm an idiot. "High school."

At noon I find her eating alone at one of the little tables that dot the campus grounds just outside of the cafeteria, earbuds in, her purple hair being blown gently about in the breeze. "May I join you?" I ask her. I have to repeat it a moment later when she pulls her buds out.

"Why?"

"I'm hungry?"

She grudgingly pulls her lunch sack over. I place mine on the table. "You call that lunch?" She grimaces as I start to take out my little containers filled with mostly vegetables – brightly colored and carefully combined for maximum taste – but vegetables none the less. I dump in the grilled chicken I've managed to keep cold and pull out a fork.

"I sure do."

"Gross."

"What are you eating?" She's not. She hasn't even opened hers up though her sack is clearly full.

"NOT animal flesh."

"Vegetarian?"

"Vegan."

"Oh, I'm sorry." I'm suddenly hesitating. I ran ten miles this morning; I'm starving. I need some protein, but I also don't want to offend Becca's sensibilities.

"Whatever. Just eat it, McCoy."

I do. And every time I put a forkful of chicken in my mouth, Becca balefully watches me chew like I just swung the ax, ripped out the feathers, threw the carcass on a hot flame and am now devouring its flesh – all in front of its children. I've suddenly lost my appetite. "So, have you always been a vegan?"

"Since I was five. My family visited a farm and the kids there were raising 4H *projects.* It was the first time I made the connection between what I was petting and what I was eating. It made me sick. I threw up all the way home."

I'm contemplating my inevitable conversion to veganism, at least during school hours, in order to survive lunchtime with Becca when Blake Michaels slides in close next to me on our bench, smelling expensive and knowing he looks good. He's flanked by two similarly styled, lanky and languid friends who apparently prefer to stand. Which is just fine, the bench is already a little crowded.

"Grace Kelly." Oozing charm, he throws his arm loosely around my shoulder and leans in. "I was wondering where you got off to. I thought you might be lost."

"Looks like you found me."

"Come eat lunch with us. Our table's just over there." He points to a mostly coupled off group of Barton's elite who are laughing and chatting with each other, some of whom are watching us curiously from behind their Ray-Bans. Whitney, strangely, isn't among them.

"Thanks, maybe another time? I'm already eating lunch today. With Becca." It's hard to tell who's more incredulous: Becca or Blake. I almost expect her to publically denounce me for the disgusting meat eater that I am and state, for the record, that I forced my company on her. But she doesn't. Instead she stares at her tattoo like her life depends on it.

"Well, all right then." Blake shakes his head as he gets to his feet. "You have fun, Grace Kelly."

"Is that really your name?" Becca finally says as she watches me playing idly with my carrot sticks.

"It is." I sigh and push whatever's left of my lunch back into its bag. "My mom had a thing for classic movies and my dad never could say 'no' to her. My friends and family all call me 'Kel' – it's a little easier to live with."

Between us, on the table, my cell is buzzing. *Kirstie Adderson, Adderson Modeling Management* lights up the screen. I quickly flip the display over and out of view as I pick my phone up. "Would you excuse me, Becca? I need to take this."

"Your casting for Tropically Kissed went well. They've expressed interest in using you as one of their swimsuit models," Kirstie says, jumping right in as she always does – why waste valuable time with hello? Tropically Kissed sells tanning products. They're gearing up to roll out a massive marketing campaign for their new, improved, sunless lotion. "This is huge, Kel. It'll mean a lot of exposure for you."

Where swimsuits are concerned, it usually does. "Wow. Okay, when and where?"

The *when* is this Friday, when I'm supposed to be in school – Dad's going to flip. Kirstie gives me strict instructions to basically not eat anything between now and then (so, no more ice cream) and to work out as much as I can. Oh, and drink more water, which I don't think is humanly possible. Twenty minutes later she sends a tersely worded text: EXFOLIATE. MOISTURIZE. WAX.

Good advice. Friday morning I'm standing stark naked and truant in a little booth, being Tropically Kissed by a tanning technician wielding an airbrush. She's very thorough. In her expert hands I'm not at all orange or streaked but have a healthy, coconut scented glow. I'm then wrapped in a robe and sent to hair and make-up and finally, handed a coral colored bikini I would wear in front of Gran.

The shoot takes up the entire day and even goes a bit long. By the time I'm done I'm rushing through traffic to make Drew's first home game; the first quarter has already started when I finally find Sam and Landry in the stands. "Westlake is up a touchdown." Landry gives me the update as they scoot to make room for me between them. "But they had the ball first. You just missed an awesome catch by Drew."

"Nachos?" Sam says offering his up. "Whoa, Squirt. You look...different."

"It's the hair." I didn't have time to brush it out so it's still very big with beach waves – and I already have enough hair on my head for two people. "Oh, yeah. I've also been Tropically Kissed."

Sam sniffs at my neck. "You smell like a pineapple."

"Coconut," I correct him as Matt throws a blistering spiral with some serious heat on it to Drew, who rises up in traffic and gloriously catches it at the four-yard line, landing one foot solidly in before being shoved out. On the next play Travon rams it through for a touchdown and Chris kicks it between the uprights for the extra point. We jump up and down and hoot and holler at the top of our lungs with the rest of the MacArthur fans through the entire thing.

"I forgot how much I loved high school football." Landry's grin is ear to ear as we once again take our seats.

The Knights end up sealing the win with a last minute, 42 yard field goal. Chris is the hero of the day.

"There'll be no living with him now," Striker grumbles as we stand around waiting for the team to come out of the locker room.

"You were AMAZING!" I tell Chris, throwing my arms around him the moment he's done high fiving and fist bumping Landry and Sam. "I was so nervous for you and you absolutely nailed it."

He blushes. "Thanks Kel. Drew will be out in a sec, coach is making him ice his ankle."

"I think we're going to split," Sam says, giving me a hug. "Landry's itching to check out a new bar that just opened downtown."

"And by 'Landry' he means 'Sam.'" Landry rolls his eyes as he kisses me on the cheek. "I'm on wingman duty. And depending on how many times he gets rejected, possibly designated driver. Tell Drew 'good job' for us?"

"I will," I promise.

I'm chatting with Matt and his girlfriend, Ginny, when Travon suddenly picks me up from behind and bear hugs me like I'm not an unwieldy 6′2″, bruising most of my ribs. "Hey girl! Hmm mmm, you smell *good.*" He deposits me in front of Drew, who's wearing a fair number of turf streaks on his uniform and even a little blood but is still smoking hot. Sweaty and tired looks good on him. "I *definitely* got to get me a woman."

"Good idea," Drew says. "Because this one's taken." I could melt in those eyes. "Hey, beautiful." He kisses me on the temple as he pulls me close. "Glad you could make it."

I wrap my arms around his waist. "Sam and Landry were impressed. They would've stayed to tell you that themselves but Sam's on the prowl."

"Yeah? What did you think?"

"I think," I say, wrapping a fistful of his jersey to pull him close and looking up at him through my lashes. "I need a shirt with your name and number on it to wear to your games. I want to make it perfectly clear you're all mine."

I may not have a lot of experience with flirting, but I'm catching up real fast.

5

"Cause you had a bad day"
Daniel Powter

"Hi, I'm Kel. Nice to meet you." I slide onto a chair next to Camila, the sixth grade student I've been assigned to mentor. She looks me up and down. She's not impressed. I'm more than a little intimidated by this twelve year old jacked with attitude but if modeling has taught me anything at all it's never let them see you sweat.

"You're...tall."

I smile at her. "It's mostly hair." Tucked into my notebook case is the list Camila's teacher just handed me of the assignments Camila is either behind on or needs help with. It's long. "Tell me a little bit about yourself?"

"I hate school. And I really hate that they're making me do this." Her arms are crossed and she's already done with this conversation.

"Fair enough. What *do* you like?"

She rolls her eyes. "Dancing, I guess."

"Really? What kind of dancing?"

"Hip hop."

"I've always wanted to learn how to dance like that. I did ballet for ten years; they're complete opposites. I'm not sure I could ever unbend enough to be that loose. You look like you'd be very good at it."

There might be the teeniest, tiniest, glimmer of movement in my direction. Let's call it glacial. "You did ballet?"

"I did, in Chicago, before I moved here this summer. Tell me about your dancing? Where do you do it?"

"Mostly with my friends," Camila shrugs. "My friend Carmen has a really big basement so we all go over there."

"I'd like to see that some time."

She doesn't believe me. She leans back in her chair. "*This rich, skinny, white girl thinks she wants to be one of us*," she says in Spanish to one of her friends and they laugh.

I took French because of ballet. It hasn't proven to be all that useful for anything else, but French and Spanish are close enough that I don't need a translation. I consider her for a moment. "I'm going to tell you something about myself that I don't tell a lot of people." My voice grows very quiet. Camila has to lean in slightly to hear what I'm saying. "My mom was killed in a car accident in January; she was hit head on by a drunk driver who swerved into her lane. Sometimes I think that's the only way she could've been taken off this earth because she was the most alive person I've ever known." I smile wistfully, that flash of pain never quite goes away. "I look at time differently now. I don't take it for granted. I want to cram as much into my life as I possibly can. Just because I've only experienced ballet doesn't mean I'm done with dance. You know how to do something I don't. Teach me."

"You said you didn't think you could do it."

I shake my head. "I said it would be hard for me. It's not the same thing."

"It would be weird, me teaching you."

"It *would* be weird," I admit. "But no weirder than me sitting here tutoring you in…" I pull out the paper. "Whatever's on this list."

"Everyone expects you to do that."

"They do?"

"Yeah. You're trying to get into some fancy college right? I'm like something you're just gonna put down on your application so you can get in."

"If we're lucky what we're doing here will get *you* into a fancy college. The hip hop is strictly for me. Trust me, I don't understand it either but college admissions boards don't seem to get the awesomeness of hip hop as a life skill." I've laid all my cards on the table. "Come on Camila, school this ballet chica. You know you can't wait to embarrass me in front of all of your friends."

She slowly grins. "I'm pretty tough."

"Yeah? I believe it. So am I."

"Okay. You got yourself a deal. When do we start?"

I push over the list. "Right now."

"So, how did it go?" Becca asks as she dumps her backpack into the backseat of the Mini in the middle of the parking lot at San Sebastian Middle School at the end of our respective tutoring sessions.

"I've got a hip hop lesson tonight."

"What?"

I fold myself into the driver's seat and buckle in. "Look for it to be posted all over the internet tomorrow," I sigh. "There's no way it doesn't go viral."

The address Camila gave me is for Carmen's house, the one with the basement. A short, elderly woman with plump, weathered edges who I assume is Carmen's grandmother answers the front door, wiping her hands on an apron as we introduce ourselves. Her graying hair is severely pulled back into a tight, little bun and she's giving me a shy smile, but she's shaking her head. "Un momento, por favor, I no speak English." She waves me in. A bunch of little boys are noisily kicking a soccer ball around the front yard.

I switch to French. *Our languages are not the same but close enough that maybe we can understand each other better this way, I think?*

She smiles at me and slowly nods.

"I work with Camila at her school and she and Carmen and some of their friends are going to teach me how to dance like they do. I hope that's okay with you?"

She grins and says in Spanish, *"If it's okay with you, it's okay with me."*

"I know it's a school night. We'll try and keep it to an hour. Thank you for letting us do this in your home, Senorita Mendes. It's very kind of you."

She shows me the door to the basement, though I could've just followed the sound of the thumping music. She rolls her eyes heavenward. "Buenas suerte." *Good luck.*

The girls are working on a routine when I walk down the stairs. One by one they stop, suddenly self-conscious. I can tell by the look on Camila's face that she's now second guessing her earlier decision. Maybe I looked less intimidating seated. I toss my backpack aside. "Hey everyone, I'm Kel. You guys look great. Camila thinks you can teach me how to dance like that. But I've got these crazy long arms and legs so you're going to have patient with me. I promise I'll try and keep up."

Camila puts me in the back row between Eren and Analy. I apologize to both of them in advance and warn them they might want to give me a little extra elbow room. We're pop and locking to Nicki Minaj's *Super Bass.* On the wall across from us, lined up close together so you can *mostly* see yourself between the framed interruptions, are several full-length mirrors. I'm so much taller than the rest of the girls it's almost ludicrous.

Camila wasn't kidding. She *is* tough. On me. For good reason. When you've had posture drilled into you your whole life it's really hard to just throw that out the window for the hunched fluidity hip hop requires.

"She's not very good, is she?" Carmen's little five-year old sister, Zoe, says. Her hands are deep in her chin as she watches us while flopped on her stomach across a beanbag chair.

Carmen blushes and darts a quick glance in my direction. "Go away, Zo."

I laugh. "She's just being honest. I'll get better at this. I have to. I can't get any worse."

Camila throws a look at me that says that's debatable. "One more time, from the top. This time, Kel, try and actually get down."

"So, how did it go?" Drew asks. I have him on speaker phone on the drive home.

"Great. I think I found something else I'm a natural at."

It's moving day.

Given that the completed house in its entirety is over 7,000 sq. ft., Dad and Uncle Bryce divided the project into phases. So while all the walls are up and windows are in, the duct work in place, and the house effectively sealed off from the elements, only the portion we're actually living in: kitchen, dining room, laundry room, two and a half bathrooms, two bedrooms, and the great room are finished in this phase. It will mean a lot of sawdust – even with the thick plastic covering separating the two remaining phases – but it's SPACE. So much wondrous, stretched out space.

The family all crowds into the kitchen and great room while Uncle Bryce gives one of his little speeches. The man missed his calling; he should've been a politician. "We gather together on this momentous occasion to celebrate a day some of us, I'm sure, were worried might not happen before she had to leave for college." He raises his glass to me. "Kel, you've been a trouper. You can thank me and Shae - okay mostly Shae - for your awesome closet later. Little brother, I'm proud of you. Wasn't sure if you still had it in you after all these years of just drilling teeth, but I guess once a McCoy, always a McCoy. So, here's to Lucas." Everyone raises Mom's Baccarat crystal to Uncle Bryce's toast. "You've made something incredibly beautiful out of something infinitely bad. And Greer would love it. Cheers."

As the rest of our furniture and belongings are taken out of storage and brought in and set up, everything feels oddly strange and new in a different space.

"I need to know where your bed is going to be," Drew says with his half grin and a raised eyebrow. In his hands he's carrying my headboard.

"Get a good look at it when we're done, McDreamy. It's the last time you'll ever see it," Uncle Bryce fires back as he disappears into the great room with Sam and our couch.

Trey and Justin walk by with my box spring. "Seriously Kel, where do you want this?"

Leaving Aunt Jill and Gran to unpack dishes without me, I follow them into my room. "How about centered on this wall? What do you think, Aunt Shae?"

She steps out of my admittedly dreamy closet, a raspberry colored sundress on a hanger still in her hand as she inspects the space. "Yes, that's perfect. I just love your view, Kel. You'll be able to see the lake first thing every morning when you open your eyes. What an absolutely gorgeous way to wake up."

Cade and Landry bring in my dresser.

By the time we call it a day, Uncle Nick is manning the boat for anyone too hot and sticky to care about his or her hair, so basically everyone but Shae. Even Pops and Gran jump in. The only other piece of the project that Dad insisted be done in conjunction with completing our essential living space is his sacred grilling area. He and Uncle Bryce are busy laying out a meatfest that would put Becca into cardiac arrest.

"So this is your mom?" Drew says quietly, sliding his arm around my waist when he feels me draw near. Everyone else has finally gone home. The house is eerily silent and still after so much activity. He's looking at the first day of summer picture of Mom, Charlie, and me I'd held onto in Chicago until the movers came. Trey helped me hang it in my room, just to the side of my bed so I could see her face first thing every morning when I woke up.

"It is."

"She's beautiful, Kel. I see so much of her in you."

"Thank you. I think that might be the sweetest and best thing you could ever say to me." I've never meant anything more. "It's weird, you know? She was such a force of nature. I miss her every day – still can't quite believe she's really gone. I don't know if you ever get over that. Maybe because we're still trying to figure it out."

Some days we do better than others. Some days the absolute emptiness feels just as raw and unbearable as when we first got the news.

Drew kisses the top of my head. "I also really like this one." He grins, pointing to a particularly telling photo Mom took of me in 3rd grade. I'm squatting next to a pond, all elbows and knees in my blue striped shirt, white denim shorts and bright red rubber boots as I hold a little green tree frog captive in the cup of my hands. There's a smudge of dirt on my cheek and a big smile of delight and wonder on my face. Because I did it by my eight year old self, my hair is in two messy, thick, lopsided braids.

"Uncle Bryce calls that my grasshopper stage. Big, buggy blue eyes; long, stick arms and legs; protruding elbows and knees. Actually I'm not sure I ever grew out of it. Sam used to say if I stood up straight, turned sideways, and stuck out my tongue I'd look just like a zipper."

"Yeah? Stick out your tongue."

Making a face at him, I do. Like the rest of me it's very long. I can touch the tip of my nose and the bottom of my chin with it – it's kind of my superpower.

Drew laughs. "That's disturbing. And strangely sexy."

"That's how I roll."

Love life: Off the charts.

School: In the immortal words of Becca Bryson – *sucks.*

People like me. Everything in my life up to this point has taught me that. Don't get me wrong, my company has never been highly sought after, I've always been a bit of a homebody and I sort of got pulled into the force of Mom's gravity so that whatever time wasn't taken up with school and ballet was often filled buckling in for one of her mad adventures. But I'm generally polite and kind and without any grating social oddities besides my tendency towards klutziness. *Worked well with others* could easily be my epitaph (but I desperately hope it isn't), so if people think of me at all it's not usually to spew venom.

So it's surreal that after I miss two more days of school for modeling jobs, one in Florida, the whispering that has followed me around since my first day at Barton blows up. It's suddenly open season on Kel McCoy.

The agency – Kirstie – wants me to be more active on social media to help *promote my brand.* They send me releases from every shoot I do for that very purpose. The trouble is, in my very short career, I've booked mostly beachwear. Posting bikini shots with a saucy Just LOVE being Tropically Kissed #glowing #whoneedssun #tropicallykissed is way out of my comfort zone.

"Stop looking at the ground Kel," is Kirstie's only response.

Reluctantly, I post a couple of pictures to Instagram the Sunday night after I get back from my Miami trip for all 257 of my followers – most of whom have known me since pre-school or are related to me. Drew helps me pick which photos to put up after we finish a hotly competitive game of Cheat with his little brothers and sister. Monday morning I wake up to 437 notifications from Instagram and a desperate text from Drew: Call me the moment you get this? Before you do ANYTHING else. I'm up. Please Kel.

Pushing my glasses further up the bridge of my nose, I sit up in bed. Charlie looks confused by this break in our routine. I'm usually lacing up my shoes at this point, not talking on the phone. Drew picks up on the first ring.

"Kel." He sounds breathless.

"Hey Drew, you okay?"

"Yes. No. Did you look at your Instagram posts yet?"

"No. Should I have?"

"You were trolled last night. It's pretty bad."

I open it up and scroll through the comments. He's not kidding. I feel sick to my stomach and violated. "I don't even recognize any of these people."

"They're probably fake accounts. Freaking cowards." Only he doesn't say *freaking* because he's freaking mad.

"But who would do this, be this awful?" I'm having a hard time getting my head around it, but even as I'm saying this, I know. *I know.*

Whitney pretty much disliked me on sight; my continual long-limbed, towering existence a shadow over her otherwise shiny universe; the one where Blake is inexplicably her sun, moon and stars. The boy is an out-and-out player. When he isn't flirting with me he's busy flirting with anyone else not named Whitney. But she doesn't see it that way. And she has a lot of friends.

Case in point: Homecoming. Blake asked me to the dance as we were gathering our books off our desks one morning at the end of English lit.

"Sorry. If I go, it'll be with Drew."

"So that's a maybe?"

"It's a hard 'no.' You should ask someone else."

"What if I only want to go with you, Grace Kelly?"

"Then I guess you stay home," I shrugged. "But you don't. And you won't."

Blake stepped in front of me, effectively blocking my exit. "I might."

I stared at him. Given that Blake already knew about Drew – had known for some time that I had a boyfriend at a different school – and nothing in my behavior would've indicated that had changed, he had to know I was going to say no before he even asked. So why do it? That's when I noticed Whitney, silent and stone-faced and without her usual posse, her arms wrapped protectively around her books as she stood at the doorway watching us. *Great.*

"Whatever floats your boat," I said, pushing past him. Whitney was gone before I took two steps. But if I'd felt like an outsider at school before she made sure I now felt like an outcast.

Ten miles at a punishing pace and a hot shower later, I dress for school with care. I've learned a thing or two from different make-up artists I've worked with. By the time I'm finished I've created a face even Shae would be proud of.

Pick a point and fix on it. Chin slightly down. I can hear the gossip and snickering, see them crowded around their phones and sliding their eyes to me as I walk by them in the hall. I'm absolutely flummoxed. Is everyone looking at the same two pictures I posted last night? In one of them I'm wearing a cropped *sweater* over my bikini top while I'm kneeling side profile in the sand. It's wet, but I'm pulling on it so it's not even clingy - only my mid-riff and legs are exposed. In the second I'm wearing a solidly sporty one piece; I look like a lifeguard.

"How was Miami, Kel?" Becca says with gritted teeth as she bursts in to chemistry, drops her books onto the counter and glares around the room, almost daring someone to say something to her.

I blink in surprise at her fierceness. "It was...busy."

"I bet." Karla Robbins, who is good friends with Whitney, smirks at her lab partner, Derek Suarez. They share a workstation with us. She says it under her breath but it's still loud enough that we can hear it. "Slut."

And just like that Becca fires out of her seat, ready to go to war. I manage to put a restraining hand on her arm and stop her from getting in Karla's face just as Mr. Frantz walks in to class.

"Thanks Bec, but I'm good," I say quietly. She stares at me in disbelief, her face almost matching her purple hair, so I smile reassuringly at her. "I'm fine, really. And I got my part of the lab done on the flight home." I slowly tug her back to our side and pull my tablet out of my bag. "Ready to do this?"

"This school *sucks*." Not exactly a direct quotation but that's basically the main idea.

Mr. Frantz, aware he might've walked in on something, looks at us all sternly but thankfully doesn't call Becca out on her language. "I've already put your supplies out for today's reaction. I hope you all did your prep for this one. And I'd advise you to be *very* careful with your measurements."

The rest of the day I wear my earbuds in between classes and listen to a recording of Drew singing the song he wrote just for me at high volume. At lunch I force myself to keep Becca entertained with the story of my disastrous attempt at vegan zucchini muffins (Charlie wouldn't even eat them and he'll eat anything). And I make her taste some of my butternut, sweet potato and red lentil stew I brought for lunch (she proclaims it edible, which is high praise from her and a sign of just how sorry she's feeling for me). I have to spend some time during my lunch hour handing in assignments to a couple of teachers and going over what I missed while I was away working, which is frankly a relief. Class is the worst. It's hard to ignore the undercurrent of snide remarks and snotty looks being thrown my way.

I barely make it home and to Mom's gray-striped couch before unleashing a torrent of hot tears. And then, because I want nothing more than to pour out my heart to her and be on the receiving end of one of her sassy, southern pep talks and lose myself in the wraparound comfort of her embrace, it quickly turns to heaving sobs. Charlie jumps up beside me where I've buried my face in the cushions and wriggles under my arm, looking worried. "Hey buddy. It's...okay...I just...had a...really...bad day." Undaunted, he licks the tears from my face as fast as they fall. And I let him.

When I've finally cried myself out and we've ended up with me flopped on my back, spent, and Charlie, quiet and still and vigilant, on my chest; I suddenly realize that I was so lost in my own drama that I didn't let him out when I got home. He probably desperately needs to pee. I'm officially the *worst.*

My phone is ringing from within the deep recesses of my handbag, still lying on the living room floor where I flung it earlier, when we get back in the house. It's Aunt Shae.

Shae's taken it upon herself to be my manager/stand in mom. She went with me to Miami for my shoot, made me coordinate with the agency for our flights and hotel reservations, arrange for ground transportation, and find places to eat. Once she was certain I was at the right location for the job, she went shopping without a backward glance until the shoot was over: *You'll need to know how to do all this for yourself soon. You might as well learn now while you have me as a safety net.* She even worked out at the hotel's fitness center with me while I was on the treadmill – and Shae hates to sweat in public. It's very decent of her. I don't think Dad would've let me go otherwise.

"Kel, thank heavens." She almost sounds surprised to hear my voice. "I've been trying to get a hold of you *all* day. Justin told me what happened. You okay, honey?"

Might as well be honest. "I've been better."

"Are these kids you go to school with?"

"Probably."

"I think you need to tell your father. He deserves to know."

"I know. I will."

"Are you home alone?"

"Dad will be here any minute." I'm looking at the kitchen clock. I didn't realize how late it had gotten. "In fact, I should probably go. I need to get dinner started."

"Dinner can wait, Kel. Trust me, Lucas will understand. I just need you to know how much I love you – how much we all love you. You've done nothing you need feel ashamed of. You're a class act, Kel McCoy. Don't you allow anyone to cause you to feel otherwise. Greer would be *so* proud of the woman you've become. I know I am."

Sometimes your light bulb moment of soul stark clarity doesn't come from books or experts with a lot of degrees tacked after their names. Sometimes it's not something new or monumental at all. Sometimes it's a truth so much a part of you that you forgot it was even there: Mom *would* be proud of me. I know this with every fiber of my being. I let my confidence in that knowledge wash over me and fill up all the places inside that had so recently shriveled and shrunk.

Dad hit the roof. Of course he did. He wanted to pull me out of Barton that very moment or at the very least storm the administration's office the next morning and demand some kind of an explanation but I convinced him to stand down. I wasn't ready to walk away. And I wanted to try and handle it myself.

Something else I learned: Just when you think the world is cruel and twisted you discover that there are always people out there who are good and kind. My Instagram was flooded both with new followers and positive comments from people I didn't even know. Chris had tagged all the nasty ones with #cleanupthemean. Travon was ready to "bust balls" for me the minute I wanted to name names. Drew stopped by as soon as he was done with football practice – which he'd gallantly tried to ditch but I wouldn't let him. "I would slay dragons for you, Kel," he said when I protested.

"I know you would. But it's too hot for you to have to run laps and I want to stay on your coach's good side. I can wait. I can."

But when I open our front door and see him standing there, still a little grimy and sweaty from practice, worry written all over his handsome face, I'm glad he didn't take the time to go home and shower first. "Look at you," he says, taking me in his arms and burying my head in his solid chest. "I hate that those losers made you cry. I really want to punch someone right now."

"Get in line," Dad says. He's changed out of his work clothes and into khaki shorts and a Spurs T-shirt. "Are you staying for dinner, Drew? I should warn you, it's vegan night. That's suddenly a thing around here. I'm grilling black bean burgers – I promise they taste better than they sound."

I know Dad feels responsible, he was the one who insisted on me going to Barton in the first place, but I feel almost guilty that he's giving me a free pass on the meatless burgers. I thought I'd have to grill them myself and serve him leftover chicken. "Sounds...interesting," Drew says manfully.

"Guys. You don't have to eat them." I roll my eyes.

"Just let me wash up first? I toweled off as best I could and Matt had a clean shirt in his bag he let me borrow but Coach worked us pretty hard."

"Feel free to take a shower," Dad says. "Use mine. There are clean towels in the cupboard, just help yourself to whatever you need. I'll start grilling."

They *do* taste better than they sound, especially with homemade guacamole. I package up the leftovers, of which there are surprisingly little – men will eat practically anything if they're hungry enough – for lunch with Becca tomorrow.

"So, tell me we have some kind of a plan here," Drew says, loading the last plate into the dishwasher. "We're not just letting this lie."

"We do." I smile at him. "Be my date for Barton's Homecoming? It's this Friday."

He grins back at me across the island. "I thought you'd never ask. I asked you to mine two weeks ago."

"I wasn't going to. There are a million things I'd rather do with you than go to this dance. But it's become necessary."

"A *million* things?" Drew says. An eyebrow shoots up as he dries his hands off on a dishtowel and makes his way over to me, a gleam in his arresting blue eyes. "I'm intrigued. Like what, Chicago?"

I squint at him. "Can you dance?"

"Seriously? Okay, not exactly what I had in mind but as a matter of fact, I can. My mom taught me. There were a lot of years between her leaving my dad and marrying Kevin. I was her go-to, push all the chairs back in the kitchen, dance partner. Why? You worried I'm going to step all over your feet when we slow dance?" He wraps his arms around my waist and pulls me close.

I slide my hands up around his neck and into his hair. "I'm more worried I'm going to step all over yours."

"Go right ahead," he whispers right before he kisses me.

The next day at school I fill out all the necessary forms and get tickets so Drew can attend our Homecoming dance. We'll be late. He has an away game that night and he has to take the bus back – team rules. Ginny and I are carpooling. I'll be tearing to get back and into my dress, but I didn't really want to spend a lot of time at the dance anyway.

"Homecoming?" Becca shakes her head as she gets out of the Mini. We're at San Sebastian Middle School for another mentoring session. "I don't get you, Kel."

I shrug. "I've never been to a school dance. It's my senior year."

"You've *never* been to a school dance?"

"Come on, Bec. I'm 6′2″ barefooted. Guys weren't exactly lining up to dance with my chin. How about you?"

"I've never been either. Not that I care." Except. Except, I could tell that she did. Maybe more than she would ever admit, even to herself.

We part at the hallway. Stepping inside the library where I usually meet Camila I quickly send Travon a text. He immediately responds with a thumbs up and a disco dancer emoji. Doesn't need to see a picture of Becca or worry she'll think it's something it's not. He just likes to be with people he cares about. I love that about him.

Camila is not herself today. She's being *nice* to me. She doesn't complain. Not once, not even when I push extra homework on her. At the end of our session she awkwardly says, "So, are you okay?"

Suddenly it all makes sense. "You follow me on Instagram?"

"Yeah. We all do. I didn't know you were a model. Carmen found out first."

"It's all pretty new. The modeling. And the abuse."

Camila is quiet for a bit, she's picking at a Selena Gomez sticker on her binder with a slightly chipped, red polished thumbnail. "I just didn't think people like you got treated like that."

I smile at her. "People like me? You mean uptight and uncool people who will never be quite as good at hip hop as their friends?"

"Yeah." She grins. "You really suck."

"I do." I hug her. "That's why I need people like you in my life."

I meet up with Becca in the parking lot. "Drew has a friend, Travon – he's a football player, so he's going to dwarf you – he'd like to take you to the dance if you want to go. We could go as a group."

"You *asked* him to take me? No thank you. I don't do pity dates."

"There's no pity involved." I show her my text: If you don't have plans after the game this Friday, Drew and I are going to Barton's Homecoming. Could use another friendly face. You could go with my friend Becca. You in?

"But he doesn't even know me."

"He will. You'll like him. He's really sweet. Would you like his number?" I text it to her.

She's staring morosely at her phone. "He probably thinks I look like you."

"I think he'll surprise you, Bec. Do you have a dress you can wear or do we need to go shopping?"

"Do I *look* like I'd have that kind of dress just sitting in my closet?"

I smile. "Shopping it is. Can you go right after school? I need to run home first and let my dog, Charlie, out. You could follow me over and we could leave from there so we'd just have one car."

Shopping with Becca is a challenge. She doesn't really know what she wants but she has some pretty strong ideas about what she doesn't. And the black and white asymmetrical number she's currently wearing is about to be pitched into that pile. "What color is your real hair?" I ask as we stare at her almost anemic reflection in the three way mirror in Dillard's dressing room. My arms are already full of her rejects and the salesgirl just keeps them coming.

"White blonde, I'm practically an albino." Her eyes *are* a very pale blue.

"You willing to try a vintage shop? My mom and I used to shop them all the time in Chicago."

I drag her to *Reflections* where I unearth a black lace, corseted top with delicate black roses printed on a white satin inset and a full, black netting tutu. "What do you think?" I say, holding them both up for her. There's only a small yellow stain on the satin and it's hardly noticeable. We could wrap a gauzy scarf around her shoulders and no one would ever know.

She grins. "Very *Black Swan*. It's perfect."

Once we lace it up tight enough that she doesn't spill out of it, it *is* perfect. She's looking at me, almost sheepishly, phone in hand as we wait for her purchases to be rung up. "Would you take a selfie with me, Kel?"

"Of course! Do you want me to do it? With these arms I'm like a human selfie stick." We bunch together and pose with our shopping bags for a couple of takes.

"Do you mind if I put this on Instagram?" Becca pauses.

"Psh. If you take a picture and don't post it, did it really happen? I'm putting it on mine."

"I wasn't sure. I thought you might be through with Instagram. And Barton, to be honest. You've been remarkably chill about this whole thing. I don't know if I would've come back."

"I'm pretty happy with who I am," I shrug, captioning my own post. "I guess that's all that matters, right?"

Dad is already home when we get back. I introduce them and invite Becca to stay for dinner but she says she has a ton of homework she needs to tackle. Dad looks secretly relieved. Vegan night twice in a row might be more than his carnivorous soul can handle.

Friday night, Becca comes to MacArthur's game with Ginny and me. She and Travon have been texting each other a lot; it was his idea. "I'm *not* stalking him," she says for like the twelfth time.

"You're talking to the girl who's wearing her guy's number on her chest." I reply, directing her toward the visitor's stands where Ginny and I spend most of the time explaining what's happening on the field to Becca, who's never been to a football game before. For all her tough exterior she can't watch Travon get hit without cringing.

MacArthur manages to pull out another close win but we don't stick around to celebrate with the team. Ginny generously whisks us back to my place so we can start getting ready for the dance. "What do you think?" Becca asks as she stares at her reflection in my bathroom mirror, her fingers absently deforming some leftover hairpins but other than that she's holding unnaturally still. She's wearing my robe, which – because I'm a foot taller than her – she's absolutely drowning in, and seated on a stool behind the vanity so I can do her make-up for her. "Nose ring. In or out?"

"I guess that all depends," I respond, checking the positioning of her fake eyelashes and then applying a bit of finishing powder to her face with a light hand and a fluffy brush.

"On what?"

"On whether or not you're the kind of girl who kisses on a first date." I stand back to get a good look at my handiwork.

"You think a nose ring makes me less kissable?"

"I think it's one more thing for a guy to have to think about if it's not something he's used to," I amend.

"For the record," she says, quickly removing her ring. "This is my first date *ever*, so it's not like I have an established kissing policy or anything. But since I might not get another chance at this, if the opportunity presents itself I'm totally going to take it."

That boy is straight up in big trouble.

I quickly change into a simple pale pink sheath I've paired with 3" nude heels and because it's fast and easy, given how many years I spent confining my hair to a bun for ballet, I pull my hair back into a low chignon – nothing too fancy, I'm saving *that* dress for MacArthur's Homecoming next week, but it'll definitely do.

Dad answers the front door so we can make a bit of an entrance. "Ladies," he says, knocking first before poking his head in. "There are a couple of sharp looking gentlemen kicking around in the entryway. Either that or they're some really lost waiters."

"Wow," Drew says with that devastating half smile of his, impossibly handsome in his tux. "You clean up good, Chicago."

"Thanks, you're both looking very James Bond tonight. Drew, Travon, this is my friend, Bec –" I start to say but Becca blows by me and marches right up to Travon, surprising us all but definitely Travon the most, grabs him by the lapels, hauls him down, and kisses him – smack on the lips.

"Sorry," she says, red-faced and a bit breathless as she readjusts her corset. "I just had to get that out of the way so I wouldn't be thinking about it all night. Who's ready to have some fun?"

Travon's laughter is explosive. "My, oh my. Well, you heard the little lady. Let's get this party started."

"Looks like someone already did," Drew whispers in my ear with a grin as we follow them out to Travon's Tahoe, Becca's arm firmly hooked through Travon's as she negotiates walking in her heels. She's a little wobbly but she insisted on wearing them: *Totally going to kill my feet but look, I'm almost normal sized!*

"You'd think so," I whisper back. "But that's Becca stone cold sober."

"Ain't no one at this school ever seen a brother before?" Travon mutters, self-consciously adjusting his bow tie as we enter the country club ballroom Barton rented for the event. "Or am I just that fine that everyone can't stop staring?"

I laugh, feeling more carefree and light than I have in some time. "Come on, let's dance."

We do. Drew wasn't kidding – he's an amazing dancer with surprisingly intuitive partnering skills. Slow dancing with him is magical and intimate and I never want it to end. "I love it when you wear heels. It makes it easier to do this." He kisses me softly on the lips and draws me in close. I can feel his heart beating against my chest.

Suddenly we get bumped from behind, even though the dance floor isn't all that crowded. "Sorry," Blake says, not looking sorry at all. He's wearing a gray tux and an unreadable expression. "Didn't see you there." He's dancing with Kendall Olson; I think she's on the golf team.

Drew nods and the moment would've passed unnoticed but Blake isn't done. "So, this must be the boyfriend. Aren't you going to introduce us, Grace Kelly?"

I stiffen, which causes Drew's gaze to narrow but I can't overcome my upbringing. "This is my boyfriend, Drew Jarrod. Drew, Blake Michaels." *He thinks he's God's gift to women. He makes my life miserable. I basically despise him.* "We're in a couple of classes together."

"I'm sure she's mentioned me," Blake says smoothly.

"Actually, no, she hasn't," Drew shrugs, his thumb rubbing lazy circles at my waist. "Kel has a life. Barton's a pretty small part of it."

My eyes widen appreciatively. Drew: 1, Dragon: 0. Not that a girl necessarily needs rescuing, but sometimes it's just nice to know your man is solidly on your side. "I really, *really* like you." I lean back in his arms slightly to gaze up at him through my lashes, Blake already long forgotten.

"Good. I'm counting on that." Smolder alert. "So, *now* can we talk about those *million things* you'd like to do to me?"

"*With* you," I laugh. "I said, *with you.*"

"Even better." He slowly grins, pulling me closer.

Travon is doing his best to look scandalized. "Y'all better cool it down out here. People are starting to talk." He dips Becca back as the song comes to an end. I've never seen her happier, even as she limps barefooted back to her chair, hanging off of Travon, her heels dangling from one finger.

"You guys ready to go get something to eat?" I say as we regroup at our table.

"I don't know, Kel. Are we?" Drew asks, his hand still firmly on the small of my back.

I survey the ballroom. Maybe not quite yet. "Give me a minute to freshen up?"

Whitney just slipped into the bathroom with two of her best friends – Kate and Ali. Kate is fussing with her hair at the mirror when I step inside; Whitney and Ali are continuing a conversation about girls too fat for their dresses from their separate stalls. Extracting my lipstick from a pearlescent clutch that had been my mom's, I very carefully and slowly reapply my color while Kate does her best to pretend I'm not there.

"I don't know," Ali laughs. "I guess it could be worse. You could be Grace Kelly. What is it with those scrawny, long legs of hers? She's like a freaking giraffe."

I press my lips together in the mirror. She does have a point. Kate is starting to squirm.

"Seriously," Whitney says. "But her boyfriend's smoking hot."

"I wonder what he sees in her?"

Whitney snorts. "Guys can put up with a lot for a girl who puts out."

Kate coughs. "Er, *Grace Kelly,* that guy you're with, didn't I see him perform at the Dotted T at some amateur night awhile back?"

I raise an arched eyebrow at her in the mirror. Really? *That's* your save? Her face reddens in response.

There's a sudden silence from the stalls.

"Yes, that was him," I finally reply and blot my lips with a tissue.

Toilets flush and then Whitney steps out looking striking in a fuchsia strapless number: her long, blonde hair in an elegant up-do held with some jeweled combs; her pasted on smile firmly in place. "Grace Kelly."

I drop the tissue imprinted with my pink lips in a nearby trash receptacle.

"Great dress. Kate, Ali, enjoy the rest of your night." I smile at them with as much sincerity as I can muster and then turn on my heel and quietly leave. Maya Angelou once said: "When someone shows you who they are, believe them the first time."

"Are we done here?" Drew asks when I rejoin them.

I am.

6

"You are the future, and the future looks good"
OneRepublic

"How are you not dead on your feet?" Aunt Shae groans, pressing a napkin to her flushed skin, her breathing still labored. Traffic into LaGuardia was a nightmare; we barely made our flight. *This is why you never check luggage*, another pearl of life experience dispensed courtesy of Shae McCoy as we sprint to our gate after an already exhausting day working in the Big Apple. She dropped a gasping: *Always...book...first class* (we rarely do), as we entered the plane – the very last ones to do so. They immediately shut the doors behind us and prepare the plane for take off.

"I don't have time?" I shrug, wriggling out of my jacket and putting my hair up into a messy bun. Digging my French textbook out of my backpack, I turn on my tablet and the overhead light. I have a midterm tomorrow. And I made a deal with Dad: I could cut school for work only so long as my grades didn't suffer. Kirstie's doing a great job of keeping me busy; my profile's been rapidly expanding and the work opportunities just seem to keep on coming, but I'm finding it increasingly difficult to stay on top of my classes. I feel like I'm gone half the time now.

"Not to add one more thing to your plate," Aunt Shae says, gratefully accepting a drink from the flight attendant. "But you should probably be thinking seriously about college applications, Kel. My boys all had theirs in by now."

I shoot her a dark look.

"Okay, fine. Sorry, you're right; I'll be quiet. You study."

But the truth is I *should* have my applications in by now. Mom and I had a plan set, a timeline for my senior year. But not only have circumstances radically changed since we received my SAT scores in the mail last fall, I have too; in ways I neither predicted nor expected. I can't decide if I want to pick through the rubble and see if there's anything worth keeping or just walk away and start over. And it feels like I'm running out of time to figure it all out.

Me: Did you get a chance to go over your flashcards?

Camila: U think after I went to all that trouble to make those stupid things I wouldn't look at them?

Me: Sorry. Functioning on 4 hours of sleep. You feel ready?

Camila: I guess.

Me: You're going to ace this, C. Good luck!

Camila: U2. French, right?

Me: Right. Thanks. I'm going to need it.

"You're awfully quiet tonight, Chicago. Not one Mickey Rooney slam. That's got to be a first for you." Strains of *Moon River* swell as a rain soaked Audrey Hepburn peppers George Peppard and a drenched Cat with feverish kisses. "The End" flashes onto the screen in case you hadn't already figured it out. I'm curled into Drew's side on our couch on a rare evening alone together (and by *alone* I mean Dad isn't hammering and sawing in the same room as us and Charlie has already claimed most of Drew's lap). "What's on your mind, Kel?"

I shut the TV off and toss the remote aside with a heavy sigh. "Just thinking about what we'll be doing this time next year. Where we'll be."

He's playing with a lock of my hair. "Made any decisions yet on where you're applying?"

I shift slightly so I can look at him. "I've narrowed it down to five: Brown, Cornell, NYU, UNC – where my parents went and where they fell in love – and of course, WDG."

"WDG?"

I smile sheepishly. "Wherever Drew goes."

Placing Charlie gently on the couch in the open spot next to us, he lies back against the throw pillows, pulling me with him as we sort out our legs so I'm now on top of him. "Any particular order to this list?"

"That depends." I tuck my head under his chin and draw little hearts on his chest with my forefinger.

"On?"

"Where Drew actually goes." I'm suddenly feeling unaccountably old and sad. "Where are you applying?"

"Applied. University of Texas - Austin, baby. I've got to stay close to home. My mom needs me to help out."

This isn't a surprise. Through two failed marriages, Drew has always been the one constant in Gabriela's life; he's as close to his mother as I was to mine but their bond has been forged through years of mutual sacrifice. I looked to my mom for everything. Drew has as many answers as Gabriela does.

UT isn't without its considerable charms: Besides Drew and Charlie, Dad's not exactly in a place where I'd feel comfortable leaving him on his own yet. Our family will step in but they won't be here late at night, every night, when he struggles the most. And then there's my closet. Every time I walk into it and the light automatically turns on to reveal a complete wraparound of floor to ceiling shelving for my shoes, handbags, and clothes; with a little island in the middle to house all my accessories and a plush bench to sit down on when putting on shoes, I hug myself. It never gets old.

Mom painted college as being this big adventure she couldn't wait for me to experience, my chance to get out in the world and spread my wings. But maybe work could be that for me. At the end of the day, if I got to come home to this boy I'd be lucky enough to have roots and wings.

"Hook 'em." I grin, sitting up and breaking out the sign for the University of Texas Longhorns with my right hand. With my left I'm indicating #1. The tightness I've been carrying around in my chest for weeks now suddenly dislodges and seemingly floats away.

"Are you serious?!" Drew throws his arms around me, disbelief clearly written all over his face. In his excitement he inadvertently sends Charlie skittering to the floor.

"I have to get in first." I laugh while being thoroughly jounced. He's squeezing me like an epileptic anaconda.

"You won't regret this. I promise." Drew leans his forehead against mine, my head cradled in his hands as he kisses me. "I love you, Grace Kelly McCoy." It's quiet and unrushed and weighty and shimmering, this gift he's just given me.

Wonderstruck, my breath catches in my throat as I press my lips against his. I don't even have to think about it. "I love you too."

Another moment: perfect happiness.

"You're applying to UT?!" Becca grimaces as we begin the day's chemistry lab. "Are you smoking something? Why would you do that? Tell me it's not because of Drew. Tell me you're not *that* girl."

"I'm that girl." I like to push Becca's buttons. Sue me. I point to the test tube Becca has suspended over our beaker. "I think we're supposed to filter that first."

"You could go ANYWHERE. What if you guys break up?"

"I'll still have my closet. Seriously Bec, stop pouring."

She doesn't stop. Apparently she likes to push my buttons too. "Fine," she glares at me. "Set feminism back 100 years. But you're still applying to other places as well, right?"

"Yes. My mom always told me to pick five so I did."

"Smart woman. Good to keep your options open."

"You should be a guidance counselor," I sigh, consulting my lab notes. Our reaction isn't turning a different color. It's supposed to be turning a different color. "And probably stay away from anything that requires any kind of precision."

"I hate chemistry," Becca huffs as she stares disdainfully at our failed result. Resigned, I dispose of it and start over. She idly taps her eyedropper on the tabletop, deep in thought, not the least bit helpful as she buries her chin in her hands. "Have you talked to Travon lately?"

"Not since MacArthur's Homecoming." The dance Becca didn't get invited to because Travon already had a date.

"Three WEEKS. And not even a text. Who does that? Well, I'm not waiting around."

"Good. You shouldn't."

Something in my voice makes her sit up straight on her stool, her pale blue eyes narrow islands in a sea of white surrounded by black kohl. "Why?"

I'm carefully weighing the compound and my answer. "Well, besides *setting feminism back 100 years,* I think he's got a girlfriend now; someone from MacArthur. Drew says Travon's liked her since they were freshmen but she's always had a boyfriend before."

"And now she has her claws in him." Becca sounds bitter.

I can't defend him; they're both my friends. "I'm sorry, Bec."

"Men *suck.*"

Setting the beaker down I pop the troll pencil topper off the end of my mechanical pencil. "Here. You need this more than I do. Just don't stick any voodoo pins in him."

"Shut up, McCoy." But she takes him and places him on her middle finger. Her hands are small enough that he actually fits.

"Nice." I roll my eyes. "Now can we *please* get back to trying to save our chem grade?"

In the break between first and second periods I discover Blake making out with Jane Gilman at my locker. And when I say *at* I mean they're slammed up against it: hip grinding, heavy breathing, serious groping, slammed up against it. To be fair, my locker is tucked away in a rather obscure location off of the choir room but to my knowledge neither of them sing – at least not at school.

"Excuse me," I say, clearing my throat. My project for world history is locked behind their writhing bodies. It needs to be turned in today. They either ignore me or don't hear me. "Guys, I really need to get into my locker. If you could just...pause. And scoot over. That would be great."

Jane is the first to come up for air, her eyes a little dazed and confused as she sees me looming over Blake's shoulder. "My locker," I repeat pointedly.

"Sorry, Grace Kelly," Blake says, smug but not moving. His hands are still under Jane's shirt but at least they've moved to her waist. "Guess we got carried away."

"Guess you did. Now, if you don't mind?"

Color is beginning to streak across Jane's face. She's just realized that a small but very interested crowd is stopping to watch – may've already witnessed – their make out session. Blake might be able to pull this off but she's done. "Jane, come on." Blake is holding his hands outstretched apologetically with his best, bad little boy smile as she walks away straightening her clothing. He doesn't follow her; instead, he leans against the locker next to mine, very aware of himself and the picture he presents in that form fitting white shirt. I've worked with male models just like him. He's too pretty for his own good.

"Wow," I say, watching her leave. "Who says romance is dead?" I'm spinning through my combination. There's a satisfying click as it unlocks and drops open. The sooner I can get my project out and be gone the better.

"I've never gotten any complaints," Blake shrugs.

I extract what I need and close the door. "Really? Then they deserve you."

He whistles. "Little judgy, don't you think?"

"If I ask you an honest question Blake, would you give me an honest answer?" My blue eyes search his gray ones earnestly. I'm wearing boots with a 3″ heel today so he has to look up slightly to hold my gaze. I like being taller than him.

"I don't know. I guess it depends on the question."

That's fair. I brave it. "What happened between you and Whitney?

He blinks in surprise. For the briefest of moments he is unarmed and vulnerable then just as quickly the wall of cockiness is back up, fully fortified. "That's ancient history, Grace Kelly. And I'm not going there. Not even for you." He wraps an arm around me, his voice rumbling close in my ear as we start to walk down the hall. "But tell me again what it is that women really want. I promise to pay close attention this time."

The second bell rings just as I wriggle out of his grasp and step inside world history. "You're late," I tsk at him over my shoulder safely from inside the classroom.

"And *you* play by too many rules, Grace Kelly." He smiles as he disappears down the hall.

"That's cheating, Kel," Q protests as I help Brody knock his croquet mallet against his ball.

"New rule: anyone under three," Noah is shaking his head at me and pointing at his chest. I quickly amend. "Anyone under six can have help if he wants it."

"I'm going to win by myself." Q makes a face.

"I'm sure you will," Sam says, surveying our game. "I've seen Kel play. Gran says you've got a five minute warning before it's time to wash up for dinner."

"So tell me about Liesel." I set Brody loose with his mallet. He's almost two; he's dragging it behind him on the lawn and heading straight for Charlie, who wisely makes a break for it.

Sam frowns. "Landry told you?"

"Is it supposed to be a secret?"

"No. Yes. I wasn't ready to talk about it. Her."

"Really?" Now he has my full attention. "Come on, Sammy. What's she like?"

His face is turning pink. I've *never* seen Sam flustered before. "She's different. Special."

"Details, please."

"She actually said she'd go out with him," Cade says, joining us. "That's different."

"I'm going to kill Landry," Sam mutters.

"After you wash up," Cade says primly, picking Noah up and throwing him, squealing, over his shoulder. "Time for dinner guys."

The first Sunday of the month Pops and Gran do a collective birthday party for everyone in the family who has birthdays that month. November is Aunt Jill, Jules (Justin's wife), and Brody. Not everyone comes to family dinner every Sunday but for Birthday Sundays we all make an effort. Which means I'm at the kids' table – one of three kids' tables, to be precise – I'm eating with Landry and Q. Sam drops heavily into the fourth chair.

"I told you not to tell anyone." He glares stonily at Landry.

"Tell anyone what?"

"Don't give me that."

"I think he's referring to Liesel," I interject helpfully.

"Of course I'm talking about Liesel. What else would I be talking about?"

Landry tears apart his dinner roll. "I'm not always sure. Pass the butter please, Q?" He's using his knife to spread it. "I didn't tell anyone."

"You're the only one I told."

"Sure about that?"

"Well, you and Ben."

I smile. Sam's eyes narrow. "When did *you* talk to Ben?"

"When I was in New York last week. He met Aunt Shae and me at my shoot. Turns out it was just around the corner from his office."

"Aunt Shae knows?" Sam groans.

"*Everyone* knows," I confirm.

"I'm going to kill my big brother."

"Killing's not nice," Q says, reaching for his milk.

Landry grins. "You tell him, bro."

"So Sammy boy, I hear you finally got yourself a girlfriend," Uncle Bryce says, leaning back in his chair. "How'd you manage that? Poor girl."

"Okay. Here we go," Sam sighs.

Drew makes it just in time for dessert; he had to work today. Gran saved him a plate piled high with food, which she's just warmed up for him. "I hope you brought your guitar, young man."

"Yes ma'am. It's in the hall. You bring yours?" He asks me, tucking into his dinner.

"I did." The McCoys can't carry a tune in a bucket; any musical talent I can claim is all Kingston. Gran has somehow maneuvered a standing two or three song concert out of this boy every Sunday after dinner. And lately I've been getting roped into it. "I stashed mine in the side guest bedroom." Hal is walking now; between him and Brody it just seemed safer. "Eat. I'll put yours with mine."

"McDreamy!" Uncle Bryce says in his booming voice as he passes me by on his way to Drew. "When did you slip in?"

Drew stands up for his requisite hug and back pounding. "Just got here."

Aunt Jill catches me in the hall and asks about New York. By the time I return to the kitchen all the guys have either pulled up chairs or are standing around the table talking football with Drew. Even Pops has joined them.

"Help me serve pie?" Gran smiles, shaking her head. "I'm afraid they're going to be at that for some time."

In accordance with McCoy family rules if you don't cook, you clean. Gran looks in at the progress I've made on Dad's sweater, Aunt Jill gives Aunt Shae pointers on her forehand, and Claire, Jules and Sarah talk politics while the men do the dishes and Justin changes Hal's diaper. I can hear them still giving Sam a hard time about Liesel as they wash up. Q, Noah, and Brody are running Charlie through all his tricks in the backyard. *I'm not ready to leave this*, I think. *I made the right choice.*

It'll still be here when you get back, a little voice, probably my mom's, slides in underneath all my surety and satisfaction, bumping it a bit so it never quite feels as solid as it once did.

Monday morning Kirstie calls while I'm getting ready for school. "I have someone I want you to meet, Kel. What's your schedule look like in the next few days?"

I stop outlining my lips. Once school started Drew moved my guitar lessons to Sundays. Homework is never ending. "I can do later today. After 4:00?"

"Perfect. Let's say 4:30 at my office."

Today is a tutoring day. Camila is sitting on top of the desk in our usual spot, swinging her legs and leaning over the dividers to chat with Analy in San Sebastian Middle School's library but she excitedly hops off when she sees me coming. "Look!" She's holding her science midterm in her hand. There's a bright B+ circled in red.

"Rock star!" I high five her, which doesn't actually require me to go all that high. Camila is really short, even for a Latina. "Good job, you! Hey Analy."

Camila's grades are slowly but steadily improving. My hip hop not so much. They're all so much lower to the ground that I just look awkward next to them even on beat. But I've taught Val and Martina how to do side splits and Elena can now pirouette seven times in a row, plus I know all the words to *Super Bass*, a song I will *never* be singing for Gran and I've picked up a fair amount of conversational family Spanish – I'm practically fluent in being able to tell someone's little brother to get lost. Extra bonus? Senorita Mendes has made it her life's mission to fatten me up. She always sends me home with tinfoil trays of her homemade tamales. Dad and Drew adore her.

I show up at Adderson's Modeling Management at 4:20, get myself a glass of ice water and chat with Rosie, Kirstie's assistant who has just returned from maternity leave and already has several framed pictures of her adorably plump, identical twin baby girls sprouting bows as big as their heads and a lot of frills at her desk. "They're absolutely gorgeous, Rosie. But how on earth do you tell them apart?"

"They put anklets on them at the hospital as soon as they were born – that helped. My husband Nate won't let me take them off; he's still worried he'll mix them up. But you can tell Nikki is a little chunkier in the face than Nora is."

I'm squinting at the picture. Must be a mom thing, I don't see it.

"Oh good, you're both here. Come on in." Kirstie says, crisp in her power suit as she opens her door at exactly 4:30. The guy folded over his phone in one of the pristine white chairs I'm always afraid to sit down in, in case I somehow get it dirty, suddenly gets to his feet.

He's just shorter than me by maybe an inch, leanly muscled and wiry with wavy brown hair and perfect Bradley Cooper scruff – just enough to let you know he could have a fairly decent beard if he wanted one but it hasn't been more than three days since his last shave. "After you," he says with a nod of his head and a bit of a smile. He's wearing a white button-down shirt and khaki pants with brown leather ankle boots. He's definitely not unattractive.

"Kel, this is Jack Donnelly. Jack's a marketing consultant and I'm making you his first assignment for the next six months. Jack, Kel McCoy. She's one of my top models and despite being a teenager, is woefully lacking in social media savvy."

I blink in surprise. Not at her assessment of my inability to self-promote, she gives me grief about that all the time. Nor am I surprised by her bluntness – it's her trademark and one of the things I love most about her. But *top model*? That seems like a real stretch. Still, if I've learned anything about Kirstie in the short time I've known her it's that she never does or says anything without a reason. I'm just not sure what it is. "Nice to meet you, Jack," I smile.

"Likewise."

"Please, take a seat," Kirstie says, indicating the chairs across from her desk.

I sit down in the chair closest to me, crossing one long leg over the other, folding my hands in my lap, and sitting up straight – slouching isn't an option. For me. Jack leans back in his chair and makes himself comfortable.

Kirstie outlines my previous miserable attempts at building my brand. Apparently they're worse than I thought. "Clients have a checklist when they're looking for a face to represent their product. Kel checks a lot of their boxes but she doesn't really have any traction when it comes to recognition. If you have to choose between two beautiful girls you go with the one who already has a built in following. I know I'm preaching to the choir here Jack, but I want you to help boost her online presence. She's already handicapped by her height; there isn't anything we can do about that. This we can change."

Jack listens impassively and then slowly turns his swivel chair in my direction. It feels like I'm on a conveyor belt going through airport security. "I've checked out your social media, Kel – at least everything I could access. You're not a big user. Can I ask why?"

I shrug. "My parents, my mom especially, wanted me to be present. I guess I just never got in the habit."

He nods. "The best way to build a brand is to build it around who you really are. Authenticity connects. Would you be okay with me spending some time with you this weekend so I can get to know who that is?"

"I have to work Saturday," I say, mostly to Kirstie. "We're shooting add-on Christmas promos for the mall."

"That should be fine," she nods. "I'll call ahead and let them know Jack will be there. I don't think it will be a problem."

I guess this is happening. "Okay. What time would you like to get together?" I ask Jack. We arrange to meet at the shoot just before it's scheduled to begin at 9:00 a.m. and exchange phone numbers.

Saturday morning I have to force myself to get up and run. I'm tempted to skip it all together but after my late night last night I'm pretty sure I'll need the energy kick running gives me just to make it through the day. Striker threw a party after the football game and Drew really wanted to go. I didn't make it home until almost 2:00 a.m.

I show up at the studio in black cropped skinny jeans; a thin, short-sleeved, white cotton turtleneck; and black ballet flats. I'm a clean slate: no make-up on, my bushy blonde hair left air-dried, hanging straight, and held back off my naked face with a black Alice band. I've got a protein shake in one hand and a water bottle in the other.

"Where's your phone?" The first thing out of Jack's mouth. He's frowning.

"In my bag," I begin defensively but then a familiar face steps into view. "Stefan!" I squeal; my hands are still full of liquids as I bend to give him a hug. "I didn't know you were on this job. It's so good to see you again! How have you been? How's Pandora?" Pandora is his dog – a *very* spoiled poodle.

"Sassy as ever." He rolls his eyes like a proud parent and pulls me into the little station he's set up. "I've got pictures I'll show you later. Come. Sit, Kel. Let me just absorb you. Gorgeous. And this skin of yours! I just want to –" Jack has followed us in, interrupting Stefan's rhapsody; Stefan raises a haughty eyebrow at him in the mirror.

I quickly put my drinks down and shrug off my bag. "Sorry! Stefan, this is Jack Donnelly – he's from the agency. He's...getting to know my brand."

All business, Stefan drapes a cape around my shoulders as Jack settles into a nearby chair. "She brought me cookies."

"I'm sorry?" Jack says when he realizes Stefan was talking to him.

"Homemade cookies. Maybe the best oatmeal chocolate chip I've ever eaten."

I blush. "I'm glad you liked them. Full disclosure – my grandma made those. The ones I brought today I made myself. You'll want to drastically lower your expectations."

"See?" Stefan says to Jack as he clips my hair back. "She bakes. And just look at this skin." He frames my face with his hands in the mirror. "Have you ever seen anything like it? It's practically poreless. *There's* her brand."

"There's my brand," I nod sagely. No wonder I need Jack's help.

Today I'm Santa's helper, a female version of Will Ferrell's too tall to fit in, elf. *Something for Everyone* is the ad campaign slogan. We shoot with the whole elf costume, a series of wardrobe changes where I'm still wearing the elf hat and posing with possible gift items from the mall, and end with me sitting on Santa's knee in a short skirt, no hat – just a good girl telling him what I want for Christmas. Santa is built like a UFC fighter and a little frisky. He's also been drinking; you can smell it on his breath.

"Not happening," I warn him while still smiling sweetly for Joe, the photographer. Santa's fingers are creeping up under my skirt on the hand that is hidden from the camera angle. I stop his progress with a tight hold on his wrist.

"You want to get together after we're done here?" He squeezes my leg and adjusts his beard.

Ew. "Tempting, but no."

"I think we've got everything we need," Joe finally says, putting down his camera. "That's a wrap everybody. Nice work today, Kel. Bruce, you can leave the costume with Nan." I quickly hop off Bruce's lap and out of his lecherous grasp.

Jack hands me my empty cookie container. "They were a big hit. I had one, it was pretty good."

"Thanks."

"Do you have time to grab some lunch? I know it's getting late but we haven't had much chance to talk just the two of us."

"Sure. Just give me a minute to change?"

He takes back the cookie container.

"Do you ever get used to people staring at you?" Jack asks, looking around as he holds the restaurant door open for me.

"My dad is 6′10″; people have stared at us my whole life."

"Two please," Jack tells the hostesses. He waits until we're seated in a booth, the waiter's given us the run down on the lunch specials and left us with plastic coated menus before leaning in, elbows on the table, his hazel eyes watching me thoughtfully. "Do you like it? The staring?"

"Would you?"

"I might."

"It makes me uncomfortable. Like they're just waiting for me to trip. Which used to happen. A lot."

"Is that why you did ballet?"

"Yes. My mom knew it would help. It did."

"You don't do it anymore?"

I'm pretty sure he knows about my mom's death. I'm not going to bring it up. "I'm a little tall for a ballerina."

We order. Jack's gaze is inscrutable as he watches me from across the table. "So then you turned to modeling?"

"Then I turned into a receptionist – for my father, so I'm not sure that counts. The modeling thing just sort of fell into my lap."

"Do you always bring cookies for the crew?"

I smile. "No. But I love to bake and we don't really eat a lot of desserts in our home. It's kind of a win-win."

"Santa seemed like a real pervert."

I blink. "You noticed?"

"Does that happen a lot?"

"Occupational hazard," I shrug, taking a sip of my water.

"How old are you, Kel?"

"Seventeen. I'll be eighteen in February. How old are you?"

He leans back in his bench. "Twenty-four."

"Why marketing?" I ask.

"I'm good at it."

"Why Adderson's?"

"I think I'm the one who's supposed to be asking the questions," Jack says gently. He pushes his glass away. "I was given two options: a modeling agency or an accounting firm. This one has a much better view."

I blush. "Well, I'm sorry you got stuck with me. Kirstie will expect results."

Jack nods. "Don't worry. We'll deliver. How do you feel about vlogging?"

"Me, personally? What would I vlog about?"

"Baking." He shrugs. "Your great skin."

"You're hilarious. Trust me, I'm really boring."

"No, you're surprisingly normal. But you're also not. Doors are opening for you. You're getting a name. Momentum for your modeling career is really starting to pick up. Why not take people along for the ride?"

"Doesn't Karlie Kloss already do something like this? Vlog, I mean." I already get compared to her a lot. Not that I'm complaining – she's awesome. But we're the same crazy height, both blonde, both athletic. We both did ballet. And we both model, although she's obviously on a *completely* different stratosphere than me. I think she even likes to bake.

"True. But you're still in high school. And just starting out. I think we'd have an audience and a fresh perspective."

"We?"

"You didn't think I was going to make you do this on your own, did you?"

"No offense Jack, but you're only here for six months. It'll probably take me that long just to convince anyone outside of my own family to watch it. And I might have to bribe *them* with brownies."

"Don't underestimate me or you. We'll get this off the ground and I promise I won't leave you hanging. It's going to be a game changer. Do you trust me, Kel?"

"There's not really a good, right answer to that." I sigh.

7

"I'm only one call away"
Charlie Puth

"Hey, good morning, Charlie." He plops down on my chest and enthusiastically licks my chin. He's a better actor than I am. "You want to go for a run, boy?" I roll over in bed and talk to the camera, no make-up on, the oversized Longhorn T-shirt I snagged from Drew a couple of weeks ago and now wear for pajamas just visible in the tangle of my blankets. "I think we're doing this."

Jack nods and then signals me with a thumbs up as he turns off the video camera. "Good, Kel." He steps into the hall and closes my bedroom door so I can change into running gear. Dad is in the kitchen, bleary-eyed and a bit grumpy at having to get up early on a Saturday, doing his best to ignore us but still wanting to be around while some guy he's never met is hanging out in his daughter's bedroom.

Jack gets video of me tying up my shoes while Charlie sits patiently at my feet and waits. He films us heading out – the sun is just starting to come up. And then, because it's supposed to look real, I sprint half a mile to work up a sweat and come back breathless. Jack films us running up the driveway, careful not to catch any discernible landmarks that might lead to someone being able to find out where I live.

Charlie is understandably confused. He is just getting warmed up when I turn us around. He cocks his head and waits expectantly for another lap but I head for the kitchen instead. When he realizes we're really done for the day, he joins Dad in long face sulking.

I take a quick shower and put on a five-minute face, my hair is piled on my head in a massive, messy bun. It's going to be a shorts and T-shirt kind of day.

"Breakfast." I slide my omelet onto my plate next to some blueberries. I top my eggs with fresh salsa. "Got to bring the heat. I'm a Texas girl now." I take a forkful, swallow, and grin. "Yeah. It tastes as good as it looks."

Jack turns the camera off.

"Did you make enough of that for me, *Texas girl*?" Dad says dryly.

"Eat mine." I push my plate toward him. "I'll make more. You might as well stay for breakfast," I tell Jack. "You gave up your morning for me. The least we can do is feed you."

"I'll help." Jack gets to his feet. "What? You think you're the only one who knows your way around an omelet? I'm a single man. I got to eat too."

"So, what now?" I pour Jack a glass of orange juice and join him at the island. His omelets are much fluffier than mine. I should've been paying closer attention to how he made them.

"You're in L.A. Thursday and Friday." Jack is spooning my homemade salsa onto his eggs. "I talked to Kirstie last night and laid out our plan. She approved the *Texas Tall* moniker for your vlog and she wants me to go with you and help kick off your social media campaign."

"Seriously?" I put down my fork. "And you're going to do it?"

"I am."

Dad looks at me. I know what he's thinking.

"Do you already have plans for tomorrow night? No? How would you like to come to a McCoy family Sunday dinner?" I say. Might as well get this over with. "The food is great and the company is...Did I mention the food?"

Not too long ago, in a rare moment of solemnity, Uncle Bryce confided in Dad and me after I made some offhand remark one night about how crazy Shae could get on our trips – she's *highly* suspicious of anyone male, especially the photographers – that she had been raped as a young woman. All those times she breezily went shopping while I was working? She had to literally force herself to leave me there alone and unprotected. "So many anxiety purchases," Uncle Bryce sighed. "Good thing you're cute, Squirt."

Giving Shae the chance to get to know Jack better before our trip just seems like the right thing to do.

Jack drives himself to Pops and Gran's. Drew and I meet him at the front door. "Hey Jack. Come on in. This is my boyfriend, Drew Jarrod, who, among other things, is a really talented musician and much more active on Instagram than I am – which I know isn't saying much. Drew, Jack Donnelly. I think Kirstie's hoping he'll turn me into clickbait."

"Classy clickbait." Jack extends his hand and Drew shakes it. "Nice to meet you, Drew."

"Kel says you're going to L.A. with her and Shae this week. I hope you like sushi."

Jack smiles. "I do."

"Come meet everyone," I say. Uncle Nick and Aunt Jill, Trey and Claire, Justin and Jules, and Cade and Sarah all had something else going on so we're a smaller group today. Pops and Gran insist on sitting Jack down with an icy glass of lemonade and chat with him about his family and his childhood home here in Austin, which in a bizarre coincidence Pops actually built.

"Kirstie's vetted him?" Shae says quietly as we watch my grandparents being their disarming, charming selves. Jack is more animated with them than he's ever been with me. "You're sure?"

"You can call her and ask, but she's the one who wanted him to go to L.A. with us."

"He seems nice enough."

"He is."

Shae nods and brightens. "Well, in any case, I'll be there."

Shae can't be there. Wednesday afternoon, two hours before we're scheduled to leave for our 6:00 pm flight, she calls to let us know that the draggy feeling she's had all day has blown up into a fever of 102° and she hasn't been able to keep anything down. Dad asks if I'm okay going alone. His surgery schedule for the next two days is packed; he's scrambling to come up with a Plan B last minute.

"I won't really be alone." I point out the obvious. Jack is picking me up any minute now to take us to the airport – we live on the same side of town.

On the other end of the line it's quiet. I picture Dad in his office, his head heavy in his hands. *What would Greer do?* Finally he sighs. "Just be careful, Kel. And promise me you won't go into his room alone or let him into yours. Be smart."

"I will. Love you."

"Love you too, kid. Travel safe. Call me when you get to the hotel."

Jack puts my carry-on bag in the back of his red Mustang and then slides in to the driver's seat. "Selfie time. Make it obvious you're in a car. Close-up. Just you," he says as he buckles in.

"I'm not going to be one of those annoying people who Instagrams everything, am I?" I already lost a thumb battle with him Sunday over filming my breakfast but I will absolutely put my foot down on this if I have to.

"Give me a little credit, Kel. Two a day is my max if you've got something big going on. One is better."

Reluctantly, I pull out my phone and take a picture of me looking out the passenger side of the window. Heading to the City of Angels. Chapstick, sunscreen & strappy sandals in hand. #survivalkit #texastall #tropicallykissed. Jack checks his feed at the first red light. "Nice."

I roll my eyes. "Just because I don't, doesn't mean I can't."

We don't talk much until we land in L.A. and we're on the way to the hotel. I have an essay to write for English lit and French, and a take home test for calculus to tackle. Jack is deep into his laptop. Sometimes I forget I'm not his only job.

"You tired, Kel?" Jack asks, the spattered glow from the streetlights and businesses we're passing flickers and illuminates different parts of him as our driver negotiates the roads.

"A little. I think I'm more hungry than anything else."

"You want to grab something to eat after we check in?"

"I have to call Dad and Drew first. Can you wait that long?" I'm rubbing at a kink in my neck.

"Call them now."

"While I'm sitting here with you?"

"I won't listen in."

"That's so not the point – and you would too, how could you not?"

"What is it then?"

I am my mother's daughter. "It's *rude*, Jack."

"It's efficient. I give you my permission to completely ignore me and talk to someone else. I promise not to be offended."

"Fine." I pull my phone out of my bag and open my favorites to select my father. "Just remember who started this. Hey, Dad. We made it."

Thanks to L.A. traffic I manage to Facetime Drew for over half an hour before we finally reach the hotel. I'm sure he wondered why I was suddenly so chatty; I don't usually like to talk on the phone. "Got to go babe," I chirp as we pull up curbside. "We're here, see?" I pan the hotel entryway for him, probably making him motion sick. I bring my phone closer to my face and make a kissing motion at the screen, which is admittedly a little too over the top. Drew doesn't call me on it but to his credit he also doesn't kiss me back. "Love you, Drew." This, I mean sincerely. "Miss you. So much."

Jack cocks his head, looking slightly amused as he pays the driver. "And *now* we can eat."

"Just as soon as I text my Aunt Shae."

Jack throws his hands up. "Okay, okay! You win."

"Thank you," I grin with a bow of my head. "But actually, I really *should* text my aunt. I meant to do that earlier but I got sidetracked being a jerk. She's worried about me being out here alone without her."

"You're not alone. You're with me."

"That's what she's worried about."

She worries about it the whole time we're in L.A. Even though I send her texts whenever I get a break and Jack has my social media hopping more than it ever has so she can see what we've been up to.

He is constantly taking pictures or video of me. He even runs a five-mile loop on the beach with me early both mornings, ostensibly so he can capture more but I actually think it's just because I told him how much I hate running inside on a treadmill because he doesn't pull his phone out once. He's a runner too; he gets it.

At the shoot he stays in the background but he's never too far away.

"Boyfriend?" Magna, the make-up artist wants to know the first day, checking Jack out with a predatory gleam in her eye.

"No. And he's single," I tell her with a smile. "Go for it."

"I will." She bites on her lower lip and rubs her hands together. "He's yummy."

But even though I try to beg off and make sure he knows he doesn't have to babysit me, that he's free to have some fun on this trip, he still insists on taking me out for sushi Thursday night just the two of us.

"All these women think I'm your girlfriend," I protest as I trail behind him in the restaurant, still smelling like a coconut and looking like I just got back from Hawaii.

"So?"

"So they don't think you're available."

"Kel?"

"Yes?"

"We're done talking about my love life."

We take a booth and Jack slides in next to me. And then we pull out our phones. I'm pretty sure if anything could disturb my mother's eternal slumber enough to raise her from the dead, this is it. Jack is carefully tracking our numbers: how many followers, how many likes, and how many comments.

"Am I actually going to have to read all these?" Most of the comments are sweet but some of them are...*ew*. Really?

"Ignore anyone disgusting or mean. Try and interact occasionally with those who seem sincere."

I open a DM that just popped up and immediately wish I hadn't. "Jack, why do guys send girls they don't even know pictures of their junk? Do they somehow think it's appealing?"

"I have no adequate response to that. I can only apologize for my sex."

He waits until we order before pulling out his laptop to show me what he has ready for me to post. "I talked to Curtis. He'll have promo releases for us from today's shoot ready for us tomorrow." He's scrolling through the pictures he's uploaded from his phone.

"I like these." I'm impressed. "They say something without being too posey."

"I think we do a mix. Tropically Kissed will want some of their shots in there. Maybe we pick one or two of our favorites, post those on Instagram and Twitter. We do this larger spread on your Facebook. I should have your first Texas Tall vlog ready for your YouTube channel sometime early next week."

Everything looks incredible – fun and glamorous but still real. I almost don't recognize my own life.

"Thank you, Jack." I touch his arm, moved. "You've really worked hard on this. At least Kirstie can't say you didn't try."

"Have a little faith, Kel." He's staring at my fingers on his bare skin, which now feels weirdly inappropriate. I quickly remove them and place my hands firmly in my lap.

"Oh, I do." I'm babbling nervously. "You definitely know what *you're* doing."

"But?"

"But I've flown under the radar for most of my life, which isn't exactly easy when you're as tall as I am. I think there's probably a good reason for that."

Jack is slow to respond. When he does it's almost gruff. "They didn't know you. They couldn't have."

We're saved from finding our way out of something that has somehow grown awkward when the waiter shows up with our food.

And suddenly, animated Jack –the one who sat with my grandparents and told stories about growing up in his childhood home with three older sisters and one bathroom – is back and by my side, making me laugh out loud through the rest of our dinner.

Friday we're shooting on the coast and it's unseasonably cold – even for early November. I spend most of my day wet and shivering in a bikini in a portion of the beach that they've blocked off but is still accessible to the public. People in down vests and jackets, who probably think I'm someone famous, stop to watch. Several are taking pictures with their phones, some with cameras with long lenses.

We have an afternoon flight back to Austin scheduled but with the cloud coverage the light is so good Curtis pushes to try and make the most of it. I'm practically blue by the time he calls a wrap. The moment he does, Jack, who has been pacing back and forth like a caged tiger, quickly pulls off his thick, navy blue fisherman's sweater and thrusts it at me. He's definitely not happy.

"I'll...get it...all wet." My teeth are chattering.

"Do I *look* like I care?"

Obediently, I slide it over my head and thread my arms through. It's still blessedly warm from his body heat. He rubs his hands vigorously up and down my arms, catching my icy fingertips in his and blowing on them with his breath. "Thank you," I shiver. "That feels…so good."

"You're frozen through. Come on, let's get you back to the hotel and into a hot shower." Wrapping his arm tightly around me he grabs my bag and, throwing it over his shoulder, half drags me to the car. "Crank the heat," he orders the driver.

When I answer his knock at my hotel door twenty minutes later, showered, dressed, and ready to go, he hands me a container of hot soup. "Eat it on the way. We're going to be pushing it to make our flight."

"I'd rather you didn't eat that in my car." Our driver frowns in his rear view mirror.

"Too bad," Jack tells him as I'm already putting the lid back on my soup. "She hasn't eaten anything since 6:30 this morning. If we spill we'll pay to have your car cleaned." He hands me a napkin. "Don't spill."

I don't. And I take my trash out with me when we reach the airport, meekly scooting across the seat and following Jack into LAX while he wheels his bag and mine behind him, one in each hand, and sprints. "Sorry, I can take that now," I say as we reach the TSA line for screening. "Jack?"

He lets go of my suitcase handle.

"Am I in trouble?"

"That depends." He pulls up our flight on his phone and shows me that it's boarding right now. "How big a deal is it to that boyfriend of yours if you miss his playoff game? Because there's a really good chance we're going to miss our flight. Learn to stand up for yourself, Kel. Curtis didn't need another hour of you crawling around in the sand, he just wanted it."

"I'm sorry."

"STOP APOLOGIZING!" He practically throws his stuff into a tray as he pushes it down the conveyor belt along with his suitcase. People are staring. I quickly place my belongings on the belt and follow him through.

We make it in but just barely. And because Aunt Shae's aisle seat next to mine is empty, Jack takes it – just as he did on the way there when things were much friendlier. Resigned, I quietly pull out my calculus take home exam and get to work. It's going to be a long flight home.

Thirty minutes of weighted silence later Jack sighs deeply and closes his laptop. "I'm sorry, Kel." He turns to look at me, pushing a hand impatiently through his hair. "I'm being a total ass. I don't know what's wrong with me. You're just a kid still, I seem to have trouble remembering that."

I stop writing. "Today sucked. I don't think I've ever been that cold before and I grew up in Chicago. But I've worked with Curtis before. I don't love that I'm just a leggy prop to him but I trust him, Jack. He's kind of a genius. I'll bet money the only shots they use for the campaign will be the ones we took today." I fish a small bag of almonds out from my snack stash. "Truce?"

He takes the package and tears it open, giving me half. "Eat something, McCoy. You're too skinny."

I pop them in my mouth. Now that the tension is gone my stomach reminds me I'm starving. Emptying out my stash, I pile all my snacks on my tray. "You want to have a picnic?" I grin.

"Yeah," he smiles back. "I do."

Jack drops me off at Drew's game. It's just started; over the sound system someone with some serious pipes is belting out the national anthem. "Looks like we made it in time." I'm staring at the bright lights of the stadium through the passenger side window of his car. Jack hasn't said a word since we left the airport. He's not mad anymore, just very quiet.

He nods. "I'll bring the rest of your stuff over tomorrow morning."

"Thanks for taking such good care of me today." It's hard to pour gratitude into words and send them out with the same force that's swelling in your heart. But you still have to try. "I know you didn't have to Jack, but you saved the day. Really. I won't forget it."

His expression is unreadable. "Anytime, kid. Now get out of here. You don't want to miss the opening kick-off."

MacArthur wins their first playoff game handily. Matt and Drew are perfectly in sync tonight and they connect over and over again – Drew's height doesn't hurt, he's a big target the opposition doesn't have an answer for. Travon grinds out the yardage; his ground game keeps the defense honest. Chris is good for the extra point every time. The guys are all euphoric.

"How was L.A.?" Drew asks once he's done spinning me around.

"Cold, it made me homesick."

He hooks an arm around my neck as we start to make our way out to Betty amid congratulations from the dispersing crowd, the bag carrying his gear slung casually over his other shoulder. "I'm glad you made it back. I missed you, Kel." He plants a kiss on my temple and gives me a squeeze.

"Me too." I pull out my phone. "Once more for a selfie?" I ask, leaning into him. This one I'm posting.

Drew blinks. "Wow. Jack's really changed you."

Yes, he has.

8

"I would rather be a comma than a full stop"
Coldplay

My dad is going on a date.

He says it's just dinner with someone he knew back in high school, but she's divorced and he's widowed and he seems pretty nervous for something that's *not* a date.

"How do I look?" He's fiddling with his collar. Again.

I smooth it down. "Really tall," I say, running my hands down the lapels of his gray sports jacket as I step back. "Handsome, Dad. You look very handsome."

"It's not too...?"

"No. It's perfect." I'm smiling brightly and nodding because I know that's what he needs right now. I'll cry when he's gone. "Now, go. You don't want to be late picking her up."

"Right."

I almost blurt out, "Keep it classy, McCoy," but that's one of Mom's sayings – so not what he needs rattling around in his head right now. Instead, I substitute an earnest, "Have fun tonight, Dad," and give him a big hug, stand on my tiptoes to kiss his freshly shaven cheek, and cheerfully push him out the door.

"He's been so lonely," I tell Charlie as we watch him drive away from our perch on the couch by the living room window. Tears spill over and trickle down my cheeks as the leaden heaviness in my chest grows. "He deserves this."

Drew has a group project tonight; I'm on my own with this one. Swiping at my face I resolutely head for my desk and the mountain of homework I have waiting for me. Being angry won't bring her back. If it did Dad would've resurrected Mom the moment his raw heart got past imploding.

Deep into my seventh color of sticky flags and four different highlighters across two gutted plays I'm halfway through my compare and contrast of *Macbeth* and *Romeo and Juliet* when the front doorbell rings. It's Jack.

He rolls his eyes at my surprise at seeing him on my front doorstep. "Seriously, Kel? I texted you."

I tuck a fallen tendril that's recently escaped from my messy bun back behind my ear and slide my glasses up the bridge of my nose. I definitely wasn't expecting company tonight but Jack's seen me like this before. "My phone's charging and I've been slightly preoccupied with Shakespeare. Sorry, come on in."

"Hey Charlie." Jack bends to scratch Charlie's ears. "I come bearing news."

"Would you like something to drink?" I ask. He's following me as I pad barefooted back down the hall and into the kitchen.

"Are we drinking water?"

Always. "I am. You can have whatever you want."

"I rarely find that to be the case. But I'm good, thanks." His hazel eyes narrow as we sit down at the island, our stools in close proximity. "You okay, Kel?"

One of the problems with being so stinking fair is that you can't hide *anything*. Definitely not cry face without the benefit of eye drops, cold water, and a makeup kit; none of which I had the foresight to use. I'm in my pajamas for heaven's sake. "My dad's on a date," I sigh, staring at my long fingers folded in front of me on the marble counter top and idly twisting around the wide silver band I frequently wear on my middle finger. "His first since my mom died."

"Ah."

"It's time, I guess. He needs to move on – he deserves that. He deserves to be happy."

"Yeah. He does. What's she like?"

"I don't know; I haven't met her yet. Her name's Erin Caffrey. They went to high school together; they used to date. She's probably lovely."

"Probably." His voice is unbearably gentle. "But she's not your mom."

Appallingly, fresh tears fill my eyes. "No. She's not."

Jack mutters something unintelligible under his breath and wraps an arm around my shoulders. "Sorry, Kel. That was clumsy of me."

Shaking my head, I clear my throat. "I'm good." I give him a watery smile. "You said you had news?"

He hands me several tissues from the box by the fruit bowl. "I do. *Fit* wants to feature you in a spread."

"Are you serious?" I stop dabbing at my eyes. "Who told you? Did Kirstie send you?"

"She doesn't know yet." Jack looks smug. "I've been working some of my contacts. The feature editor just called me late this afternoon with the green light."

"You got me this?"

"*You* got you this. I just pointed them in the right direction."

"This is insane! I can't believe it. I don't know what to say." I'm beaming at him as I give him a big hug. "Thank you, Jack."

"No thanks necessary. Unless it's more cookies. Then, please, thank me all you want."

I grin. "Done."

"Good. So, what were you doing before I showed up at your doorstep unannounced?"

"You mean besides sitting here feeling sorry for myself? Homework. I've got an essay due tomorrow."

He shakes his head in disbelief. "You're *always* doing homework. I swear I don't remember my senior year being this hard."

"Maybe it wasn't. I'm always playing catch up."

Jack gets to his feet. "No, I think I just spent all my time playing."

"And now you work all the time."

"Do I?"

I look at the kitchen clock. "It's after 8:00, Jack."

He shrugs. "This isn't work."

"What is it?"

"Indentured servitude. Don't get up; I'll see myself out. See you tomorrow, Kel."

"Tomorrow?" I call out. I don't have anything agency related on my calendar.

He smiles at me over his shoulder. "After Kirstie finds out about the shoot."

Since the Homecoming dance I've managed to somewhat thaw through the ice at Barton – not entirely, Whitney and her posse still treat me like a communicable disease, but everyone else at least talks to me now.

"You're practically famous," Becca shrugs and sounds slightly disgusted as we stretch out lazily on a bench outside at lunch. She lifts her cat eye sunglasses up off the tip of her nose so I can see the disdain in her pale blue eyes. "Carter Vandenberg has a Tropically Kissed ad of you in a bikini hanging in his locker."

"Carter Vandenberg? Isn't he a sophomore? And like 5′6″?"

"Exactly. He knows we're friends. He's always hanging around and asking about you. It's *really* annoying."

I grin. "I hope you're nice to him."

"I'm not."

You have to give her credit. She does ornery like no one I know. I raise a water bottle to her. "Never change, Bec."

She shifts slightly and pulls up the legs of her shorts to expose more of her pasty white skin to the sun. "Ugh. Is this year just dragging or what?"

"Is it?" To me it feels like it's approaching light speed and I'm strapped in, slammed back in my seat with G forces sucking at my face, holding on for dear life.

"You're lucky. You're never here. I wish I had a legitimate get out of jail card."

I'm not dumb enough to point out I don't have a life because I constantly have to make that time up. Becca already scorched me once for complaining about it. She kind of has a point. "Be an actor," I say, looking up at the cottony white clouds and then closing my eyes and just enjoying the sensation of the sun's warmth on my face. She definitely has a flair for the dramatic.

"I'd have a better chance at being a pop star."

I open one eye. "Do you sing?"

"Not at all. But that doesn't seem to stop anyone else."

My phone is still on vibrate from being in class. It's buzzing in my purse. I don't even have to look to know who it is. "Hey Kirstie."

"Can you stop by the office after your last class this afternoon?"

"Sure." I wait for her to break the big news but she doesn't.

"Good. I'll see you then."

"The agency?" Becca says, sitting up as I toss my phone back into my bag. "Let me guess, *Sports Illustrated* wants you for their swimsuit edition? It must really suck to be you."

"You're funny." I make a face as I study her. "What *do* you want to do, Bec?"

"What do I want to be when I grow up?"

"Exactly."

She moistens her lips. "A life coach."

I laugh. And then realize too late that she's being serious.

"What?" She bristles. "Not everyone has your golden life, Kel. You wake up and roll out of bed looking like that. I know; I subscribe to your YouTube channel. Guys throw themselves at you. People pay you money just to *wear* their clothes. Maybe people don't want to be me but at least they can relate. I'm living proof that you can actually survive pain and isolation – and in the world we live in that's a life skill you can take to the bank."

If only Charlie could talk, I think, throwing my long arms around her and giving her an affectionate squeeze. "Sorry Bec, I didn't mean to laugh. I bet you change a lot of lives. You've absolutely changed mine."

Muttering, she leans into me. "You start singing anything from *Wicked* right now and I'll end you."

As instructed, I head straight to the agency after school. Rosie hurries to hold Adderson's glass door open for me the moment she spots me stepping out of the elevator. She looks anxious as she ushers me inside. "Kirstie's waiting."

"Seriously? I came as soon as I could." That woman needs to cut back on her caffeine. Running a quick hand through my hair, I smooth my skirt, straighten my top and with an approving nod from Rosie, sail into Kirstie's office. "Jack. What a lovely surprise."

He winks at me and gets to his feet. "Nice to see you, Kel." He kisses my cheek. That's new. "Act surprised," he whispers, his breath tickling my ear.

"What's this about?" I say, taking the chair Kirstie indicates is mine with a royal wave of her French tips.

"As you know, we've been getting some serious mileage with your Tropically Kissed campaign. Between your Texas Tall vlog and the considerable boost in your online presence, people in the industry are starting to sit up and take notice." Kirstie's eyes gleam expectantly. "*Fit* wants you for a feature spread."

"Really?!" My grin is real, Jack's about to make me laugh out loud. I hope it comes across as giddy. "That's amazing, Kirstie. Did they say when?"

"They want to capture a bit of your school life since they're hitting the teen angle hard. I've been given permission from your Head of School to schedule the shoot a few days before school lets out for winter break."

That wipes the smile off my face. "They want to shoot at my school?"

"Is that a problem?" Kirstie frowns.

Absolutely. I close my eyes. "I guess not."

"Good." Kirstie leans forward in her leather chair. "I don't need to tell you what this could mean for your career and the agency. I'm really proud of you, Kel. You've completely justified my well-placed faith in you. You've worked incredibly hard for this. You both have. Congratulations."

Jack bows his head. I guess that's all the public acknowledgement he's going to get for landing this monster fish. I give him my best apology face. It's one he knows well.

"One more thing." Fingertips from both her hands meet in a mirror reflection, her elbows are on the table, her chin tilts slightly, and those brilliant blue eyes are x-raying me. That's never a good sign. I shoot a nervous look at Jack: *What now?* He shrugs: *You're overreacting.* Kirstie continues, "I would like you to start working out with a trainer, Kel."

I raise an eyebrow at Jack: *Who called it?*

She hands me a business card. "Tony is expecting your call. Set something up as soon as you can. Let's see what he can do for you."

Tony Ardestrani – Personal Trainer, Fitness Coach. Shaping lives one session at a time. The "T" in Tony is a stick figure man holding dumbbells. Blech. In what I consider an Oscar worthy performance, I smile at her. "Okay. Sure," I say, tucking the card serenely into my purse.

"Do NOT mock me right now," I fume as Jack follows me, close on my heels, down three flights of stairs out to the parking lot and the Mini. "Why am I being punished for this? It's *supposed* to be a good thing."

"It's not like you weren't already working out." He gets out of my way as I throw open the car door and stormily toss my bag onto the passenger seat. "This will just be with someone watching, possibly yelling at you, to make you do more."

"Fine. Whatever. Still not loving it. But they're coming to my school."

Jack scratches at his perpetual 5:00 stubble and crosses his arms as he leans against the hood, getting comfortably situated for the coming rant. "I thought I caught some discontent when Kirstie dropped that bomb."

"I was *finally* starting to fit in, Jack. They got over my freakish height and the fact that people take pictures of me." Now I'm just whining. "I don't want people taking pictures of me there."

"So what are you going to do about it?"

"I don't know. SOMETHING." I open the trunk, pull out the container of cookies I made for him earlier that morning, and abruptly push it against his chest. "Here...thank you."

"For me? You shouldn't have."

"I need to go."

"Hot date?"

"You could say that. Drew has a game." I slide in behind the wheel. His football season ended last weekend in a heartbreaking loss in the state finals. Monday the basketball coach had him running wind sprints in preparation for their first game with the team this Friday.

"McDreamy, still?"

"I knew I was going to regret introducing you to Uncle Bryce."

Jack shrugs. "He your Disney prince, Kel?"

Despite the recent storm cloud, a reluctant smile makes an appearance. "Yes. He is."

"Cheer loud," he says and he closes my door.

I sit with Ginny and Tanika, Travon's new girlfriend, on the bleachers in MacArthur's packed and spirited student section – they're already on their feet chanting and cheering and the game hasn't even started yet. I zipped home from the agency and changed into a white shirt, skinny jeans and Drew's away jersey, but by now everyone knows I'm Drew's girlfriend. They even know my name, which I can't quite get used to, but Drew is in the popular crowd at his school. I guess I shouldn't be surprised.

He's out on the floor warming up with the team but he busts out his heartbreaker smile when he spots me in the stands. We could be the only two people in the room. I smile back at him with my heart in my eyes. *Yeah, I love that boy.*

At half time, Ginny goes with me to help navigate MacArthur's hallways and show me where I can find a restroom in her school. Then she patiently waits with me while I fill my water bottle back up at the water fountain so we can do this all again just as soon as the game is over because that's my life.

"Don't turn around Kel," Ginny says slowly, lowering her voice and angling her body slightly so her face can't be seen. "But that guy over there won't stop staring at you."

"I'm kind of a freak of nature, G. It happens. A lot." I shrug.

"I don't know. He followed us out of the gym. I thought he was just getting something from the concession stand but he's been standing against that wall and watching you since we came out of the bathroom. It's like he's waiting for you. He's giving me the creeps."

"Where is he?" I'm carefully and deliberately screwing the lid slowly back on my water bottle.

"Gray shirt, Cowboys ball cap, over by the trophy case. Your 5:00."

We turn around in unison but the second we make eye contact with him he immediately pulls his cap down low and quickly walks away. "See?!" Ginny grabs my arm, her eyes wide. "Sketchy, right? Do you think we should tell someone?"

"And say what? It's not illegal to stare. But thanks for cluing me in. I tend to be oblivious to that sort of thing. And you're right – that was a little weird."

She takes me firmly by the hand. "Well, I'm not letting you out of my sight. And you should definitely tell Drew."

"TELL DREW NOW." I have the feeling that if Ginny actually knew my full name she would've whipped it out already – maybe twice; she's gone into full mothering mode. The look currently on her face means she's not messing around. "If you don't Kel, I swear I will."

"Tell Drew what?" Drew says, his hair still wet from his shower as he and the rest of the guys emerge from the locker room. They're all smiling. It was a good night for MacArthur. Drew had a triple-double and ended the night with 27 points in their runaway victory. "Hey beautiful." He kisses me twice in succession, the second time he lingers. "Why does it always feel like I'm just getting you back?"

"You know what they say about absence?" I say softly against his lips.

"It stinks?"

"Yeah." I lose myself in his arms.

"Drew, Kel has some creeper following her." Ginny says, interrupting our moment.

"What?"

"Staring," I quickly amend because the smile just left Drew's face. Ginny suddenly has his undivided attention. "He was just staring. It's probably nothing."

Ginny glares at me. "Or he could be a stalker. And if we're not careful we'll hear about him on the news years from now. *After* he's abducted you and made you his sex slave."

I blush. She's continuing an argument we had during the fourth quarter when the game was comfortably in hand. *The Room* and Elizabeth Smart were just the tip of Ginny's evidential iceberg. I Googled "men who stare but are harmless" as a rebuttal but she remained unmoved and unimpressed. And Tanika had annoyingly taken her side.

"Start at the beginning G," Drew says. "What happened?"

Ginny lays out the scene again, this time for the boys, although she's improving on her story every time she tells it. By the time she's finished Matt, Travon, and Chris are pretty much wearing the same deadly serious expression Drew is.

"Have you seen this guy before, Kel?" Drew asks.

Ginny rolls her eyes. "She didn't see him tonight. Not until I pointed him out."

"Come on G, I'm 6′2″. People are *always* staring at me."

"Girl, you think they're looking 'cause you're tall?" Travon shakes his head. "She does. She really thinks that. Drew, my man, your woman needs protecting. And maybe a mirror."

"Guys, really. I'm fine. If the four of you don't scare him off, Ginny definitely will. Can we go celebrate already?" I look at Drew, pleading. "Please?"

"Okay," Drew says, throwing his hands up. "But just to be safe, I'm driving with Kel." He tosses his keys to Chris. "You've got Betty tonight. Meet you all back at the Dotted T?" That's the plan. Everyone loads up into their separate cars and drives away, the victory party now very much back on.

"You sure you're okay babe?" Drew asks as we make our way across the parking lot hand in hand. I wasn't able to find a spot close to the gym.

"I'm *fine*. Ginny was definitely more freaked out about it than I was. Things kind of got blown out of proportion. We'll probably never see that guy again." But I'm wrong. There he is, standing inexplicably by my car and peering in the windows.

"Is that him?" Drew's grip on my hand tightens. With his other hand he shifts his gear bag from his shoulder to his fist.

I have a bad feeling about this. "Yes."

He steps in front of me as we silently approach the Mini. "Looking for something?" he says in a voice I've never heard him use before.

The man slowly turns around and just as slowly pushes up the brim of his hat. "I was."

Drew freezes and his face drains of color. "Dad?!"

9

"I've got friends in low places"
Garth Brooks

"What are you doing here?" Drew's breathing is ragged and angry.

"I came to watch your game. You've got a pretty sweet three point shot, son," Andy Jarrod says quietly.

"I shut you down and your play is to stalk my girlfriend?"

"She seemed like my best chance at getting to you."

"Unbelievable! You *never* change. This is between YOU and ME. Not Mom. And definitely not Kel." Drew grabs my hand, whisking me away from his father and around to the passenger side of the car. "You stay away from her." He's biting out each word like a finger emphatically jabbing at Mr. Jarrod's chest.

"I just want to talk, Drew."

Drew opens the door for me. "Too bad. The world has always revolved around what you want, *Dad*." He practically spits the word out. "To hell with everyone else." He's stormed back to the driver's side, furious, and in his father's face. "Well, I don't want to talk to you. I don't want you watching my games. I don't want you in my life. And if I ever find you anywhere near Kel again, I promise you'll regret it." Drew is still carrying all his muscle and bulk from football. He's taller, he outweighs his dad by roughly forty pounds, and he's got a lot of years of white hot rage built up inside just waiting for a spark; it's not an idle threat. "Have I made myself clear?"

Mr. Jarrod holds both hands up in surrender. "Perfectly."

Drew says nothing as we speed away but his jaw is clenched so tight I can see the muscle working in his cheek and his knuckles are white on the steering wheel. Deep within the recesses of my purse, my phone buzzes.

Ginny: U want us to order for u?

Me: Something's come up. Don't wait for us.

Ginny: R u being held hostage rn?

Me: Give it a rest, G. But if we don't show, don't worry.

Ginny: Srsly?

Me: We might need some alone time.

Ginny: ?

Me: xo

"Ginny. I told her not to expect us," I report quietly. Drew just nods. I'm not even sure he heard me.

He's taking us out of the city, an unexpected road trip. I open up a playlist Drew recently uploaded to my phone and let the sounds of Jason Mraz, Colbie Caillat, Ed Sheeran, and Jack Johnson –as well as several other local acoustic artists he follows – work their soothing, mellowing magic as their music fills the car. He meant for it to sing me to sleep on the nights I grew tired of listening to his voice. "Inconceivable," I'd grinned, kissing the tip of his nose to thank him for his gift while smugly slipping in a *Princess Bride* reference– his favorite of the movies I'd introduced him to. Maybe his playlist hadn't been used as intended but it *had* gotten me through the stress of some pretty grinding homework sessions. It seems to be having the same effect on Drew now; his tight grip on the steering wheel has lessened, the tension in his body is slowly easing away.

"My father's not a good man," Drew finally says, finding my hand in the darkness, our fingers intertwined as he rests them on his lap. "Things have always come too easy for him – women, money, the next high. He doesn't have a lot of self-control and he's a mean addict. I'm pretty sure my mom would've left him long before she did if it hadn't been for me. You don't know what he did to her. I don't even think I know most of it – I was young and she won't talk about it – but what I do know sickens me. The Jarrods are definitely nothing like the McCoys," he finishes bitterly.

I squeeze his hand and will him to believe me. "You're not your father, Drew."

"That might be the sweetest and best thing you could ever say to me," Drew says wryly. My heart hurts for his. "He can't be trusted, Kel. He's proved that over and over again. Promise me that if he's stupid enough to try and get to you, you'll just walk away?"

"Okay," I say, and I can tell this is a big deal to him. "I promise."

"Good."

Not to change the subject – because I'm pretty sure it's no coincidence that his father suddenly showed up out of nowhere now, but because I'm anal and I've got a few last minute details to iron out – I smile winningly at him. Thursday is Drew's eighteenth birthday and I've got big plans for this boy. "So, Coach Baylor's got to be happy with how you played tonight."

"I think the football rust is finally starting to fall off," he nods, obviously relieved to talk about something else, and then grins. "Well, maybe not for Travon." He fouled out. "But he'll get there."

"You think Coach B will still want extended practices?"

"I guess we'll find out Monday."

I tuck this information away to revisit later and gaze out my window and up at the scattering of stars overhead. "Drew?"

"Yeah, babe?"

"Where are we going?"

"Not Chicago, sorry." He looks down at the dashboard; the low fuel warning light just came on. *Get gas* had been on my to-do list. I'd just planned on doing it on my way home after the game. While still in Austin. When

I'd already been coasting on fumes and a prayer. "We're probably good for another ten miles. This road loops back to the 290. We can stop in at Dripping Springs."

Turns out Dripping Springs, a little town just outside of Austin, not only has a gas station, it's also the wedding capital of Texas. It must be. It says so, right there on the poster. I'm intrigued.

"Yeah, we love us a good wedding here in Dripping Springs and we do more than our fair share of them, that's for sure. We're like a classier Las Vegas." The woman with heavily sprayed and teased blonde hair behind the register at the gas station beams as she rings up my bottle of water and Drew's Gatorade. Drew is still out at the pump. She nods in his general direction. Her hair does not move. "That man of yours ever decides to put a ring on it y'all might just want to come on back and check us out."

To be fair, I'm no longer wearing Drew's basketball jersey – I returned it to him after the game so he'd have it on hand for his next game Tuesday night, I didn't have time to paint my face, and unless Ginny rubbed off on me I'm 100% glitter free so nothing about me is screaming *high school* right now. Still. *Yikes.* I smile at her. "Thanks. We will."

"Hey Chicago," Drew says tucking a thumb into my belt loop and drawing me close as I meet him at the Mini and hand him his drink. "Here we are, out of the city, just the two of us. I can't remember the last time I had you all to myself. We should do something to celebrate."

I smile up at him. "It's been awhile. What did you have in mind?"

He opens my door for me. "Dinner. And then...who knows? Feeling adventurous?"

Me: "Absolutely."

Also me, not forty minutes later: "We can't go in there, Drew. We're not old enough; we'll get caught." We just ate BBQ at a little café after wandering the streets of downtown Dripping Springs, hand in hand. Now we're standing outside of a bar that has karaoke. Inside, someone is singing a very off-key but earnestly committed version of *I Can't Live*. And Drew's grin couldn't be bigger.

"If people are giving us marital advice, I think we're good to go. Please, Kel?"

That gives me an idea. Quickly, I pull him around the corner so we can't be seen through the bar's windows. "We're married." Slipping my thumb ring off, I work it onto his left ring finger and move my wide silver band to mine. "It'll make us look older."

He's staring at our hands. "Married? Just like that? You really *are* the perfect woman. Okay. Let's do this."

"Wait. I'm going to put my hair up. People always say I look older with my hair up." Digging in my purse I retrieve a hair tie and a few bobby pins. I'm critically inspecting my reflection in the window of a parked car as I quickly pull out a few pieces. *I could legitimately pass for someone in her early twenties.* I hope. "Just please don't try and order anything that could get us carded. I'm a terrible liar."

When a waitress approaches the little table we've taken near the stage Drew orders a cranberry juice for him and still water for me. "Training. Sorry," he tells her apologetically, turning on the full force of the Jarrod charm when she still tries to sell us on what's on tap. "This is our first time in Dripping Springs, *Arlene*." He reads her nametag featured prominently on her chest and puts his devastating half-smile and those cheekbones to work. "Are most of these people locals?"

Arlene is only human. She blushes and stammers under the direct heat of Drew's unfiltered blue gaze. "A few are. Mostly they're tourists. We get a lot on weekends."

"I can see why. We've really enjoyed our stay here, haven't we honey?"

I smile at them both. "We have."

"Sing with me?" Drew begs as soon as Arlene leaves to get our drinks.

"No. In front of all these people?"

"They're complete strangers, Kel. Block them out. Just look at me."

I look at him. "I can't believe you're making me do this."

"*Please?*"

Arlene isn't the only one who is powerless against those blue eyes. Suddenly I realize that Drew doesn't take advantage of being Drew nearly as often as he could. "Fine," I sigh. "What are we singing?"

"Be right back."

Left alone so near the front of the stage it comes as no surprise that I find myself being serenaded to by a man with a beer belly and a white Stetson. Apparently I'm one of his exes who live in Texas. Give him credit; his George Strait is not half bad. We're halfway through a strident rendition of Aretha Franklin's *Respect* from a bushy-haired woman raging about the floor on 4″ red heels when Drew finally returns. "We're singing *Lucky* and we're up next. The ladies in front of us in line let us cut ahead. If anyone asks, it's the song we sang at our wedding."

I shake my head at him. "We are going straight to hell."

"Yeah," he grins. "But at least we'll be there together. Come on."

Lucky is a Jason Mraz, Colbie Caillat duet that we have actually performed before for my family. It's disconcerting not to have a guitar in hand this time; I have nothing to hide behind. Drew gives me a microphone and a reassuring wink and then he's at his intro and he's singing, his voice caressing the notes, love and confidence behind every one. We blend well. He's right, there is something freeing about just singing for each other. His voice elevates mine. As our last note ends he leans over and kisses me, to the delight of the other patrons who are all clapping enthusiastically and whistling their approval.

Our wedding rings are on full display. We're the feel good act of the night.

We leave a big tip for Arlene and slip away, hand in hand.

On the way home Drew doesn't bring up his father; it seems like such a closed subject I wonder if he ever will again. But he doesn't turn the music back on either. After a long stretch of quiet he suddenly starts to sing a cappella – something he frequently does, something I love about him, something that makes me melt. But this time he's singing a song I haven't heard him sing before, *Desperado*, by the Eagles. It's raw and poignant and wistful and beautifully sad and I realize he hasn't stopped thinking about his father at all.

"How would you feel about me inviting Erin over for dinner Sunday night?" Dad says as he walks into the kitchen Saturday morning where Charlie and I are both gulping water just as fast as we can after our run.

"As in meet the whole family or just me?"

Dad smiles. "I don't think anyone's ready for that yet – do you? I thought we could just barbeque some ribs here. Invite Drew."

Deep breath, Kel. "Sounds fun. I can't wait to meet her. What time are you thinking? 6:00?"

At 5:30 Sunday night the doorbell rings. It's Drew. He has the bouquet of fresh cut flowers I asked him to stop and pick up, his guitar for lessons later, and he's still wearing his wedding ring. "I can't get it off."

"Did you try soap?"

"And butter. That was Travon's idea."

"You're going to freak Dad out," I whisper, taking the flowers from him.

He leaves his guitar in the hall and follows me into the kitchen. "Maybe he won't notice."

I take down a vase. "He'll notice."

"Drew, nice to see you," Dad says, giving him a hug. As he pulls away he glances at the ring on Drew's left hand. But he doesn't say anything because for the first time I realize he's no longer wearing his own wedding ring. Immediately I'm reliving the day. Was he wearing it this morning? When did he take it off? *And why does the room suddenly seem to be spinning?* I drop the flowers on the counter and quickly sit down before I fall down.

Just as quickly, Drew gathers the bouquet back up and places it in the vase.

"It was time, sweetheart," Dad says quietly.

"I know."

"It's what your mother would've wanted."

"I know."

"I'm sorry, Kel."

I look at him with tear filled eyes. "I know."

"Come here." He wraps his arms around me. "Are we okay?"

"Yeah." I lay my head against his chest. "I know it doesn't look like it, but I'm happy for you Dad."

"Really?"

"Really."

"Thanks." Dad's voice has grown thick. "That means a lot, Kel." He kisses the top of my head, straightens up and then clears his throat and looks sternly at the two of us. "But don't think this means you're getting out of explaining that ring on your finger, young man."

Drew grins. "It's a great story. We'll save it for dinner."

"Good idea," I say. "Then he can't kill us."

Erin Caffrey is a slim brunette with dark eyes, a great smile, and a quick wit. She wrinkles her nose whenever she laughs and she laughs a lot. So does Dad when he's around her. He's lit up from the inside again.

"So, what do you think?" Drew asks, sliding his arms around my waist as he steps in behind me while I start the dishwasher. Dad is walking Erin to her car.

"I like her."

"You think he's serious?"

"He wouldn't have asked her to have dinner with us if he wasn't."

"How do you feel about that?"

"I'm not sure. Give me time; I'll get there."

We finally get the ring off using a YouTube trick with dental floss. "I think the universe was trying to tell me something," Drew says, flexing his now bare but much abused finger. We're sitting on my bed, a mishmash of long limbs.

I tug on his shirt and cock my head. "Marriage isn't for you?"

He leans over and kisses me. "Next time bring a bigger ring."

A text pops up on my phone, which is currently lying on my nightstand.

Jack: Tony's tomorrow, right? Good luck with that.

"Tony?" Drew says, handing me my phone. "Sorry, didn't mean to look."

"Tony. It's been a *really* long week."

Tony Ardestrani is short and bulky. He's balding so he's just given up and gone full cue ball, which is sad; he can't be any older than 35. He's wearing a muscle shirt and cut off sweatpants at the knees and carrying a clipboard when I walk into his facility Monday after school. On his biceps he has inked some Chinese characters. I make a mental note to figure out what they mean.

"Tony Ardestrani. You must be Kel McCoy." He's squinting up at me.

"I am. Thanks for agreeing to meet with me, Tony."

"Kirstie said there was some urgency."

I set that aside. For the moment. "I've never had a personal trainer before. I'm not sure how this works."

It starts with a lot of measurements. Modeling, you get used to complete strangers handling your body. With the exception of a few pertinent private inches, Tony now knows me as well as my mother did. And he's taken pictures. He plugs it all into his computer program and turns me into a spreadsheet.

Then we work out: forty-five minutes of plyometrics and an hour of boxing and he pushes me harder than I've ever been pushed before. He leaves me planking while he prints out my diet and workout schedule for the rest of the week. "Any questions?"

I slowly get to my feet. Several things hurt already, but I've done ballet for ten years; I've got grit to spare. "I'll let you know."

I hate him.

"I hate him."

On the other end of the line Jack laughs. "I think you mean that."

"Oh, I do." I'm lying flat on my back in my bed. I've got him on speaker because I don't have the energy to hold onto the phone. "He's got me on a strict diet. I have to weigh in every time he sees me. He wants to reduce my body fat by 2% before the *Fit* shoot."

Jack stops laughing. "Seriously? Has he seen you?"

"He spent three hours with me today Jack."

"Where the...where does he think you've got 2% to spare?" He's angry.

"He has a spreadsheet I'm sure he'd love to show you," I sigh. "It's fine. The shoot is in less than a month. I can do anything for a month."

"Whatever. Don't think I'm dropping this – I'm not, but I actually called you for a reason. Have you looked at your Instagram lately?"

"Um, define *lately.*"

"Grace. Kelly. McCoy." Pretty sure if Jack ends up with TMJ it'll be all my fault.

"What? I've had midterms." There is a long pause broken only by something that sounds suspiciously like more teeth grinding on the other end of the line. "All right. Don't say it. I know, I'm lame."

"Yeah. You are. *Look* at it."

"Right now?"

"No. Next month." Someone's getting grumpy.

"Fine." I roll over and open it up on my phone. 500,097 followers?! Whoa. That's over half a *million* people. "Half a million?" Dropping the phone back onto my chest, I lick at lips that have suddenly gone dry and push my hair back off my face. "When did this start snowballing?" The last time I checked we'd barely cracked 80,000 and that was *after* I worked the beach volleyball tournament Tropically Kissed sponsored in Miami where Jack had been manically pimping out my socials. "Is this for real?"

"Apparently your Dopamine Dressing segment got name dropped on *L.A. Lit* last night and it was picked up by all the major entertainment news carriers. Subscriber adds to your YouTube channel have been skyrocketing." He's like a kid on Christmas morning. "Kel? You still there?"

"Dopamine Dressing, huh?" It's hard not to sound the teeniest bit smug. If I had the energy I might even gloat.

"Okay, fine. I'm man enough that I can admit when I'm wrong." Of course he can, he so rarely is.

We argued over what to call our latest Texas Tall vlog for a good hour but I wanted this title so bad I even made it personal and proposed dragging my reluctant father on camera to give us a punch of fun chemistry context (Jack: How many teen-age girls even know what dopamine is? Me: We're *not* stupid. And we have Google).

He finally caved because I've become passionate about finding and wearing clothes that make you feel good about yourself and I really sold it. Dad's dry sense of humor was pitch perfect for his brief cameo. Hands down, it was my favorite piece we've ever done.

"We make a good team, Donnelly."

"Yeah. We really do."

"Half a million people. Kirstie should give you a raise."

"Actually, you pay my salary."

"I do?"

"You do."

"Hmm. How are you at holding up flashcards?" I ask, eyeing the stack of French vocab I still have to get through before I can call it a night.

"Go hydrate, McCoy."

The next morning I'm aware as I wake up that a large portion of my body is already sore. Moving just confirms it. I run anyway.

"A less graceful Grace Kelly?" Blake says as I shuffle into English lit. The heat from running and a hot shower that had offered my aching muscles a temporary reprieve is now officially over. And the ibuprofen has yet to kick in.

"Not today, Blake."

"And submissive as well. What's going on?"

I sink carefully into my desk chair. It's always a toss up – just get the excruciating pain of sitting down, engaging those screaming quads, over with all at once or handle it gingerly? I breathe through it. "Personal trainer. I don't want to talk about it."

Tactical error on my part because of course, now his interest is peaked, but I'm not myself at the moment. He follows me around all day long. Even to the parking lot when school is over and Becca has long abandoned me for some online gaming tournament she cut sixth period to make. "Victoria's Secret?"

"What?!"

"Just tell me. You know I'm going to find out."

"No."

"No, it's not Victoria's Secret or no, you won't tell me?"

Scrud. Andy Jarrod is waiting for me by the Mini. *At. My. School.* SO many red flags. "Blake, stop talking." I drop my voice but it's urgent and possibly a little frantic. "Will you do something for me without asking any questions?"

He regards me intently, the cockiness drops away. "Okay."

"See that man standing by my car, he's been following me. I don't think he wants to hurt me but I don't want to talk to him. Will you just walk me to my car and help me get away?"

Eyeing Mr. Jarrod suspiciously, Blake nods and puts his hand on the small of my back, positioning himself so he's between me and Drew's father, who has backed away from the Mini looking irritated. "See you tomorrow," Blake says when he's sure I'm safely belted in. Then he closes the door and watches me lock it and drive away.

Who knew? When push comes to shove Blake could be a good guy. *What am I going to do?* If I tell Drew about his father showing up at my school he'll lose it. If I don't and Drew finds out...I better tell him. Later. He has a game tonight. I don't want him distracted.

"BURPEES!" Tony is spitting in my face. Well, actually, it's more like my collarbone – he can't reach my face when we're both standing. Not unless he gets a stool.

I glare at him. If this is a battle of wills he should know mine is being jet fueled by my intense dislike for him. I don't like the way he stabs his meaty finger at my chest when he's trying to make a point. I hate being called "Barbie." And I can't stand the way he sucks air through his teeth when he's thinking. I'm almost excited for boxing just so I can direct some of my aggression at its intended target. Not that he couldn't lay me out with one punch, but he won't. At least I don't *think* he will. The hatred might be mutual. I suspect that it is.

Not thirty minutes later Jack unexpectedly strides in with one of Tony's assistants trailing unhappily behind him. "Hey Kel."

"You'll have to wait outside," Tony says, lowering his boxing gloves and glowering. I'm doubled over, panting, and evilly considering throwing a cheap shot at that iron jaw while he's distracted but it would probably break my hand.

"Sorry, Kirstie asked me to stop by and check on our client."

"And you are?"

"Jack Donnelly. I'm head of Kel's personal team."

That musters a smile out of me. What that boy won't do for more cookies.

Tony frowns. "This isn't part of our arrangement. Do I need to call Kirstie?"

"I don't know. Do you?" Jack isn't backing down. He takes a seat and pulls out his laptop, making himself comfortable. He's here for the duration.

"Again!" Tony barks at me. We resume sparring, which consists mostly of Tony egging me on, telling me I punch like a girl and pushing me around the ring while he yells at me to hit him already. We finish with me jumping rope at a quick clip for twenty minutes. "Tomorrow I expect you to work harder." Again with the finger jab. "We go full out or not at all. Do I make myself clear, Barbie?"

I don't have the breath to answer him. Instead, I throw up on his shoes, something I find *supremely* satisfying. And in some sick and twisted way, so does he. Smirking, Tony hunkers down on the floor, removes his shoes and socks, and leaves them in a pile by my vomit for someone else to clean up and walks away.

"Are you okay?" Jack asks staring hard at Tony's departing back as he helps me to my feet. Jimmy from the front desk is already on his way with a mop.

"Dandy." I swipe weakly at my face with the bottom of my sweat soaked tank and head straight for the water fountain to rinse out my mouth. "What are you doing here?"

"After we talked last night I did some research on this guy. Talk to Kirstie, tell her what's going on here Kel; I'll back you up. This is just wrong. I get that he gets results, but no one deserves to be treated like this. It's inhuman."

"He wants me to quit. He doesn't think I can take it."

"Are you kidding?!"

"One month." I grab my water bottle and my bag. "I'm going to go home and make a paper chain, one link for every day I have left with him. He's *not* going to win this."

Frustrated, he shakes his head.

"What? Just say it, Jack."

"Why are you doing this? Look at you, Kel. You're already in great shape. You got this feature because you're real – not some unrealistically cut, fitness freak who lives her life in a gym. You don't need this. You don't need him."

"Kirstie thinks I do."

"Kirstie's wrong."

"You going to tell her that, Jack? Because I'm not. She wasn't wrong about me needing you."

Jack glares at me. "I'm not Tony."

"No, but I didn't want you either in the beginning. And look at us now."

"Yeah? Well, you make me crazy."

I smile at him and bump him with my hip. "Psh. You know you love me."

10

"If I could turn back time"

Cher

"Kel?"

Startled, I jump. My hand flies to my throat as I spin around on my heel. It certainly doesn't occur to me in the moment that a mugger or rapist probably wouldn't know my name. Drew's father – *again*. The parking lot at Barton is practically deserted. I came in early to do a make-up lab since I have to be gone the rest of the day for work. Besides being caught off guard, I'm more than a little freaked out that he is here waiting for me when school doesn't officially start for another hour. "Mr. Jarrod? I wasn't expecting you."

He puts both hands out in front of him, palms up. I guess to show me he's unarmed, which is not always the case in Texas. "Sorry, didn't mean to scare you. I just want to talk."

Tucking a container of cookies under my arm, I lock the Mini and start briskly making a bee-line for Barton's front doors. "You should probably talk to Drew."

I'm not the only one with long legs; we're practically the same height. Mr. Jarrod has no problem keeping up with me. "I would but as you saw the other night, he refuses to talk to me."

"Then you can understand why I can't talk to you now."

"I'm just trying to apologize to my son; I need to make things right. I don't expect it to change anything between us. I just want the chance to be heard."

Keep on walking. Ignore the obvious desperation in his voice. "Then write him a letter." It sounds cold, even to me.

He grabs my arm, so abruptly the cookies slide around in their container. "Would you give it to him if I did?"

I'm a bit frightened at how tight his grip is. "If you think that would make him more likely to read it, you don't know your son at all."

"I've seen the way he looks at you. If you ask him to read it, he will."

"Please let go of me. I'm going to be late for my lab."

He steps in front of me, stopping me altogether. "I screwed up Kel. I've done nothing *but* screw up where Drew and his mom are concerned. Nothing I can do or say will change that. But they should know that I'm sorry. That's all this is. Does that seem like a bad thing to want?"

I hesitate and then feel myself give way. Those Jarrod blue eyes are endlessly my undoing. "I honestly have a lab I'm going to be late for and then I'm gone for the rest of the day. If there's a letter waiting on my windshield when I come out – and you'll only have an hour – I'll give it to Drew. I can't promise anything more."

He lets go of my arm. "Thank you."

An hour later I emerge victorious from another successfully made up chem lab. I had to bribe Mr. Frantz into coming in early using Gran's oatmeal chocolate chip cookies and Becca slept through most of it, but the important thing is I have just enough points now that I can still squeak out an A if I ace the final. Which is a good thing. I wasn't looking forward to trying to explain to my father why his only child, with his love and mastery of chemistry clearly coded into her genetics SOMEWHERE, could only manage a B.

My euphoria is short-lived. From the front steps of the school I can clearly see an envelope tucked under the wiper on the driver's side of the Mini. I really hoped there wouldn't be. I still haven't told Drew about the first time his dad was waiting for me at my school. I have no idea how I'm going to explain this. But I know someone who might.

"Kel?" There's a long silence behind the surprise in Jack's voice. I know exactly what he's doing right now; he's pulling up my schedule on his laptop and squinting at the screen because that boy refuses to get glasses. "You're supposed to be on your way to Archer Darby. Don't tell me you're using your cell phone *in the car*?"

"Of course I am, Jack. Don't be a pain; I'm hands free. I need some advice."

"Well, since you asked me so nicely...hang on." His voice is muffled. Someone has stopped by his desk to chat. That someone is female and flirty and slow to take a hint. "Sorry, I'm back. What can I help you with?"

As I continue to negotiate traffic I explain everything, beginning with Drew's basketball game and ending with the sealed envelope I now have sitting in my purse, an undetonated bomb. Jack just listens quietly without interrupting once. "So, Wise One," I finish. "What should I do?"

"First of all: Always say 'Wise One' with awe and reverence. What do you really know about this guy, Kel?"

"Drew's father?" I choose my words carefully. I don't want to betray any confidences. "He was in the Air Force. Apparently being faithful isn't really his thing, neither is paying child support. I think he's lived life on the edge. Drew and his mom figured out how to get by without him pretty early on. Why?"

"Let me just recap so I make sure I've got this right: Drew's father cyber stalks you when he figures out you're his son's girlfriend. He knows your name and what you look like. He knows what car you drive, even though we've been painstakingly careful to make sure there are no existing photos of it across both your socials and Drew's.

He not only knows what school you go to, he's shown up there twice – a grown man who should have a job and a life, neither of which should include harassing a minor. He physically restrains you and practically forces you to carry a message to his son, who so far has refused to have anything to do with him and in all likelihood is going to be furious with him and you for doing so. Did I miss anything?"

"So, you think Drew's going to be mad?"

"Did you hear *anything* else I just said?"

"Yes. But you're thinking like you. I was wearing Drew's away jersey at the game. It has his name and number right on it – pairing us up wouldn't require much of a leap. A surprising number of people know my name at Drew's school. Mr. Jarrod could've asked any one of them for it. And we were late getting out after the game was over. We had to wait for the team to come out of the dressing room and then Ginny sucked everyone into her drama. By the time Drew and I finally made it out to the parking lot there were only a couple of cars left. That's probably why Mr. Jarrod was peering in the windows; he was trying to figure out which car was mine."

"And showing up at Barton?"

I'm parallel parking and frowning. "Okay. *That* was weird." Then I remember Whitney. "But, maybe not. After I was attacked on Instagram, Drew and his friends rallied the support of everyone they knew. I'm sure the name of my school came up – Barton already has a reputation for being insufferable. That's the sort of thing people remember."

"He was there an *hour* before your school started."

"I think he just wanted to make sure he could get me alone."

"Which is not creepy at all."

"He's desperate, Jack. You should've seen his face."

"I don't trust him."

"Neither does Drew. Which brings me back to the real problem: How do I tell Drew I've got a letter from his father for him?"

"After he specifically made you promise not to have anything to do with him." Jack reminds me. Because he's comforting like that. "Yeah. I don't know, Kel. You better bake the biggest batch of cookies ever and come in wearing your heart on your sleeve."

"He's going to be furious, isn't he?" I turn off the ignition and thunk my forehead against the steering wheel.

"Probably," Jack says quietly. "We don't know their history, but whatever happened between them it was bad enough for Disney Prince to threaten physical violence against own father."

The pit in my stomach is only growing. "Ugh. I can't think about this right now. I've got to go work." I sit up straight and take a deep, cleansing breath. "Thanks Jack."

"Kel?"

"Yes?"

"Drew *will* forgive you."

"How can you be so sure?" I sound as miserable as I feel.

"Loads of experience." Jack's voice softens. "You're annoyingly impossible to stay mad at. Good luck today with Archer Darby. Let me know how everything goes?"

I step out of the Mini with a composure I'm far from feeling. "I will."

Archer Darby is a husband and wife design team that recently moved from New York to Austin but they've kept shops in both places. They specialize in high end business to evening wear. I walked for them at the Couture Fashion Show in Dallas a few weeks ago as part of Dallas Fashion Week where they showcased some of their more formal pieces. They asked me back today to model a private preview of their spring collection for a major potential client. Along with two other girls, I'm required to sign several non-disclosures before we're taken back and dressed. The buyers are male, the music is quiet, and the pace is slow. Beyond the initial impact, there's a great deal of interest in the details and drape of each garment. While sipping tea from exquisite fine china, the gentlemen comment openly on what they like while an assistant takes notes.

"That all went very well," Pippa Archer says with her pleasant upper crust English accent and pleasant smile as she thanks everyone for all their hard work. She places a slim hand on my arm as she turns to leave. "Kel, may I have a word with you before you go?" This feels considerably less pleasant.

I gather my handbag and scarf and follow her into her office, my heart pounding.

"Would you mind closing the door behind you? Thanks. Please, sit. Don't look so worried. You've been quite a find for us, Kel. Even our buyers commented on it. Possibly because they snapped up almost everything you wore. Thomas and I are hoping you'll open our show for us in February during New York Fashion Week."

I'm nodding. I hear myself tell her I'd be honored but it feels like I'm watching someone else do and say these things from under water.

"I'll talk to Kirstie then, shall I?"

"Please," I finally manage, breaking through the surface of my shock and drawing breath. "Thank you for this incredible opportunity, Pippa. I won't let you down."

"Of course you won't." She makes a discreet gesture and her assistant brings in a wrapped Archer Darby box. "Often when I design I have a certain woman in mind. I must've been thinking of you with this piece. When you stepped out from behind the curtain with it on we all caught our breath just a little. I'd like you to have it Kel, as a gift from me and Thomas. Consider it a thank you for a job well done today."

I take the box home and carefully unpack the gorgeous, ice blue sheath from its bed of tissue paper. The top is fitted and it has a swingy skirt with the exception of one panel, just above my left knee, that's shorter – giving the illusion that there's an underskirt, drawing attention to my long legs. The coloring of the dress makes the blue in my eyes pop. Staring at my bare-footed reflection in my closet mirrors feels oddly like déjà vu. Wistfully my fingertips search for the skirt of the little black dress Mom found for me a lifetime ago. I still remember that day vividly. It was the day I finally saw what she saw when she looked at me.

Thursday morning I wake up so sore from Tony's ab workout the night before that I have to grit my teeth to reach for my phone but I'm ready to celebrate. It's Drew's birthday.

Me: Hey handsome, Happy Birthday! Can't imagine my life without you in it. Good job you, for being born. And for growing so tall. Love you truly, madly, deeply xx

Charlie is ready to run. "Not today, buddy." I tell him. He's confused. I'm putting on sweats and shoes – it *looks* like we're running. Until I start hauling four huge garbage bags stuffed full of balloons out of the living room.

"You off?" Dad says, stretching as he wanders into the kitchen.

"Yeah. Thanks again for blowing all these up. Erin must really like you."

"Maybe she just likes you."

"Maybe she just likes Drew," I grin at him.

"Get out of here. I'll take care of Charlie."

"Be back with your car in about an hour."

Ryan left Drew's keys to Betty under the flowerpot by the garage for me. I quickly stuff the cab with Hershey Kisses and balloons and decorate the outside with window markers and streamers. And then take a picture of me grinning next to his truck and hang it on his rear view mirror attached to a posh necktie and a voter's registration card with a little note that says, "Sorry, only one of us is an adult here – and it's not me. Happy Birthday!"

At lunch I have eighteen pizzas delivered to him at MacArthur.

After school, Tony abuses me for two hours while Drew practices with the team. Gabriela is preparing a special birthday dinner with all of Drew's favorites and I'm absolutely ditching my "fuel plan" (Tony's euphemism for "diet of broiled chicken and steamed vegetables") tonight. Miraculously, I make it to Drew's house before he does. His little five-year old sister, Daisy, offers to let me hide his present in her closet. We're setting the table together when Drew finally walks in the front door.

"Hey you," he says with his easy grin. "You're in trouble."

"Yeah? Well, I'm not the one who's late."

"Drew. Shower." Gabriela takes off her apron as she walks out of the kitchen. "You can kiss Kel later."

"Later." I put a finger to his lips and wink at him.

"Or *never,*" Will gags. "Gross."

"Ha. I'll remind you of this conversation in about five years, dude." Drew messes up his little brother's hair. "Be right back."

Dinner is a smorgasbord of dishes that have nothing in common except for Drew's love of them individually and universally – he's in birthday boy, second helpings heaven. At the end of the meal, Gabriela triumphantly brings out a double layer, chocolate frosted cake; candles aglow, as is her face as we ooh and aah over her masterpiece. Ryan's been assigned chief photographer duties and he's wildly gesturing for us to all crowd in a bit closer as we enthusiastically sing "Happy Birthday" but just before Drew can make his wish and blow out his candles, the doorbell rings – bringing our Norman Rockwell moment to a screeching halt.

"Are you expecting anyone mi hijo?" Gabriela asks, carefully placing the cake down on the table.

Drew shakes his head and excuses himself to answer the door. I'm filled with a sense of foreboding. *He didn't think I was going to give Drew the letter right away - did he?* Apparently, he did.

"Happy Birthday, son," Andy Jarrod says, his smile somewhat uncertain as he stands in the doorway. I don't know how I didn't spot the family resemblance right away. In this light it's strikingly obvious that Drew, even with Gabriela's olive skin and dark hair, is an upgraded version of his father.

Drew frowns. "What are *you* doing here?"

Mr. Jarrod looks past Drew's shoulder to me. I shake my head slightly, just enough that he knows I haven't given Drew his letter yet. "You promised." It's accusatory and angry.

"I'm sorry." I can feel the color flooding my cheeks. "I was waiting for the right time."

Drew turns to me in confusion. "Kel?"

"He wanted me to give you a letter." My voice is small but I square my shoulders and own it. "I told him I would."

"When?!"

"Yesterday. At Barton."

Incredulous, Drew rounds on his father, slamming him up against the house and pinning him there. "You went *to her school?!* I told you to LEAVE HER ALONE!"

"Children, go in the other room and watch a movie," Gabriela says quickly, nodding at Ryan.

Their eyes are huge. Daisy looks like she might cry. "Come on guys." Ryan hurriedly puts his arms around his younger siblings and ushers them into the TV room.

"Drew," she says quietly, placing a gently restraining hand on her son. With a final angry push, Drew releases him and steps away. But he stays between Gabriela and her ex-husband and he looks like he could plow a fist into his father's face at any moment. "You need to go, Andy. Now."

Andy is defiant. "I don't get a say in this?"

Gabriela's shakes her head. "You gave up your right to have a say with us a long time ago. You're no longer welcome here."

"You can't shut me out, Gabi. He's my son, too."

Drew's blue eyes, so like his father's, are practically sparking. "I have news for you *Dad.* I'm officially an adult now; I can make my own decisions. We're done. Don't come back. And stay away from my girlfriend. Next time, Mom might not be here to save you."

"I just wanted..."

Drew shoves him, knocking him over, and then steps back and slams the door shut with a ferocity that echoes throughout the house and startles both Gabriela and me.

"Mi hijo," Gabriela cautions and she softly adds something else in Spanish I can't quite make out.

"You're getting a restraining order against him, Kel." Drew grabs his truck keys; he's clearly disgusted with me, his father and maybe even himself. "I need some air."

I help Gabriela and the kids somberly clean up the kitchen. The candles have all melted into wax puddles on the cake and gone out. When he doesn't return after an hour, I pull the letter out of my purse and leave it with Gabriela.

"Give him time, Kel. He'll find his way back to us."

I numbly nod. On the way home I call Jack.

"Hey Kel. What's up?"

“Tell me again how impossible it is to stay mad at me.” My voice is tremulous and wire thin. I’m not sure how much longer I can keep the tears at bay. “Please, Jack.”

11

"When you're dreaming with a broken heart,
the waking up is the hardest part"
John Mayer

"McDreamy working tonight?"

"He had other plans," Dad says, his hand on the small of my back as we walk into the kitchen where most of the family has assembled. "It's just us today."

I try my best to smile. "Need any help, Gran?"

Sam's brought Liesel. She's tiny, barely 5′ tall, with a dark pixie cut, a little button nose, and big brown eyes with crazy long, spiky lashes. "Oh my gosh, you're Texas Tall!" she squeals and then punches Sam in the thigh. Mostly because that's what she can reach. "Why didn't you tell me she was your cousin?"

"Who's Texas Tall?" Sam looks confused.

"Seriously?" Liesel says.

"We love him anyway," I smile. "I'm Kel. It's nice to meet you, Liesel."

"I bought all the products you used for your natural face video." She leans in and points to her cheeks. "See, dewy, right?"

"Nice. You have amazing skin."

"Where's Drew?" Landry says, hauling in chairs. "His fantasy football team is totally kicking...it," he finishes sheepishly when he notices Gran archly watching him with a dishtowel in her hand and an eyebrow raised.

"I'm not sure." He hasn't returned any of my calls or texts. He's been radio silent for three days now. I'm trying to give him space but I feel wobbly and lost and scared that he even needs it. "Did you want this asparagus in spears or bite-sized?"

"Spears." Gran hands a salad to Aunt Jill for tossing. "We're grilling it."

"You're even prettier in real life. What's it like being a model?" Liesel asks, climbing up onto a stool to supervise Sam's potato mashing.

"A lot of hard work," Aunt Shae says, putting the finishing touches on her fruit platter. "And not nearly as glamorous as you'd imagine. Kirstie told me Archer Darby wants you to open their show for New York's Fashion Week. Congratulations, Kel. That's huge."

"Thanks."

"Up." Hal is tugging on my leg.

"Let's leave Kel alone," Jules says, scooping up her son. "Look, she's making your favorite vegetable."

"Really?" Liesel makes a face. "I couldn't face asparagus until I was a senior in high school."

"She was kidding." Sam rolls his eyes.

"Samuel Mann McCoy," Gran scolds.

Trey hoots and snaps the length of his forefinger against his middle finger several times, making a clacking noise. "Somebody's in the doghouse, Sammy boy. Pops says the steaks are about done. Anyone seen Brody?"

Sam looks chastened. "Sorry, Liesel. It's just, you know, no one likes asparagus when they're a kid."

"Haven't seen him," Cade says, walking in with Brody on his shoulders. He puts his hands to his mouth. "Bro–dy. Bro–dy."

"He's up there," Noah giggles, pointing at his grinning little brother who is hanging on tightly to fistfuls of Cade's hair.

I make my way out to the back porch where Pops is manning the grill with Uncle Bryce, Uncle Nick and Dad. "Asparagus. I brushed it with olive oil and kosher salt. It's ready to go."

"Thanks sweetheart." Pops takes it from me and hands it to Uncle Nick. "Where's Drew tonight?"

"With his family," Dad says quickly. Maybe too quickly. Uncle Bryce is suddenly watching me very closely. I'm not sure I'm going to be able to keep this up. Dad rescues me. "Kel, would you please grab one more platter for us?"

I return to the kitchen. "Claire, we need one more platter for the meat. Is there anything left in the cupboard?"

She stops putting rolls in breadbaskets and checks. "Big or small? Actually, take this one." She removes the last three rolls off her now empty tray, dusts it for crumbs, and hands it to me.

"Hey Q." He's hunkered down scratching Charlie's ears. *Sorry, buddy.* "Would you please take this out to Pops? Try and keep your hands off the top of it. If there's any dog hair in the meat Gran will have both our hides."

Sneaking back through the hallway I make my way to Gran's cell phone basket. Digging mine out I slip out the side door and into the rose garden and the relative privacy of the stone bench and text Drew: At Pops and Gran's. Everyone keeps asking about you. Don't know what to tell them. Wish I did. Mostly I'm just missing you. So much. I love you Drew Jarrod. Don't forget that.

I sit and stare at my phone, willing three little dots to appear but they don't. *Don't cry. Don't cry. Don't cry.*

"Kel, awe you sad?" Brody. The kid gets around.

"No," I sniff.

"You awe cwying." Nailed by a two-year old.

I swipe at my eyes. "Are you hungry Brody? I'm hungry."

"I'n hungwy too."

"Let's go eat."

He puts his chubby little hand in mine. "No phones," he sings, pointing at my contraband. "No phones!" I smile in spite of myself. I almost wish Jack were here to witness it: *this* is why I am the way that I am.

Monday night as I'm climbing into bed I get a text, but not from Drew.

Travon: What's up with our boy? You guys okay?

Me: Wish I knew. Haven't heard from him since his birthday party.

Travon: Dude looks baaad. Don't think he's slept in days. What's up with that?

Me: His dad showed up. They had words. Drew shoved him up against a wall. If his mom hadn't been there he probably would've taken him out.

Travon: Scrud.

I take a lot of abuse for my vocabulary. Mostly from Travon.

Me: Exactly! You've got his back, right T?

Travon: Always.

Me: Miss him like crazy.

Travon: He misses you too.

Jack is now a fairly regular observer of *Torture by Tony.* They must believe I really do have a "team," no one even bats an eye anymore when he just shows up and settles in to do some work. Except for Nessa, one of the trainers. She bats both eyes at him every chance she gets and fetches him glasses of ice water. She's always finding an excuse to touch his *muscle groups*, which seems like a thinly veiled excuse to grope him. "Someone likes you," I tease, laying a towel down to absorb my sweat before I plop myself down on the table next to his laptop. Either I'm getting tougher or Tony's gone soft, it's no longer excruciating.

Jack leans back in his chair and places his hands behind his brown wavy hair, which he's taken to wearing quite short. The scruff will always be there. "Of course she does. I'm very likeable."

"Do you like her too?"

"What is this, Kel? Sixth grade?"

"You're here all the time." I point out the obvious. "And your apartment smells better." I'm actually guessing on that; I've never been to Jack's place but it can't smell worse.

"Yeah, but you can't beat the entertainment value. I think I'd actually pay money to watch you do squats on a Bosu ball," he says, closing his laptop. He's done talking about Nessa. "Kirstie wants me to go with you to New York to shoot footage for your next vlog."

Shae is visiting her sister in California; I was going to do this trip solo. It's an overnighter, but Jack's gone with me before, it shouldn't be a problem. Truth be told, I could use the company right now. "Sweet. I get aisle this time. My legs are longer and you never have to go to the bathroom." I hop off the table. "Which reminds me, I should probably go inform Tony I'm out Thursday and Friday."

"Try and look a little less giddy when you do," Jack advises dryly.

We're shooting a promotional video in New York for Archer Darby to play on a loop at their stores. And we have an early flight out. The darkness is still heavy when Jack's

Mustang pulls into our driveway. I leave a note for Dad on the kitchen counter and strict instructions with Charlie not to wake him as I turn the alarm off and slip out with my luggage.

"You know there's a weight limit, right?" Jack says hefting my backpack into his trunk.

"Homework," I shrug. "But if you want me to do the heavy lifting just let me know. I work out."

"Get in the car, McCoy."

Jack videos me in the airport as we sit off in a corner by ourselves while we wait to board. "Heading to the Big Apple today." I grin and make a face. "It's *really* early." I pull out my phone and flash the display on my screen for the camera to see just how early it is. A big 4:27 a.m. floats boldly over a selfie I took of me on Drew's back, my arms thrown around his neck as I'm leaning in to kiss him on the cheek. I drop the cheerful façade. It's been a week today.

Jack puts his camera down. "Still no word from Disney Prince?" he says quietly.

"No." It's small and tight. Not a lot of room for expansion.

"He's going to come to his senses Kel."

"Maybe he already has," I say flatly, turning to stare out the window at the planes emerging whole from the darkness as they approach the terminal. I wonder if he's up, what he's thinking. I'd text and ask him but at this point it's starting to feel naggy. I don't ever want to be that girl.

Jack disappears for about ten minutes. When he returns his arms are hidden behind his back. "I got you something. Pick a hand."

I humor him. "Right."

"You suck at this."

"The other right."

He produces a bottle of water. "Ta-dah!"

I smile faintly and roll my eyes. "Gee, thanks."

"Okay, maybe you were right the first time," he grins. There's a box of three Godiva dark chocolate truffles in his outstretched right hand now dancing around my nostrils. He knows me so well. They're my absolute favorite.

"I can't eat those, Jack."

"I won't tell Tony if you don't."

"He'll know," I sigh. "He's probably downloading satellite pictures of this even as we speak." But I take them anyway. "Thanks, that's really sweet of you." Our zone is being called for boarding. Carefully tucking the chocolates and water bottle in my bag, I gather up my belongings and my breaking heart and follow him dejectedly onto the plane.

"Hang on just a sec, Dad?"

Jack is knocking at the door of my hotel room. We're going out to dinner together after a very long day of shooting. "Come on in. I'll just be a minute," I tell Jack, waving him in. I've got Dad on speakerphone so I can finish getting ready. "You look nice," I whisper with a smile and go back to my conversation with my father while putting a few pins in my hair. "I can't believe you told Uncle Bryce about Erin. What were you thinking?"

"Thanksgiving is next week. I couldn't put it off much longer."

Thanksgiving. There will be no escaping the inevitable questions about Drew this time. *What am I going to do?* In the long ensuing silence Dad finally clears his throat. "Drew stopped by earlier this evening on his way to a game."

My heart leaps. "He did?"

"He didn't know you were in New York."

"How did he look? What did he say?"

Dad sighs. "I don't want you to read anything into this; the two of you really need to talk face to face. But he had the guitar you gave him for his birthday. He wanted me to return it to you. He probably would've held onto it until you got back but I think he was worried it might get stolen if it was left in his truck and he didn't have time to go back home with it."

The handful of hairpins I was holding scatter as I lean staggered over the bathroom sink. *He returned the guitar. It's over. We're over.* My brain can't process it. *We can't be.*

"I'm sorry, Kel. Just promise me you won't jump to any conclusions. Give him a chance to explain. I gave him your flight information. He asked if he could be here when you got home. You can get this all sorted then."

I'm nodding and mutely crying.

"Kel?"

"I heard. I've got to go," I finally manage and I end the call.

Jack already has tissues in hand. "Come here," he says, taking me into his arms. I can't talk about it. Mostly because I don't really understand what happened. So I just sob all over his jacket and ruin his dress shirt. And he lets me.

"You sleepy?" Jack asks some time later when I'm all cried out. We're stretched out on the bed in my hotel room against propped up pillows, under a few blankets to keep warm, his jacket's off, his sleeves rolled up, his shoes are by the door, my hairpins are gone and my hair is down, I've cleaned the mascara streaks off my face, my contacts are out, glasses on, and I'm lying curled up next to Jack barefooted in my dress, my head on his chest, his arm around my shoulder while we watch Jason Bourne nail someone with a stapler. Our room service dishes are still sitting by the TV. The empty Godiva box is in the trash.

"No," I say. I'm exhausted. But I don't want him to go. It feels a little less lonely with him here.

He runs the back of his finger tenderly across my cheek. "You sure, Kel? That was some pretty heavy breathing coming from you a minute ago."

"Hello. Matt Damon."

"He's short."

"So are you."

"6′1″ is *not* short."

My eyelids are growing heavier and heavier as I nestle into him. "Jack?"

"Hmm?"

"Promise *you* won't leave me."

"I won't," he sighs and kisses the top of my head. "I can't."

I wake up in the morning, momentarily disoriented and confused. There's a solid arm draped across my waist and the body heat I'm feeling along the length of me isn't coming from Charlie.

Jack. New York. No Drew. My eyes are wide open now but I still can't see. And I don't want to search for my glasses in case I wake Jack up. I don't know what time it is but my 7:00 a.m. alarm hasn't gone off yet.

Jack snuggles in tighter and then his breathing pattern changes slightly and I can almost gauge the moment he's fully awake because he immediately lets go. I shift slightly in his arms, suddenly a little shy. "Good morning."

He's quick to put some distance between us. "Morning."

I sit up and find my glasses on the nightstand. I'm pretty sure my hair is a tousled mess; the blankets are pooled at my lap. "Did you sleep okay?"

He rubs at his eyes. "Well, you don't snore."

Something in his voice makes me ask. "Do I kick?"

"Like a mule."

I laugh. "I do not."

He pulls at his scruff and smiles sleepily at me. "Why do you think I was spooning you McCoy? Those long legs of yours can't do as much damage from close range."

I blush. "Sorry."

He props himself up on an elbow. "How are you?"

"Resigned, I guess." It's strange, this newfound intimacy between us. It feels different. *We* feel different. I now know Jack's a cuddler. I'm not sure how to find my way back to familiar ground. Mom believed manners were the perfect answer to any social difficulty. I reach for them now. "Thanks for last night, Jack. Maybe one of these days you'll be the needy one and I can return the favor."

"Maybe," Jack says, as if it's a real possibility. It's kind of him not to laugh it off outright. He tugs on my blanketed toe; his hazel eyes are searching my bespectacled ones like he wants to tell me something but he's not quite sure how to begin. He doesn't get the chance. My alarm goes off and he runs a hand impatiently through his hair as I reach to quiet my phone. The moment's gone. "I guess we better get this day started," he says, sitting up and throwing the blankets aside. "I'm going to go back to my own room and shower. The car's scheduled to pick us up at 8:00. We should leave enough time to eat something before we go." He heads into the bathroom briefly and then retrieves his jacket and tie.

I meet him in my badly wrinkled dress at the hotel room door and hold it open for him. "I'll hurry. Thanks again, Jack."

He reaches out and gently touches my hair. Possibly because it looks like a haystack and could use a good patting down. "Any time you want me to spend the night with you again, Kel; just let me know." He leans in and kisses my cheek; his whiskers skim my jawline as he nuzzles his way to my ear and whispers, "I'll be sure and bring shin guards next time."

My hair is still in an elegant chignon from the final wardrobe ensemble for the shoot and I'm wearing considerably more make-up than I normally do; I almost feel underdressed boarding the plane at the end of the day in my turtleneck and skinny jeans. The businessman sitting across the aisle from me has put down his *Wall Street Journal* and is eyeing me appreciatively. I've pulled out my copy of Joseph Conrad's *Heart of Darkness* and spread out my usual assortment of sticky flags and highlighters across my table tray.

"You like Conrad?" he asks.

I put my finger down to hold my spot so I can politely give him my full attention. "So far. This is my first time reading him."

"Oh, did he write anything else?"

"I think he was fairly prolific. *Heart* might've just been his most renowned work." I return to my book.

"You reading it for a class?"

Beside me Jack is getting irritated. I put my finger back down on my passage. "I am."

"English major?"

"Not exactly." I pick my book back up and do my best to look deeply engrossed in it.

"Humanities?" he continues, oblivious to my body language.

"High school," Jack says pointedly. "You want to give her some space? She's got an assignment due."

I smile at Jack.

"What?" he mutters.

"Nothing," I shrug. But a moment later I draw a little orange heart on the back of his right hand with my highlighter.

Betty is already sitting in our driveway when Jack pulls in.

"You okay?" Jack quietly asks as he puts the Mustang in park.

"Part of me never wants to get out of this car," I confess, suddenly terrified of what's about to happen. Right now, nothing is definite; nothing has ended. In a few minutes that could all change. Then I see Drew. He's walking out to meet me. In the sudden glare of the motion sensor security lights all I can see in that tense, tired, beautiful face is that he still loves me. And I can't get out of the car fast enough.

"Hey Kel," he says hoarsely. Travon's right; he looks terrible.

I throw myself into his arms. "Drew Jarrod, don't you *ever* do that to me again."

12

"Hello from the other side"
Adele

"I've told myself I'm not him, I'm nothing like him, for so many years that I actually believed it," Drew says. We're sitting on my bed, our legs tangled together, both my hands are touching him; I can't seem to let go. "Turns out I'm just like him, only sober. At least he had an excuse." He sounds so bitter and self-recriminating I can't bear to hear any more.

"Look at me." Words can hurt, break, blister, and punish but they can also lift, restore and heal. *Find those words. Use those words.* "You've taken care of your mom and your brothers and sister your whole life, not because you had to but because it's who you are. You're big-hearted and brave and extremely loyal. People depend on you because they know they can. This, losing your temper with your dad – someone who has hurt people you love – doesn't make you a monster; it just means you're human."

"I saw the look on your face, Kel. You were scared of me."

"No. No, I wasn't. I was scared *for* you. It's not the same thing at all. You asked me not to have anything to do with him. I promised I wouldn't. But I did it anyway. If anyone should be apologizing, it's me. I'm sorry, Drew. Really, I am."

Drew pulls me onto his lap. "That's my line."

"I forgive you." I smile and kiss him soundly. "See how easy that was?" Then I spot the Taylor Signature guitar I got him for his birthday, sitting in the corner of my bedroom. "Now mister, about your birthday present. You have some explaining to do."

He watches me watching him. "I loved it. It's the most beautiful guitar I've ever seen. And the sound is amazing."

"So?"

"It cost thousands of dollars, Kel. It's too much."

"This may surprise you, it still surprises me, but I actually get paid a lot of money to have my picture taken."

"Save it for school."

"My parents set up a college fund for me when I was born. It's already paid for."

"Buy yourself something nice."

"I did. And I gave it to you." I extract myself from his arms, retrieve the guitar and place it on his lap. "Happy Birthday, Drew. I hope this inspires you to always follow your dreams."

"You inspire me," he says quietly. "But thank you, Kel."

I kiss him gently. "Right answer."

Erin has daughters. Two, if we're getting specific. Ava is sixteen and Bella, thirteen. They're all coming to Thanksgiving dinner at Pops and Gran's. Dad thinks we should do a trial run on a smaller scale and invite them over for Sunday dinner at our place to ease them into it before we go the whole McCoy.

"Ava's a vegan," Dad announces, making her my assignment as he walks by with a basket full of freshly folded laundry.

I look up from my shopping list. "Are you serious?"

"What? You've sort of already eased me into it."

"Once a week." And Dad never complains about it but there's a visible sagging of shoulders and immediate air of resignation whenever he wanders into the kitchen and discovers it's vegan night *again.* If things between Dad and Erin continue as they have been there's a definite possibility we could all be family one day. Neither of us has actually said it out loud yet but that's the collision course we're on. I pull up a recipe for an apple nut quinoa salad I tried a few weeks ago and quite liked; it will go well with the pork roast already on the menu and we have almost everything we need to make it. My list transfers automatically to my phone; I close my laptop and hop off my stool just as Dad re-emerges with his keys in hand. "Have you met them yet?"

"Just once. They spend every other weekend with their father in Dallas."

"What are they like?"

"Teen-age girls."

"What's *that* supposed to mean?"

"You'll see." He shakes his head at Charlie. "Sorry bud, not this time. Can we try and keep it to a two-stop shop? Bryce and Justin are coming over this afternoon to help me lay down some flooring upstairs and I need to do some prep work before they get here."

I have to spend my afternoon with Tony. Jack is nowhere in sight, which is completely understandable – it's the weekend and he has a life. But I miss his sardonic grin all the same. I'm not the only one. "Jack's not with you?" Nessa says wistfully when she realizes I've come alone, that I haven't just hidden him behind me. She checked.

She waits expectantly for me to tell her where he might be, what he might be doing but he hasn't texted or called since he dropped me off last night. With a start I suddenly realize I was in such a tear to get to Drew I completely forgot all about Jack. No: *Good-bye, Jack.* No: *Thanks for letting me cry all over you, Jack; and eating room service when you REALLY wanted to go out, Jack; and then putting up with me kicking you all night when you could've been comfortably asleep in your own bed, Jack.* After everything he'd done for me in New York, I'd left him in an instant without a backward glance, without another thought. I didn't even remember my luggage in the back of his car. Dad must've brought it in for me.

"Stop dawdling, Barbie!" Tony barks. "You've missed two workouts and it already shows. Nessa, I want her stats. You. Start jumping rope."

I deserve Tony today.

When he finally gets bored with trying to kill me off and releases me, I dive for my phone. I have to keep wiping my sweaty hands and smeary screen on my sweaty shorts but I can't take the time to shower and change. I'm a horrible person.

Me: I owe you SO many cookies! When and where? I'll deliver.

Jack: Unnecessary.

Me: Nonsense. You were a saint. ARE a saint. Please? I know how much you love freshly baked cookies still warm from the oven...

Jack: I'm out tonight.

Me: Breakfast?

Jack: Might be awkward. Not sure how I'd explain that.

Me (blushing): Right. Of course. Sorry.

Jack: You and Drew kiss and make up?

Me: Yes!

Jack: Thought so. Happy for you, Kel. Got to go.

Me: Thank you for everything, Jack! Thank you again. And again. And again.

He doesn't respond.

Sunday night, Dad, Charlie, and I are waiting at the front door all cleanly dressed and pressed, ready with big smiles to greet the Caffreys: the McCoy Family Welcoming Committee. Mom trained us well. "Ava, Bella, this is my daughter, Kel," Dad says as he ushers everyone inside.

"It's so nice to meet you," I say. Nice, but also weird. Charlie barks once to remind us he's there and then patiently sits down and expectantly waits. "This is Charlie. Don't worry; he's really friendly."

"May I pet him?" Bella asks shyly, bending down to his level but looking up at me. She has Erin's dark eyes and a flash of deep dimples in her rounded cheeks. Her soft curls are the color of milk chocolate. She hesitates to make sure he's okay, that we're okay with her in our space. I feel a rush of warmth toward her and realize, maybe for the first time, that I'm not the only one facing big change here.

"He'd be crushed if you didn't," I tell her, joining her on the floor and showing her where Charlie likes most to be scratched.

Ava proves much harder to win over. Any attempts I make at starting a conversation with her are met with a terse reply and an immediate return to her phone. The last time it's accompanied by a heavy sigh and rolling of eyes. She takes her hair tie out and lets her hair fall forward, effectively curtaining off her face from us. Obviously, I'm annoying her; I'm having Whitney flashbacks. I look to Dad for guidance but he just shrugs. I can tell that he wants me to keep trying but I'm not sure I'm that masochistic.

Then Drew arrives, fresh from his shift at Strings, with that face and those blue eyes and it's like a switch flips. Suddenly Ava's out of her phone. She's sitting up straight, smoothing her hair back behind her ear, and smiling. At him. But it's revelatory; she's actually quite pretty when she's not scowling. "Boy, am I glad to see you," I whisper in Drew's ear as he leans in to kiss me. "Ava hates me. Go, be charming."

He does. At dinner I seat him next to Ava. I sit across from him and next to Bella. Dad and Erin are at either end of the table: one big, awkward, happy-ish family. Drew draws her out. Through him we discover she plays tennis, hates the rain, wishes there were more holidays, and thinks licorice is disgusting. When it's apparent that dinner is winding down I casually say, "Drew's a very talented musician. I bet if we ask him nicely he'd sing for us."

Gran does this to him all the time; I know he won't mind. "You singing with me, Chicago?" he asks with his half-grin, his blue eyes dancing.

I hesitate a beat, and in that space Ava rushes in. "I will."

No one looks more surprised than Erin. "There you go," I say, standing to start clearing the table. "Drew, you know where my guitar is. Let me know if you need anything else." *Bless you.*

Dad places two stools from the kitchen island out in front of the open space in the great room for their performance. While the rest of us clean up from dinner, Drew and Ava pick a song and go off by themselves to practice it quietly a few times. Dad and Erin are on the loveseat. Bella, Charlie and I are on the couch; Bella has Charlie gathered in her arms, her chin tucked between his ears and looking for all the world as if the two of them are the best of friends instead of newly made acquaintances.

Drew and Ava perform Taylor Swift's *Style* and even nervous, Ava knows every word by heart – it's obviously one of those songs she's sung endlessly into her hairbrush at the top of her lungs. Drew harmonizes beautifully and it covers the few times she's not quite on key.

"Did you record us?" Ava breathlessly asks me when the clapping has ended and we're all gathered around congratulating them.

"I did. I thought you might want a copy."

My first smile. "I do. Thanks, Kel."

We end the night as we began, at the front door, this time to wave good-bye.

"I don't know what we would've done if you hadn't shown up," I tell Drew, leaning back against his solid chest.

He wraps his arms loosely around my waist. "Ava? She seemed nice enough."

"Oh, she was. To you. I was getting nowhere, fast."

"Erin says Ava's had a hard time with the divorce," Dad sighs. "We might have to bear the brunt of it for a while."

"How long's a *while*?" I ask him skeptically.

"Eventually she'll go away to college," Dad shrugs, closing the door; the tail lights from Erin's Rover are no longer visible. "Until then, Drew, don't go anywhere."

Thanksgiving day I get up early enough to squeeze in a ten mile run. I've got two turkey dinners to plow through and there's no way I'm skimping on pie. If you're a McCoy, the holiday actually starts with an early breakfast at Pops and Gran's. Along with the usual suspects, my cousin Ben is home from New York and Jake is back from M.I.T. and he brought Rachel – apparently long-distance is working out just fine for them.

"Looking good, Squirt," Jake says, giving me a bear hug. "Nice to see you again, Drew."

"Hey Rachel," Landry says walking into the front hall, hugging her. Then he slaps his little brother on the back. "Eat quick you two. Everyone else is done and we're about to start picking teams."

"Who put Q and Noah in charge this year?" Sam appears in the doorway, looking sulky.

"I did," Gran replies crisply, wiping her hands on her apron; her tone brooks no argument. She didn't raise four rowdy boys for nothing. "Jake and Rachel, come and eat some breakfast while it's still hot. Catch me up on what you've been up to."

Q and Noah have us all divided up by the time Jake and Rachel make their way out to the backyard, hand in hand. Thanks to Cade and Landry's coaching we're pretty evenly matched. "We've got Rachel," Cade says, tossing the football in his hands. "And the ball to start. May the best team – mine – win."

Probably not a shocker, given the McCoys hail from Texas, but we're a family that takes our football very seriously and to make matters worse we're fiercely competitive and mostly athletic – the perfect recipe for several bruised bodies and an occasional trip to the ER. It's glorious fun. We play for ages.

"Next touchdown wins," Uncle Bryce says, panting, his hands on his knees. "Shae just gave me the signal we're needed in the kitchen."

We have the ball. Landry nods and gathers us into a huddle. "Let's end this. I'm going long to Uncle Lucas. Justin and Kel be ready in case he's not open. Everyone else stay at home and block. On three. Team!"

Jake snaps it back to Landry and Dad, Justin, and I tear down the field. Drew is matching me stride for stride. Trey is covering Justin and Uncle Nick is on Dad. No one is on Jake so he starts running. Landry sees he's open and throws a hard spiral right to him and Jake tucks it in and moves faster than I've ever seen him move. Which now means we're blocking for him.

"Sorry, Kel," Drew says and he shifts to the left as Jake runs by us. Drew puts on a burst of speed and lunges for Jake but he's off center. I throw my body on him and take him out.

"Me too," I say when I land heavily on top of him. Jake scores.

"Where did you learn how to do that?" Drew says laughing breathlessly, his hands in my hair.

"She's a McCoy," Landry beams proudly, helping us both up. "It's in the blood."

"Next year you ladies need to trim your nails first," Trey says, holding up his left arm and showing us the angry red streak just above his elbow. We're bunched together outside the bathroom in the hall, waiting for our turn to wash up.

Cade shakes his head. "That was Ben. He got me twice."

The front doorbell rings as we're comparing battle scars. We all lean to the left so we can see who it is. The Caffreys are being welcomed in by Pops and Gran and Dad. Gran is sweetly explaining the house rule about no cell phones and showing Ava her wicker basket already filled with ours. Ava looks horrified. You'd think she'd been told she had to cough up a kidney. Erin and Bella cheerfully add theirs into the pile; Ava clings stubbornly to hers until Erin whispers something in her ear. When she does let go, it's not willingly. She storms by us on her way to the back porch and outside where there are considerably less McCoys to irritate her.

"Wow," Sam says, stepping out and nudging me with his shoulder. We'd all glued our backs to the hall walls to let Ava through. "Is she always like that?"

"I've only met her once," I reply. "But unless you're Drew, yes."

The guys all turn and stare at Drew. "What?" He shrugs. "She likes me."

"I bet," Landry grins. "That's not at all awkward."

Bella found Charlie right away. Or maybe he found her, which means she's an immediate magnet for Noah, Brody, and Hal. On his own, Charlie is naturally a little more wary of their sticky fingers; obviously, he's trusting in her to save him from any abuse. I scoop Hal up and place him on my knee so there's room for me to sit down on the step next to her. "You doing okay with this lot?"

"Yes," she replies softly. "Your family is very tall."

"And loud. We can be kind of overwhelming. Stay out of the fray as long as you want. I need to go peel potatoes."

"Do you need any help?"

"No. You and Charlie – and Noah," I wink at him. "Are keeping the littles occupied." I kiss Hal on his very kissable round cheek and plop him back down beside Bella. "That's huge."

Dinner is noisy and laughter filled, except for our table. Ava is still sulking about her phone and beyond the occasional smile in Drew's direction, refuses to respond to our overtures. Bella is so obviously happiest when she's not being engaged that we eventually stop torturing her by trying to bring her into the conversation.

"I never see you at the ACC anymore," Rachel says gathering a forkful of Gran's amazing stuffing.

"No time," I sigh.

"Well, you're obviously doing something right. You look incredibly fit."

"Thanks. I'm still running."

"And she's working out with a personal trainer," Drew adds. "Tony Ardestrani – Kel hates him."

"How did the launch for the new addition go?" I ask.

"Great. You should come check it out. You're plastered all over the front entrance."

"She's not kidding." Jake makes a face. "She took me by on the way here. It's oddly disconcerting to see yourself looming that large. I had no idea my legs were so hairy."

"I told you to wax," I grin.

"You should stop by and see it for yourself. We've added seven more walls. You know you have free access for life. It's not like they won't recognize you at the door," Rachel smiles.

"Do you know what? I haven't climbed in ages and I really miss it. What do you think, Drew? Could we fit it in tomorrow morning?" I ask.

"My first game isn't until 3:00," Drew nods. "Coach wants us there at 2:00." He looks apologetic as he takes a sip of water. "Holiday basketball tournament."

"You don't do Black Friday?" Rachel says grinning at me.

"Yeah, *no*. But I'd love to spend some time with you guys; it's been too long. You're coming too, right Jake?"

"You mean, instead of getting in the way of my mother's Christmas decorating? Yeah. I'm in."

And because I must like banging my head against a brick wall, I try once more. "Ava, Bella, you want to join us? It's really easy and a lot of fun."

Judging from her immediate and visceral recoil there's nothing Ava would like less. "Are you serious? No!" Jake blinks in surprise at Ava's vehemence and Rachel stares uncomfortably at her plate. Ava's unrepentant until she notices Drew's frown. With a flushed face she finally adds, "But thanks for asking."

To our relief, the doorbell rings. Jake pushes his chair back as he stands and tosses his linen napkin on the table next to his plate. He's closest to the door. "I've got it, Gran." Moments later he reappears with Jack, of all people, dressed in a sports jacket and tie, already apologizing as he walks into the kitchen.

"Sorry to interrupt your Thanksgiving, Mr. and Mrs. McCoy. I promise I'll be quick."

"Nonsense. Please, come in, Jack. We're about to eat dessert," Gran insists. Dad's ready to fetch another chair. "Won't you join us?"

"Thank you, but I can't stay; my family is expecting me. I just need to steal Kel for a moment, if I may?"

I'm already on my feet but I can't read his face. I hope nothing's wrong. "Of course. We can talk in here." I indicate the direction of the living room with a wave of my hand. "Excuse us please, everyone."

Jack pushes a hand through his hair; his other hand is on his trim waist. He gets right to the point. "Kirstie's been trying frantically to reach you all morning. Apparently she doesn't know about your grandmother's no cell phone rule."

"So she made you come track me down? On Thanksgiving?"

"Not a big deal. She called asking if I might know where you were. I was heading over to see my parents; this is kind of on the way. Not the point, Kel. Go get your phone."

He follows me back into the front entryway. "How was your date the other day?" I ask, looking at him over my shoulder.

"It wasn't a date."

"Okay. How was your evening out?" I gently turn Gran's wicker basket on its side and empty its contents onto the sideboard table. We were one of the first to arrive; my phone is at the very bottom.

"She didn't kick if that's what you're asking."

I blush. Jack's in a foul mood. Obviously he and Ava could be besties tonight. I have seven missed calls and three voice messages from Kirstie. And she texted me twice. I call her back. She picks up on the first ring. "Kel? *Finally*. I've been trying to get a hold of you all day."

"Sorry. That's what Jack said. What's up?"

"You need to be on a plane in a couple of hours. Your casting for Bentha's came through. They want you in Milan for their show this weekend."

Milan? As in Italy? I'm staring numbly at my reflection in Gran's antique oval mirror. Still me. *How is this my life?* Kirstie hasn't stopped talking. "I'm sending Jack with you. It's your first international job. I think it will be good for your vlog."

"Wait, what?"

"You two make a great team." Even though I can't see her I know Kirstie's beaming; it's in the sing-song quality of her voice. "Let's get some serious mileage out of this on your socials."

She tells me she's sending me the details and we end the call. Jack's hazel eyes are hooded and distant as we both stare at my phone. "I'm sorry, Jack."

"For what?"

"You probably had plans."

"So did you. But this is our job." He sighs and straightens his tie. "I've got to go. I promised my mom I'd eat turkey with them before I left; she's been baking for days. I'll see myself out. Pick you up at your place in an hour?"

I nod. *I'm going to Italy.*

Might as well announce it to the whole room; they're all staring expectantly at me, waiting. For once there's quiet. "I am...I'm going to Italy. Like right now. I've got to go pack." Drew nods and puts his napkin down.

Sam is the first to break the silence. "Psh. She'll do *anything* to get out of doing the dishes."

"Kel, I can't," Aunt Shae starts to say, looking stricken and suddenly overwhelmed. She has a huge charity event she's in charge of tomorrow night. Drew and I had tickets to attend after his last game. He even borrowed Landry's tux.

"I know. Don't worry about it. Jack is going with me." I kiss Dad on the cheek. "You stay. Drew will take me home. Pops, Gran, thanks for the amazing dinner. Love you all. Happy Thanksgiving, everyone! Ciao!"

"Play something for me while I pack?" I ask Drew as I flick on the light to my bedroom and head straight for my closet. "Please? This is all a bit surreal. I'm feeling a little frazzled."

He picks up my guitar. "Got your passport?"

"I do now." I smile at him and extract it from my desk drawer on my way to the bed, suitcase in hand. "Thank you."

He joins me, moving his knee to make room for my open case as he leans back against the pillows and begins strumming. "I guess this is your life now, Chicago."

"It's *part* of my life." I'm getting pretty good at packing for quick trips. I've streamlined the essentials and have got in the habit of keeping everything I need for a fast getaway clean and accessible. Italy is throwing me a bit but I stick with my strategy of layers. Until Drew starts to pick out the opening chords to, "When You Say Nothing at All."

I should be cramming stuff into my suitcase, Jack will be here any minute, but I sit on the bed, a pile of clothes in my arms, and listen to every beautiful word he sings. "Have I told you lately that I love you, Drew Jarrod?" I say with a wobbly smile when the last note fades.

"Every time you look at me. Come here." He buries my head in his chest. "Go. Be beautiful and smile pretty for the camera, Kel. I'll be right here when you get back."

The doorbell rings.

"That'll be Jack." I wipe my eyes on my sleeve. "I still need to change. Will you tell him I'll be out in ten?"

Quickly, I finish packing and change out of my grass stained clothes into an outfit I can sleep in but still walk off a plane the next morning looking ready to go. I'll fix my hair in the airport.

"That's it?" Jack says with a raised eyebrow when I wheel out my carry-on and tote. "No homework this trip?"

"Not this time. I'm actually caught up for once." Mostly because I'd planned on spending every free moment I had with Drew over the holiday weekend.

"Great. We might actually make weight for once." He takes my case from me and leaves so Drew and I can say good-bye.

"Drew."

"Yeah, I know. Me too."

I kiss him and hand him a hastily scrawled note. "For your mom. Tell her I'm sorry about dinner?"

"I will. Be safe, Chicago. Text me when you land."

It's very quiet in the car. Jack isn't talking as he steers us toward the airport. After a bit I finally say, "So, did you get to eat enough of your mom's turkey?"

"Don't."

I look over at him in surprise. "Don't what?"

"*Don't* feel guilty. *Don't* apologize."

I rest my head against the passenger window and reluctantly smile. "You mean don't be me?"

"Exactly."

"Are you mad at me, Jack?"

He sighs. "Did you hear anything I just said?"

For the first time since we've flown together, Jack drinks. "Hydrating," he says when he orders his third whiskey. "You should try it sometime, Kel." And he downs the entire contents and grimaces. The flight attendant is still smiling at him. Maybe this isn't unusual after all.

"Just water for me, please."

"She *really* likes water," Jack grins.

He follows me off the plane at JFK where we are catching our connecting flight. While we're waiting to board he flirts with an Australian woman with big, brown eyes and a broad smile. Jack's a surfer. Who knew? "We should get a picture of this, right Kel?" He pulls me out of my book. "She's a model," he says to his new friend.

"Hi, I'm Kel." I wave awkwardly. I don't know what else to do.

"Donna. Nice to meet you."

"Is this your first trip to Italy, Donna?" I ask.

Jack's hanging his head in his hands. "No. I've been there a few times," she says. "You?"

"It's my first time. I've heard it's incredible; I'm excited to see it for myself."

"She's a model," Jack reasserts.

"A model?" Donna says politely since this is obviously the direction Jack wants the conversation to go. "What's that like then?"

I hesitate. *Breezy answer or truth?* I doubt I'll ever meet her again. I take a deep breath and smile. "You said you love to surf, Donna? I'm sorry, I was eavesdropping earlier. Did you always know you wanted to surf?"

"Yeah. I grew up on the Gold Coast. It's kind of a way of life there. I've been surfing for as long as I can remember, maybe as soon as I could walk. It's just what we do."

"Sounds amazing. I grew up in Chicago – big lake, no ocean. No one I knew surfed. Wanting to surf never even crossed my mind. Modeling is kind of like that for me. The fact that I'm here, sitting in an airport, ready to fly to Milan because someone thinks my long legs and face work for their look still feels so unexpected and strange."

Jack chuckles. "You should see her in a swimsuit."

Donna stares at him and then me with obvious confusion. I ignore him and smile at her. "What's the Gold Coast like? I've always wanted to go to Australia."

By the time our zone is called and I get Jack settled in his seat on the plane I'm genuinely worried for him. He wandered off to the bar just across from our gate while Donna and I were chatting. He's moving a little slower and sloppier now and his speech is starting to slur.

"Has the flight attendant come by with drinks yet?" He wants to know.

"I think you've had enough."

"Cutting me off, Kel?"

"I am. You'll thank me tomorrow. Try and get some sleep, Jack. We've got a full day ahead of us."

He reaches out and grabs my wrist. "Don't leave me," he mumbles. His fingers seek out the solidness of my arm, just like I did to him in the hotel that night in New York. And suddenly I realize as he drifts off to sleep that he's hurting and lonely. And I'm clueless.

13

"Girls just want to have fun"
Cyndi Lauper

"*Who* is Ava Caffrey?" Becca demands Tuesday morning as she pushes into chemistry and drops her books with a loud thud onto the countertop of our station. "She's after your boyfriend."

I'm jet-lagged and nursing a pounding headache. "Take it down a notch," I beg. "And don't be ridiculous. Her mom is dating my dad. Of course she knows Drew."

Becca climbs onto her stool and blinks at me. "You're wearing glasses."

"My eyes were too dry for contacts this morning."

"Can you still see in those things?"

"Of course I can."

"Really? Because I think you might be blind. Did you see her Instagram posts from Drew's tournament over the weekend?"

"Okay. She likes him. Happy now?"

"Are you?"

"I'm not worried if that's what you're asking."

"Where were you when she was taking all these selfies with Drew? You didn't answer any of my texts."

I take a restorative swig from my water bottle. "I was on a plane. Coming back from Milan."

"Seriously?" Becca's eyes widen. "When did that happen? You didn't say a word about a trip to Italy before the break."

"It was very last minute. I had to work. They don't celebrate Thanksgiving in Italy."

Mr. Franz walks in just as the second bell rings. "I need details," Becca whispers, reaching for her safety goggles.

So does Kirstie. I'm weighing the opportunity to legitimately wriggle out of Tony's grasp against having to sit in the same room with Jack for any extended period of time when she tells me she expects to see me in her office promptly at 4:30.

Fueled by the green vegetable power smoothie Becca humanely brought me after school and several doses of ibuprofen I slink into Adderson's wishing I could just curl up on one of those overstuffed white chairs and hibernate. "Rough trip?" Rosie says sympathetically, handing me a glass of ice water.

"You have *no* idea. Thanks Rosie, you're a lifesaver."

Jack walks in looking damaged and wearing dark sunglasses, even his scruff is bedraggled. He winces noticeably when Rosie greets him with her usual loud enthusiasm. "Sorry. Wow. You guys look awful." You can always count on Rosie for the unblemished truth. That was something we used to laugh about.

He slowly removes his glasses and takes a seat across from me. "Kel."

Now we're talking? I cross my legs and fold my arms. "Jack."

"There's my power couple. Come on in you two," Kirstie beams. "Sit down. I know, those transatlantic flights are the worst. So, tell me all about it. I want to hear everything."

I moisten my lips and avoid looking at Jack. "I think it went well. The Bentha people seemed really happy with my work. They even invited Jack and me to their afterparty. And it was pretty exclusive."

"Good. I hope you got some great footage."

Jack clears his throat. But before he's able to make a full confession I interrupt him. "We did." I hand her my tablet. "I couldn't sleep on the flight home so I got a head start putting it together. I'm sure it'll be much better after Jack's final edit but I think you can get a fairly good idea of where we were going with it."

Jack stares at me as Kirstie watches the series of videos I filmed of my trip while he was out being a total jackass. "This is great. How soon can we have it up?" she asks Jack as she hands me back my tablet.

"I can have it online tonight," he finally replies.

"Good. Sounds like the trip was a resounding success."

"I think it was. We learned a lot, didn't we Jack?"

He silently nods. The moment we're outside of Adderson's I hand him my tablet; he already has my password. "I'm sorry, Kel," he says.

"Good. You should be. I didn't deserve that, Jack. Don't do it again."

Drew is waiting for me at home; he has a code to our front door so he can just let himself in. "Hey babe." He kisses me and takes my face in his big hands. "You look exhausted. You sure you don't want to just crawl into bed and crash?"

"My body is so messed up, Drew. I need you to help me stay up until at least 7:00."

"Come on." He threads his fingers through mine. "I've got *A Christmas Story* ready to go, popcorn made, and all the ice water you could possibly want."

I curl up on the couch next to him and Charlie, who's always down for popcorn and a movie. "I should be studying for calculus right now," I sigh. "But I just don't have the brain cells for it."

"So, let it go." He puts his arm around me and kisses the top of my head as we settle in amongst the cushions.

My eyes fly open when the alarm system indicates the garage door has opened with a discreet but audible beep. "Well, well, look who's awake. Hey beautiful," Drew moves my hair out of my face. I'm lying on top of him next to Charlie, who leans over and promptly licks my now uncovered nose.

Blinking, I find my glasses – which Drew must've taken off – and my phone. It's 6:37. "You let me fall asleep?"

"Hey, I tried. Electric shock wouldn't have kept you up, Kel. You were practically in a coma."

"Glad you're still here Drew," Dad says, walking into the living room from the kitchen already loosening his tie and carrying a plastic bag that is bulging with little white boxes. "I went a little crazy with my Thai order. Can you stay for dinner?"

"Sorry, wish I could – that smells amazing – but my mom has to work the late shift at the hospital tonight. I'm needed at home."

"You hungry Kel?"

"Not really. But Charlie is." I get out of his way as I sit up and stretch.

Drew takes out his phone and opens his Instagram. "I took a picture of us while you slept. I hope that's okay. I kind of wanted to make a statement just to keep things crystal clear."

I look at the picture he posted of me snuggled up against his chest, my long, blonde hair splayed everywhere. When the girl you love falls asleep in your arms it's a good day. #jetlagged #sleepingbeauty #luckyman

"Where was Charlie?"

"He left for a stretch. UPS delivered a package; they must've left it on the front porch. I think he went to investigate." He kisses the tip of my nose. "So, Milan? You still haven't told me much about Italy."

"There's not much to tell. It was mostly work, hotel, work, airport. Jack and I got invited to a party after the show. He drank too much and chased anything in a skirt. I learned how to say 'I have a boyfriend' in Italian. We were a big hit. Sorry about Ava. Was that uncomfortable?"

"Not really. The guys gave me a hard time. You have to walk a thin line with her – nice, but not so nice she gets the wrong idea. I think she just wanted her friends to see she knew a senior from a different school."

"A hot senior," I tease.

He grins. "Well, yeah."

Tony has his eyes on the prize. With less than two weeks before my *Fit* shoot and me in New York a couple of times a week now, he's pushing me fiercely every chance he gets. Jack no longer comes to watch, things between us have settled into brisk professionalism and brief communication. It's almost too bad. He would've appreciated this moment.

"Move!" Tony barks. He's been spitting in my face for almost three hours. My muscles are trembling; I'm dehydrated and having difficulty performing at the same proficiency level as fatigue takes over. At some point I'm at high risk for injury – I'm a dancer; I've had plenty of experience with this. But Tony isn't letting up. "Stop being so lazy!" he screams at me amidst a stream of expletives.

I stop cold. I always imagined my rant, when it finally came, would be much more powerfully delivered. But I can barely catch my breath. "You work for me."

"*What* did you say?"

"I said: You. Work. For. Me." I glare at him, gathering steam. "I am *not* lazy and I've put up with a lot of your crap because Kirstie's right – you do get results. But here's a newsflash for you Tony. I would work just as hard – maybe even harder – without all the shouting, cursing and degrading insults. So either dial it down or I walk. I'm done for today."

The impulse to text Jack on my way out is practically irresistible. And the fact that I don't only makes me sad. It's at times like these, when I'm out of my depth and floundering, that I really miss my mom and her pithy but compassionate wisdom the most. *I think a guy loves me the way I love Drew. How can we still be friends? Because I miss him like crazy.* And she would know. Me, I'm at a loss.

He's at the *Fit* shoot. We start the second day at Barton, early, three hours before the first bell is scheduled to ring. Mrs. Gallins, our Head of School, gave her permission for us to shoot into the first hour of class if needed but no more. Talia, the chief photographer, has everything storyboarded. She knows exactly what she wants and she's efficient with getting it. We wrap fifteen minutes after the second bell rings.

"So this is Barton." Jack stayed behind and waited for me to thank everyone, change back into my own clothes, and remove most of my make-up. He's leaning against a row of lockers in a now empty hall – even the crew has picked up all their equipment and left.

"In all its glory." I'm still sorting out my hair.

"I'm glad I saw you here. In your uniform. In this environment."

"What? High school?"

"Yeah. High school." He shakes his head as he straightens up and pulls on his scruff. "It's easier to picture you here, hauling around your stack of books."

"I don't actually haul them all. That's what my locker's for."

"Right. And I'm keeping you from class. I should probably go before we both get detention." He smiles at me, the first real smile I've seen from him in a while. "Have a good day, Kel."

"You too, Jack." I watch him leave. He doesn't look back.

I slide into English lit and ongoing drama. Blake has a girlfriend who just started at Barton; she's only been here a couple of weeks. Her name is Giulia Altadora and she's tiny and dark and fiercely Italian. Whitney might've met her match. I've already witnessed a couple of screaming matches between them in the parking lot and I'm rarely here.

"You're welcome," Blake says softly in my ear, smirking as he watches me watching Whitney and crew coldly snub Giulia in class.

"You're despicable."

"Maybe I'm in love."

He says it so seriously it stops my blistering retort in its heated tracks. *Is he?*

"Are you?"

Blake's grin curls. "Of course. Giulia's a *great* girl."

"You make my skin crawl."

He laughs. "Works for me, Grace Kelly."

At lunch I learn Becca's stepfather is taking them to Bermuda over the Christmas break. "He thinks I should be grateful." She's scowling at her black bean and sweet potato chili and stabbing at it repeatedly with her fork.

"Aren't you? It sounds amazing."

"You know my skin only comes in two shades – white and extra crispy."

"So, wear sunblock. And a big hat."

"Right. Because every guy wants to hit that."

I stop doing my calculus homework. "Are you looking for a vacation romance?"

"Vacation. Gas station. Check-out line. At this point I'll take whatever I can get."

"Really, Bec?"

"Not everyone is meant for true love and a happy ending, Kel."

"You can't mean that."

"I do."

"Because you haven't had a boyfriend in *high school* you think it's going to be like this your whole life?" I shake my head. "Becca, we go to Barton. Our entire student body is less than 250. It's a private school; this is not a cross section of real life. The yin to your yang is out there. Don't give up. And don't settle. You, Becca Bryson, are meant for happy endings. Don't you forget it."

"Yes, mom."

"I'm being serious."

"I know you are." Becca looks at me with real affection. "You're doing that pointy thing."

Sheepishly, I put my finger down. "Eat your chili."

I haven't been to Strings in months. The shop is decorated for Christmas with enticing gift giving suggestions on display everywhere. Country Christmas music is playing softly in the background. Jesse is wearing a Santa hat at a jaunty angle on his grizzled, gray head and bent over an acoustic guitar, tuning it, when I walk in. Jesse is a Willie Nelson wanna be, even down to the long braids. He looks up and breaks into a wide grin when he sees it's me. "Well, well, well, if it ain't Ms. Kel McCoy. You're certainly a sight for sore eyes, young lady. But if you're looking for that man of yours pretty girl, you just missed him. He left to pick Daisy up from a birthday party about – what? Twenty minutes ago?" He looks at Hardy for confirmation.

Hardy nods. Hardy is loose limbed and reedy and has terrible posture but his smile is incredibly kind; it starts in his eyes and sort of wraps around your heart. "Hey Kel," he says shyly from behind the rack he's stocking. And that's a long sentence for him.

I smile warmly at him. "Hey Hardy. I like that color on you – you're looking very festive."

"Don't you let him off the hook, missy. He's supposed to be wearing the hat." Jesse points to his own head. "I got one of these for everyone who works here. And I'm the only one wearing it. Everyone's so worried about his hair. Where's the Christmas spirit? That's what I want to know."

I fondly tap the fluffy, white ball at the end of his hat with my index finger and set it swinging. "Well, you're rocking it, Santa."

"That's right. I am." He puts the guitar down. "Might as well pull up a chair and make yourself comfortable while you wait." Hardy has already gone to fetch something from one of the studios. Jesse crosses his arms and squints up at me. "Drew says you've been to Italy? I guess that must make you some kind of supermodel now?"

"You'd think so. But sadly, no. I *can* say 'I'm 1.88 meters tall' in five different languages though. Thanks, Hardy." I tuck my long legs under me as I sit down. "What have you been up to, Jesse? You still trying to two-step your way into Miss Reba Ann's heart?"

"If that woman could cook I'd ask her to marry me."

"If you could cook she'd probably say yes."

Hardy grins appreciatively. "Don't you have something to do?" Jesse scowls at him as the store door opens and a couple of customers walk in. "And you, Ms. Sassypants, make yourself useful." He scoops up a Santa hat from behind the register and throws it at me. "Put that on."

I do. When Drew returns with Daisy they find me perched on a stool, wearing my Santa hat, and playing *Silent Night* on the guitar for a couple of kids while their parents plot with Hardy about delivery of the instruments they've clandestinely ordered for them for Christmas. "You're shameless, Jesse," Drew says over his shoulder before he leans in to kiss me. "Nice hat."

"You should try it sometime." I wink cheekily at him as I wrap up my impromptu concert – my audience is being claimed by their parents. "Here, you can have mine."

"I have my own." He takes my hat and tucks it under his arm. "Thanks for this Kel. I should be off in a couple of hours."

"No problem. Daisy and I are going shopping."

"At the mall?" Daisy asks hopefully.

"Sure. Why not?"

Why not? It's the week before Christmas; the mall is packed. It takes us ages to even find a parking spot. In the crush of people I'm clinging tightly to Daisy's hand.

Tonight's top news story won't be: *Girl Loses Boyfriend's Little Sister Entrusted to Her Care.* "What would you like to look at first?" I bend to ask her, and immediately get bumped sideways from behind.

"Sorry, didn't see you there," a guy in a red pullover, jeans, and running shoes says as I turn around. I've got maybe eight inches on him in these ankle boots. He blinks up at me in surprise. "You're the elf."

I'd completely forgotten. Sure enough, hanging from the ceiling and strategically placed on the floor are enormous foam core tiles with my picture plastered across them. "That's you!" Daisy says excitedly. "Look, Kel – you're everywhere!"

"Shh. I see."

"Can I get a picture with you?" Red sweater wants to know; he's already taking out his phone. People are starting to stop and stare. "The guys won't believe this."

"Um, okay. Sure."

We get stopped a few more times on our way to the American Girls store. It must be easier to get in line than to be the one initiating because I'm being asked to take pictures in clumps. "You're like a Disney princess at Disneyland," Daisy grins as she takes my hand again.

I'm rethinking our day. "How do you feel about miniature golf?"

But Daisy has a list and all her carefully hoarded allowance tucked safely away inside her little purse; she can't be dissuaded and she doesn't want to shop anywhere else. I pull up the mall's store map on my phone and we escape to a somewhat secluded bench so we can strategize her Christmas shopping in proximity to where we parked the car: video games, athletic store, department store. This is no time for wandering.

"Kel, when I grow up will people want to take pictures with me?" Daisy asks as we finally leave with purchases in hand, me hurrying, her skipping by my side through the parking lot.

"Of course." It's right up there with food and air in Maslow's *Hierarchy of Needs* 2.0. "Careful of that car Tonks, it's backing up."

She skips a little faster. "Would you take a picture with me?"

"When you grow up?"

She giggles. "No, now."

I smile at her. "How about when we get to the car?" Pulling her close to the Mini and out of the danger of any traffic, I dig my phone out of my purse and squat down beside her so we're almost the same height. "Make sure we get all of our bags in so we can show off all our hard work. There we go. Nice smile! One more. Perfect."

As I stand back up a truck packed with obnoxiously overblown testosterone slows down. Windows unroll and I'm being loudly propositioned with several crude comments and catcalls. Uncertain, white-faced, and with huge eyes, Daisy looks to me for guidance, slipping her little hand into mine for safety. I open her door and force myself to smile reassuringly at her. "Just ignore them, Daisy."

They don't give up. With head held high, I make my way around the front of the Mini between parked cars, to the driver's side, quickly get in, and lock the doors. Thankfully, they drive off, laughing. "Did they do that because they like you?" Daisy asks, confused. Her fingers are pleating the handle of one of her shopping bags.

"They did that because they're morons. You okay?"

She nods.

"Hey, we did great today, didn't we? We got everything on your list; we should celebrate. You feeling like ice cream?"

"So, how did it go?" Drew asks, meeting us halfway down the front steps of his home in his bare feet. "Looks like you bought out the store, Tonks."

"Don't peek!" she squeals, grabbing my arm. "Come on, Kel. We need to hurry and hide everything."

I grin apologetically at him. "What she said. Distract Ryan and Will?"

Drew throws open the door and gets out of our way. "They're not back yet."

Daisy has a big cardboard box in her closet that she's labeled: "SEEKRET – STAY OUT" and covered with a lot of Xs and mean looking frowny faces so it's clear she means business. We stash everything inside and I help her close it back up and cover it over with a stack of clothes – which also conceals all her painstakingly posted warnings but she knows her brothers better than I do.

I find Drew in the living room, picking out chords on the guitar I got him for his birthday. "Working on something new?" I join him on the couch.

"I am. I *was*." He puts his guitar aside. "Now I just want to make out with my girlfriend."

"Is Drew a moron too?" Daisy asks curiously as she walks into the room hauling Oscar, the corpulent family cat, heavily in her arms. She – and Drew – are both looking at me expectantly, waiting for some kind of an explanation.

I blush to my roots. "No. No, he's not."

"But you said..."

Seriously? I'm in way over my head here. I look to Drew and heaven for help. "Er, Daisy is referring to an incident that occurred when we were getting ready to leave the mall today. A bunch of guys in a truck were...harassing us. They were pretty crude. She asked me if they did that because they liked me. I told her they did it because they were morons."

"Ah." Drew is quiet for a moment. "Daisy, guys like that *are* morons. Don't give them the time of day – ever. No guy worth knowing treats a girl like that."

"Kel didn't like it," Daisy says quietly. "I didn't either."

"I bet." He tugs on her arm and pulls her and Oscar onto his lap. "I think that's how you can tell. If someone notices you – even if it seems like they like you – but you don't like what they're saying or how it makes you feel then walk away. If they won't leave you alone, tell someone. Tell me. Promise?"

Daisy solemnly pinky swears and then grins when she hears the sound of the front door opening. "Mom's home!" She scrambles off Drew's lap, dumping Oscar unceremoniously onto the carpet.

"You want to be my big brother?" I ask, slipping onto Drew's vacated lap.

"No." Drew nuzzles my neck. "I think the neighbors would talk."

14

"We're on each other's team"
Lorde

"Kel. Good to see you. Come on in." Mr. Sanders, my guidance counselor, waves me into his office that smells faintly of disinfected lemons and shoe polish and closes the door. The motivational posters on his walls are all in Latin: Per Aspera ad Astra (through hardship to the stars); Veni, Vidi, Vici (I came, I saw, I conquered). Busts of William Shakespeare keep his books upright. On his desk sits a framed *South Park* cartoon to show he's a man of the people and a brass nameplate, in case he forgets who he is. "Please, take a seat."

I do. I'm only two days into the new semester and I've been here for both of them, I'm not sure what this is about. He smiles at me as he eases his bulk into his massive wooden chair and leans forward with his elbows on his desk. "Don't worry, you're not in trouble. I just wanted to check in on you, see how things are going."

"Fine. I think." I've managed to keep fairly stellar grades, despite my frequent absences and heavy course load. Maybe he knows something I don't. "My teachers last semester were all really great about working with me so I could stay on top of my school work."

"I guess that's what I want to talk to you about. I understand your modeling career is really taking off. Your picture's everywhere these days. I even saw you over Christmas, out shopping with my wife. You were the elf."

I blush. "Sorry about that."

"I'd say congratulations are in order, if fact I should probably ask you for your autograph but that's not what this about. I pulled up your attendance record." He hands me a copy. "Do you notice a trend?" He has a green line connecting all the dots for the days/week I was at school and a red line for all the days I wasn't.

"The amount of time I'm absent has increased." I didn't need a graph to tell me that.

"I noticed that too. Do you see this trend continuing?"

I spent most of my Christmas break in New York doing castings in between the three jobs I booked. And I already have a trip to L.A. tomorrow and Thursday. I have to be honest. "Probably."

"You've got another ambitious class schedule ahead of you, Kel; looks like three AP classes. Thankfully, none of them require a lab so at least we won't have to work around that this semester; but still, they're going to be a challenge. And you're signed up for choir – that's weighted heavily on participation."

I sigh. "You think I need to drop it?"

"Are you willing to risk your GPA?"

I love singing. I've been in choirs of some sort since kindergarten; this one hurts. "Okay. I'll pull out."

"I think that's a wise decision. I've spoken with all your teachers and they're willing to assist you with a lot of curriculum access on-line, provided of course, that you continue to meet deadlines and perform well in your classes."

"I will. Thank you, Mr. Sanders."

"Of course. Can't have it said that we stood in the way of you becoming the next Gigi Hadid now, can we?" He's grinning as he gets to his feet.

Becca leans heavily against the locker next to mine. She probably only weighs 95 lbs. soaking wet so it barely registers but she's scowling like a pit bull and looks ready to sink her teeth into the administration. "So? What did Sanders want?"

"He wanted me to drop choir."

"*That's* why you were called to the office?" She deflates. "As if I needed any more proof that you and I are polar opposites."

I give her my best delinquent face. "Hey, he also called me out on my attendance."

She snorts. "Right. Was your dad there?"

"No."

"Did you have to come up with an Action Plan for Improvement?"

"He made me promise I'd turn stuff in on time."

"So *not* the same thing." Becca folds her arms in front of her. "Were the words expulsion or suspension mentioned *at all*?"

"No."

"I rest my case."

I hook a long arm around her exposed neck – she cut her blowsy hair into a short pixie cut over the break, only her spiky tips are still purple – and give her an affectionate squeeze. "Action Plan for Improvement, huh? Is it working?"

"Shut up, McCoy."

My phone is buzzing; I dig it out of my purse. *Kirstie*. "You got *Vogue*! Did you hear me, Kel? You did it! You're going to be a *Vogue* girl."

I sit down on an ordinary, empty bench in an ordinary hall, suddenly weak-kneed and light headed. It had seemed like such a long shot. "When?"

"Next Thursday. I've already talked to Shae; she's freeing up her schedule. And I'm sending Jack with you to L.A. tomorrow."

"Why?"

"I don't particularly like the photographer on this shoot; he has a reputation for being handsy. You know how Shae gets. Jack will be able to be a physical presence without the meltdown."

"I don't need a babysitter, Kirstie. I'm a big girl; I can take care of myself."

"I'm not doing this for you, I'm doing it for Shae. You'll be eighteen next month. We can revisit this then."

I sigh. I know that tone. "Okay."

"Good news or bad?" Becca wants to know. "I couldn't tell; your face was all over the map."

I brighten. "The best. You're not going to believe this Bec, I just booked *Vogue!*"

"Of course you did. How are we even friends?"

Jack waits until we're airborne and I've spread out across my tray table before gently placing a small box wrapped in ornate gold foil and tied with a gorgeous black bow on top of my open copy of *The Blank Slate: The Modern Denial of Human Nature* by Steven Pinker – required reading for my psych class and just as fun as it sounds. I stop highlighting. "What's this for?"

He shrugs. "Late Christmas, early birthday. Just because."

"Wow." I carefully remove the bow and ease my fingers under the folds of the paper and lift them slowly apart one by one.

"Christmas morning must take forever in your home."

"The paper's so pretty I don't want to rip it."

"Are you *saving* it for something?"

"I might." Of course not.

He rolls his eyes. I grin at him, elated that we've found our way back to a space where we can simply be Jack and Kel.

"Oh Jack," I breathe as I lift the box lid. Nestled inside is an exquisite antique silver locket necklace. With trembling fingers I open the clasp, on the right hand side is a black and white picture of Mom, the left side has an engraved inscription, a quote by Abraham Lincoln: *All that I am, or hope to be, I owe to my angel mother.* My eyes are swimming in tears as I lean over to kiss his cheek. "It's beautiful. I'll treasure it always. Thank you."

"I've had it for a while," he says quietly. "I just wasn't sure when to give it to you – especially after you gave me a surfboard and I'd only given you Godiva truffles. But it was your first Christmas without her, I guess I was worried it might be too much."

I slowly nod as I dab at my eyes with the napkin Jack hands me. "It was harder than I thought it would be – and I thought it would be pretty hard. My mom *loved* Christmas and she never did anything halfway. Dad found Charlie's jingle bell collar when we were unpacking the tree ornaments she'd collected over the years. He had to leave the room." Charlie went from sad eyes resigned to tail wagging relief as he watched me resolutely tuck it back into another box of many boxes of decorations we couldn't bring ourselves to put up this year. The tree felt necessary. "We mostly tried to keep ourselves crazy busy."

"I noticed."

I slip the necklace on over my head and gather up my hair and drop it over the top of it so the chain is lying cool against my neck and next to the delicate silver filigree necklace Drew gave me for Christmas that simply says *Grace*. "Hawaii looked fun."

"It was. I needed that."

"Can we talk about the cute blonde you had your arm around in most of your pictures?"

"No."

"I don't even get a name?"

"No."

"Did *you* get her name?"

"Don't you have homework you should be doing?"

"Always."

"Don't let me stop you."

"Jack."

"What?"

"Thanks again for the necklace. I really love it."

He goes back to his laptop. "You're welcome."

"David Tennant." There's no hesitation.

"I'm surprised you didn't say Matt Smith." Jack scoffs as he waits for me to get out of our ride. We're heading for sushi after a long day with a particularly creepy photographer – Kirstie wasn't kidding. Even without him physically touching me I had to take an exfoliating shower the moment I got back to the hotel just to feel clean again. "I thought you were all about the dreamy?"

"Matt Smith is *not* dreamy. He's a good actor and he made a good Dr. Who but come on, Jack, be serious: David. Tennant."

"So, Tennant's a better Dr. Who because he's dreamier?"

"No, that's just a bonus. How shallow do you think I am?" I shake my head as we climb the stairs to the second floor of the little strip mall on Sunset Boulevard that houses heaven. "Never mind. Don't answer that. I need you to be nice to me tonight."

"Jack?!"

I've seen shock before: the draining disbelief on my father's face when he'd been trying to reach Mom for over an hour with no response and then suddenly two police officers were on our front doorstep quietly asking if we were the family of Greer Kingston McCoy; Drew, when he discovered it was his absentee father inexplicably peering into the windows of the Mini; and my friend Maggie in downtown Chicago when we inadvertently ran into her mother and the man it turned out she was having an affair with coming out of a hotel. From the hunted look on the thin, pale face of the woman standing in front of us completely out of place in a Stella McCartney sleeveless, black sheath and sleek Louboutin heels it would appear Jack was the last person on the planet she expected or wanted to run into tonight.

"*Lily*?" I can feel the tension rolling off Jack in waves. Lily is wearing a wedding ring. The plot thickens.

Neither of them seems capable of speech so after an interminable silence I turn into my mother. "Lily? Hi, I'm Kel McCoy. Jack and I work together." This is meant to be soothing and friendly but she seems instantly stung. I'm rattled but my mother's persistent belief in manners being able to save the day runs deep. "We were just about to grab a bite to eat. Would you like to join us?"

She starts to shake her head *no* but then surprises us all. "Yes, I think I would."

I squeeze Jack's arm. Wordlessly, he opens the door to Sushi Park for us. Still smiling, I sit between them, a long, leggy Switzerland. Even our waiter, who is quite good-looking and very flirty at first, quickly abandons me for the safety of a hasty retreat. I pretend to study the menu I already have memorized while Jack and Lily continue to breathe the same oxygen.

"Would you please excuse me for a moment?" I whisper to Jack once our order has been taken, desperate to escape the table and give them some privacy. He doesn't move.

"Why are you doing this, Lil?" He finally says.

Her eyes flicker woodenly to mine and back to his. "Curiosity, I guess."

"Satisfied?"

She pulls a hundred dollar bill out of her purse to cover her order and throws it on the table as she gets to her feet. “Not for a long time, Jack. But I think you already knew that.”

“Don’t.” Elbows on the table, Jack buries his forehead in the palms of his hands when it’s clear she’s gone.

I put my arm around him and lean my head against his shoulder. “Do you want to get out of here?”

“I promised you Sushi Park.”

I hunt down our waiter and return as quickly as I can. Jack is still staring unseeing at his plate. “They’ve packaged up the first three. I’ve settled our bill.” I look at my phone. “Our ride will be here any minute. Come on.”

Jack follows me up to my hotel room but he stays in the hall. “Aren’t you coming in?” I ask.

“No. Enjoy your sushi, Kel. I need to clear my head. I’m going to go for a run.”

“Give me a minute, I’ll change and run with you.”

“Thanks, but I think I need to be alone.”

There’s a sadness I can’t shake as I nod and hold him tightly. “Promise you’ll text me when you get back? Just so I know you’re safe?”

He wraps a finger around a lock of my hair and sighs. “You’re doing it again.”

“I know. I can’t help it.”

Resting his forehead against mine I feel him leave before he’s actually gone. “Night, Kel.”

The next morning we meet at breakfast; Jack looks tired but thankfully not hung over. I hand him a glass of freshly squeezed orange juice. He takes a sip and grins wryly. "Someone's been busy."

"Just drink it."

"Did you run on the treadmill?"

"I did."

"Sorry. I just couldn't drag my butt out of bed this morning."

A waiter is approaching our table carrying plates. "I ordered your omelet for you."

Jack cocks his head. "Careful Kel, we're starting to feel like an old married couple."

"Good. You ready to talk about Lily?"

"No."

"Eat your breakfast. The car will be here in twenty minutes."

He picks up his fork. "Too bad they didn't have any..."

I push the little white covered bowl next to my plate over to his. Lifting the lid, he sheepishly dumps the rest of the salsa on his omelet and gives me his cantaloupe. Maybe we do spend too much time together.

Camila: Carmen's abuela got shipped off to a detention center!

What? Quickly, I turn off the chicken I was in the middle of stir frying for dinner and call her. "Camila? What happened?"

Camila has a bad habit of switching to rapid fire Spanish when she's excited so it takes me awhile to sort it all out but apparently Senorita Mendes was caught in an ICE raid while visiting the home of a sick friend who had a son with some legal troubles that weren't just limited to documentation: wrong place, wrong time. "Do something, Kel." Camila is crying now. "All of her family are here. She's old. It's not fair."

"I know. I'm so sorry, Camila. I love her too. My cousin Ben is a lawyer in New York. Let me call him and ask him for his advice. Let's see what he says."

"Was she here illegally?" Ben gets right to the point.

"Technically, yes. But she's been here for over fifty years. She's had three children here. She's paid into the system. They've paid into the system. They're all hard working, law abiding people...with the exception of that one little form."

"Sorry, Kel. That one little form is a deal breaker. The best thing you can do at this point is to start the application process for naturalization. If she's as sweet as you say, the family should be able to get her released on bond while she waits for her hearing."

"Sometimes," I tell Charlie morosely as I end my call. "Life is *not* fair."

The detention center is in Taylor, forty miles away. Dad lends me his car so I can haul all the girls there for a visit. It's like walking into a prison. Senorita Mendes is brought in shrunken and gray, her step slow and unsure, in an obnoxious orange jumpsuit that's rolled back at the arms and legs but still swimming on her.

Carmen immediately gets to her feet but the security guard gives her pause. We wait for him to step back; it's obvious he enjoys this little play of power. *"Senorita Mendes, how are you?"* I ask in Spanish and I touch her arm. "*Here are the girls. They miss you too."* My Spanish is still not great but at least it gets them talking. Tears are trickling down her cheeks. Now everyone is crying.

"*We will get you out of here,"* I whisper in her ear as I lean down to hug her before we leave.

"Jack, what would you think of me using my social media platform to draw attention and maybe apply pressure to an unfair situation?" We're sitting at my kitchen table after dinner, the faint sound of the dishwasher quietly running a cycle in the background. He's editing our latest vlog I did with Jasmine, my hair stylist and a good friend, with all kinds of quick and easy styling tips for wash and wear hair. My chin is deep into my hands, my elbows resting on everything I could find on immigration law.

He looks up at me. "Like what?"

I tell him about Senorita Mendes.

He listens impassively and waits until it's clear I'm done. "No. Don't do it."

"Why? What's the point of having any kind of influence if you can't use it for good?"

"Not everyone sees good the same way you do, Kel. Once you get political you risk offending someone. You can't afford that."

"Seriously? I'm a model; I'm not running for public office."

"You may not have noticed this – your focus is always on getting to know the people you're working with at shoots – but quite frequently, along with the model's name on the callboard, they post how many followers she has. It's just sitting right there for everyone to see. But even if it's not that in your face, you're kidding yourself if you think this doesn't matter."

"So only take a stand on moisturizers and the best beach waves?" I indicate his laptop screen with a touch of disdain and a wrinkled nose.

Jack shrugs. "It's what the people want."

"Do they?"

"Have I ever steered you wrong before?"

I sigh. "I don't like you very much right now."

"Psh. You know you love me," he grins.

"Yeah," I reluctantly smile back at him. "Well, you make me crazy."

Things between Dad and Erin have cooled slightly. They've decided to slow it down, take their time, not rush into anything; parental code for *Ava is being a colossal pain.* To be fair, the holidays didn't help. Memories of Mom were inescapable and oh so vividly threaded through even our barest of bones Christmas – and January 26th still has to be faced. Maybe Dad realized his heart wasn't as free as he thought it was. But my money's on Ava.

She keeps showing up at Drew's games.

"Why is *that girl* here again?" Ginny frowns, giving me a hug and scooting to make room for me on the bleachers. She knows Ava's name; she just refuses to use it. Ava is laughing three rows below us with a couple of friends she brought with her – their glossy heads are frequently bent together. They're wearing MacArthur colors and she's painted Drew's number on her cheeks.

"Maybe she just really likes basketball. Hey Tanika! Great earrings."

Ginny won't let it go. "I'm pretty sure her school has a team."

Drew nails a three pointer from way outside the arc and the MacArthur fans are on their feet. I have to shout to be heard. "THEY DON'T HAVE DREW."

"NEITHER DOES SHE!"

At half time Ginny, Tanika and I get out to stretch our (okay, my) legs and go to the bathroom (I've converted them all to drinking more water – even Striker, though he'd never admit it). Across the gym in the visitor's section I'm startled to spot Drew's father sitting alone in the crowd. He's almost unrecognizable from the last time I saw him at Drew's birthday party; he's wearing a ball cap but it's obvious his hair is all gone – it's unnaturally white where his hairline used to be. His face seems pinched and pale and from the way his clothes are hanging on him I'd say he's lost a lot of weight. My stomach lurches. "You're coming, right?" Ginny says, pulling on my arm.

Matt's parents are out of town for the weekend; everyone is heading over to his house after the game. See, I *was* paying attention. "We are." Andy's still looking down at his phone.

"What are you staring at?" Ginny stands on her tiptoes, trying to follow my gaze.

I quickly shake my head and drag my eyes away from him. "Nothing. But I'm not sure how late we'll stay tonight, G. Drew has to open the store tomorrow."

"What are you guys, eighty?"

When we return to the gym Ava and her entourage are standing in the aisle chatting, effectively blocking our path back to our seats. "Hey Ava," I say.

I expect the usual scowl and dismissal of my person but she's beaming at me. She tosses her hair and I wonder, not for the first time, if she and Whitney are secretly related. "Kel, these are my friends, Brynn and Jessica. They're big Texas Tall fans. I told them you'd take a selfie with them."

"Oh, hi." Beside me Ginny is seething. The girls already have their phones out. I smile at them. "I'd love to. Brynn, right? Do you want me to take it? I've got these crazy long arms; they've got to be good for something."

"That girl's got some nerve!" Ginny glowers when we finally get back to our seats. "Why do you put up with that?"

"It's so not a big deal, G." I'm scanning the room for Andy. He's gone from his earlier spot; he's nowhere in sight. The second half is about to start. The referee blows his whistle; MacArthur throws the ball in and the spirited student section is already on their feet, loud and proud. I lean over, close to Ginny's ear. "Excuse me, I'll be right back."

"Where are you going?" Ginny and my brain want to know.

It's a good question. One I don't have an answer for. I find him sitting on a bench by MacArthur's front doors looking exhausted and frail. "Mr. Jarrod? Are you okay?"

He hesitates before answering. "I guess I'm a little more tired than I thought I'd be."

"Is there something I can do? May I get you anything?"

He shakes his head. "I've got a car coming to pick me up."

I sit down beside him. "Does Drew know you're here?"

"What do you think?"

"I think your relationship is complicated," I sigh.

"Did you ever give him the letter?"

"I left it for him the night of his party. I don't know if he read it or not."

Outside a car has just pulled up. Andy gets unsteadily to his feet. "Do me a favor? Don't tell him I was here."

"Seriously?"

"I don't want his pity." I see now where Drew gets his stubborn streak. He looks back at me as he slowly pushes the door open. "Take care of him for me, Kel?"

"I will." I wonder if anyone's taking care of Andy.

Much later, deep from inside Matt's house, music is thumping; the sound slightly muffled until the balcony door slides open and the golden goodness of Beyonce spills out into the night.

"There you are," Drew says, joining me on the back porch. "Thought I lost you. What are you doing out here by yourself? Aren't you cold?"

"Hmm? Just thinking."

He wraps his arms tight around my shoulders and kisses my neck. "About what?"

I relax against him and wait a bit before answering. "Did you ever read that letter your dad wrote you?"

He immediately stiffens. "No. Why?"

"He was at your game tonight," I quietly say and turn around in his arms so I can see his face; storm clouds are already gathering. "Drew, he's sick."

"What did he do?" The muscle clench in Drew's jaw is back.

"No, I mean seriously physically ill. I almost didn't recognize him. He had to leave at half time. He looked exhausted."

Drew takes a step back. "Why are you telling me this? Did he talk to you?"

I raise my pointy chin at him. "I needed to make sure he was okay."

"And what? He asked you to try again?"

"No. Actually, he asked me not to say anything to you at all."

"Then why are you?"

"Because I'm done keeping secrets from you, Drew. And your father's really sick. I just thought you should know." I reach up and kiss his cheek. "I'm going to call it a night, babe. I'm tired; it's been a long week. See you tomorrow?"

"Tomorrow," Drew echoes, his hand lingering on mine. He's staring out at the black expanse of Matt's unlit backyard, a frown creasing his brow. I guess now we both have some things to think about.

"You've changed, Kel."

I look up from my physics homework spread across my table tray. We're on a plane bound for New York and my *Vogue* shoot. Aunt Shae is staring thoughtfully at me. "I have? How?"

"You're so much more confident now, much more polished. You're not our little Grace anymore." Shae sounds almost wistful.

I smile at her. "I don't think I was ever really *little*."

"You know what I mean. A year ago, could you see yourself here?"

A year ago, for at least three more days, my mother was still alive. My life was consumed with ballet, choir concerts, hanging out at home, and perfect attendance – you got a medal at the end of the year if you pulled it off and I've always been reward driven. Ironic that I give Jake a hard time about being a nerd, I'm as nerdy as they come.

"No." I wonder what Mom would think of her latest of late blooming daughter shamelessly trading in on her genetic good fortune. Mom was not unaware of the way she looked; she just was uninterested in it defining her. I put down my mechanical pencil. "Do you think Mom would approve?" It's a question I've been asking myself a lot lately.

"Of course she would. Greer was your biggest fan."

I swallow hard. "It's not the same thing though, is it?"

"Are you happy with your choices, Kel?"

"Most of the time."

"Then believe me, as a mother and as someone who also loves you, that's all Greer ever wanted for you."

"Really?" I can't help but feel skeptical. "I've given up on almost everything she encouraged me to do."

Shae puts her hand on my arm and gives it a gentle squeeze. "Moms have a tendency to direct their children to things they think will help them grow. Maybe it works, maybe it doesn't, maybe it does and they discover they've learned all they could from it and it's time to move on to something else. The goal is always to get your children to the point where they are armed with a skill set and enough experience to make good decisions for themselves. You're not just book smart, Kel; you're intuitive. Trust that. Greer would've."

Shae's words are still ringing in my ears later that afternoon when I'm sitting on set with four other models as the lights are being reset.

"So, wait, you live in Austin?" Daphne's dark eyes are rimmed with purple and she's propping up the stars twisted throughout her gravity defying hair with a hand heavy with gaudy rings.

"I do." Scotty is carefully powdering down the shine on my face. I've been under the lights the longest and beads of perspiration are ruining his handiwork. I'm careful not to move while he checks on the rhinestones glued to my cheekbones.

"And you fly into New York every time for work?" Gretchen makes a face. She's painted in white so it comes off a little Day of the Dead. "Doesn't that get old?"

"Sometimes," I admit. "What did you do?"

Gretchen shrugs. "I got my GED and moved here just as soon as I could."

I'm trying to imagine a conversation with my father that included his daughter and a GED. I can't even make believe him go through it.

"You graduate in May?" Kieko softly asks. Since Scotty has moved on to Daphne, I'm free to nod. "That's not so bad then." At fifteen she's the youngest of us – she's been modeling since she was twelve. She has a tutor and is living in Soho with her grandmother.

"Are any of you going to university?" I ask.

"What for?" Brigitte asks, rolling her eyes. The fake eyelashes she's wearing are overly elongated and quite thick so the effect is pronounced. "You can't make this kind of money going to school." She's Danish so she purses her pouty lips when she says the "oo" in school. "You're the sunless tanning girl, right? And the new face of Archer Darby? How many shows are you walking in for Fashion Week next month?"

"Nineteen." I don't know if that's a high or low amount. They just nod.

"You don't need school Kel," Brigitte declares, rising gracefully to her feet as they call us back to set. "You need an apartment here in the city. And a good accountant."

15

"Who run the world? Girls"
Beyonce

It's March 31st; Jack's six month assignment with Adderson's is officially ending and I've never needed him more. I convinced him to let me take him out to dinner as a thank you and to celebrate his freedom. I even picked him up. For the record, his apartment smells *much* nicer than Tony's gym.

"You okay?" Jack leans back in his chair and regards me curiously with his hands folded in front of him on the restaurant table. In case I don't mention it enough, Jack cleans up well. I've always admired his taste in clothes and tonight he's looking especially sharp in a form fitting, white button down and trim, black tailored slacks. Bad sign that I'm feeling nostalgic; we haven't even given our order to the waiter yet and I already don't want this evening to end. "You're being weird."

"I need some advice."

"Don't cut your hair."

I blink, momentarily distracted. "Why not?"

"Two words: Keri. Russell."

"You watched *Felicity*?"

"I had the flu," Jack huffs. "For an *entire* week. You owe me at least four seasons of *The A-Team*."

So *not* where I was going with this. "Fine. The next time I'm sick I'll binge it." I'm struggling to retain an air of casual indifference. "So, I've now heard back from all five of the universities I applied to."

"Let me guess; you got in to all of them, even the Ivies."

I stare at him, surprised. "I did. How did you know?"

"Are you kidding? I've seen your homework. Why do you care? I thought you'd already decided on UT?"

I sigh and stare at the clean, smooth surface of my gleaming white dinner plate. "I thought I had too."

Jack's hazel eyes are watching me closely. "What happened to change your mind?"

Back to the beginning Grace. I take a deep breath. "I may've mentioned this before, but the only reason I started this whole modeling thing, *huge* ego boost aside, was because it slightly terrified me and pushed me out of my comfort zone. I didn't actually expect it to turn into...what it has. Everything just happened so fast. No one, not even Shae if she's being honest, saw it coming. I know we all worked incredibly hard for this but really I just got *so* lucky."

Jack waits.

I realize I'm twisting my napkin into knots. I place it firmly on my lap and set my hands on the table. "I don't want to do it anymore."

"I'm sorry? *What* did you just say?!" He's squinting at me like somehow if he just does it hard enough it will help him see things clearer. "Are you being serious right now?"

"Come on Jack, we both know the only reason I exploded on social media was because of you. I can't keep that up on my own. I don't want to. It's not who I am. My whole life I've pretty much been two things: tall and smart. I need to be more than a glorified clothes hanger. I want to go to law school. I want to be able to help shape public policy one day. I didn't know this about myself until I took psych and philosophy this semester and it's like every day as I studied and read, little pieces of my puzzle started to come together and then Senorita Mendes was put in that awful detention center and researching immigration law something suddenly just clicked for me and I finally made sense. I want this so desperately and I'm terrified I've already screwed it up. How's anyone supposed to take me seriously when they've seen me hawking Tropically Kissed products in a bikini?"

He rolls his eyes. "Don't be so dramatic, Kel. Everyone has to pay for law school somehow. Just lead with your brains like you always do." He pulls at his scruff. "Have you already told Kirstie this?"

"I haven't told anyone yet. You're my litmus test."

"How am I doing?"

"You're not yelling at me. That's a win."

"I don't have a signed contract with your name on it," Jack reminds me.

"I went over copies of all my contracts last night." I stop extracting documents from my tote and make a face at him. "My Tropically Kissed contract is actually up for renewal. I'm supposed to have it signed, sealed, and delivered to Rosie first thing tomorrow."

"Yeah? My flight doesn't leave until 3:00. Can you please wait until after then to let it all hit the fan?"

I ignore him. "I have another year on Archer Darby but I actually don't mind that; Pippa and Thomas are lovely and their stuff is always highbrow. I'll just have to figure out how to work my school schedule around whatever they need."

He slowly nods.

"Everything else I can wrap up between now and the end of summer. See?" I'm laying everything out chronologically for him. "I can do it, Jack." I lean forward, almost whispering now. "Legally. I can walk away."

His hazel eyes skim the contracts I've papered our table with and then back up at me. "This is really a big deal to you, isn't it?"

"Yes. It is."

"Well, if you're not going to UT, where *are* you going to become the next Amal Clooney?"

I blush, gathering everything back up and reattaching the clip. "Brown. And then hopefully Harvard."

He straightens and reaches for the pitcher he'd hastily moved to the side to make room for contracts. "Of course. I don't even know why I bothered to ask. Would you like some more water?" I slide my glass over his direction. "So what does Disney prince think of all this?" He stops pouring when he sees the look on my face. "Ah, that's right, I forgot. Litmus test."

"UT isn't really practical," I say quietly.

"I know," he says gently.

"You do?"

He reaches out and gives my fingertips a little squeeze. "Sadly, I've found that what I want and what's best for me are rarely the same thing."

"So, what do you do?"

"You make the hard choice and trust that in the end it was the right one."

"What if it wasn't?"

"I don't want to know."

I stare at his well-shaped, oh so familiar hand in mine. "I'm really going to miss you."

He casually reaches for his glass, releasing my hand to do so. "I'm not going anywhere, Kel." Not true. Jack is leaving Austin for New York City tomorrow. He was just hired to work on the marketing team for the Miss Universe Pageant system; apparently his help with the successful launch of my career hasn't gone unnoticed. It's a great opportunity for him and probably a dream job, given he's all about the view – and that's about as good a view as it gets for a heterosexual male. He won't have time for me now. He'll be too busy promoting *world peace.*

Our waiter suddenly appears at our table like a mirage, but a grumpy one that just wants to know what he can get for us already. *An attitude adjustment,* Jack's raised eyebrow indicates at the waiter's obvious disapproval that after all this time we still haven't figured out what we want to order. *Don't get me in trouble. And don't make me laugh,* my blue eyes plead as I hastily pick up my menu. Jack winks at me; *I don't know what you're talking about*, as we get down to business.

At the end of the evening, Jack invites me up to his apartment. "I have something for you."

I park the Mini in his visitor spot and retrieve the package I wrapped earlier for him from the backseat before we head upstairs.

"You first," I say, handing him his present as he joins me on his couch – one of the few things left not boxed up or covered in moving blankets. I took considerable pains finding the perfect paper and complimentary ribbon and I tucked in all the edges and taped it together so none of the tape is showing. It's altogether very elegant and looks as good as any of the finished versions from the YouTube demonstrations I watched several times. He doesn't need to know this was my second attempt. Jack sighs as he takes it in his hands.

"You're going to make me open this carefully so the paper doesn't tear, aren't you?"

"It's your present. Do whatever you want with it," I shrug, not taking my eyes off my pretty wrap job.

"Do you have a curfew?"

"No."

"Good. We might be here all night."

I slip out of my kitten heels and tuck my long legs underneath me on his sofa. "Please, don't let me stop you."

Given the insane number of photos Jack has taken of me over the past six months, I only have three pictures of the two of us together. My favorite was taken in Central Park at the end of a run. The sun was just starting to come up and our cheeks are still flushed from the brisk morning air and our recent exertion. Jack is wearing a beanie over his bed head; I've got my hair up in a high, chunky ponytail and am sporting a furry white ear warmer. We're both grinning madly, our heads bent close together. I had the photo blown up and framed. Attached to the back is a silver engraved plate: *We had a good run, you and I. Thanks for going on this crazy journey with me, Jack. Love you always, Kel.*

"I forgot about this," Jack says softly as he stares at our radiant faces. "That was a really good day. Thanks, Kel. This is going with me in my suitcase to New York." He leans in slowly and kisses me on the cheek. I hold onto him a little longer and a little tighter than I probably should. I hope he knows how much he means to me.

Maybe if you actually told him. "I hope you know how much you mean to me," I sniff in his ear.

"You're so predictable." I can hear the smile in his voice. There's a rustling of paper and then, in my blurry line of vision, a snowy white hankie dangles from his fingers.

I pull away as he hands it to me. "Since when do you carry a hankie?"

It's monogrammed. With my initials. "Since I learned I wouldn't be around to keep you in tissues for a while," Jack says. There's a gift bag next to him containing eleven more. "Don't worry, I'll stock up whenever you come to New York."

"Psh. You won't have time to see me."

"Yeah. You're probably right." He wraps a finger around a lock of my hair and gives it a gentle tug. "Call me anyway. I know I'll never see you on Instagram again. Promise?"

"Promise."

But I realize as I drive home that I also promised Drew I'd go to the University of Texas – Austin with him this fall. Apparently my promises don't mean a whole lot.

Me: Free for dinner tomorrow night at my place?

Drew: Is it vegan night?

Me: That was yesterday.

Drew: Love to.

"Something smells good." Dad bends to greet Charlie, one hand already loosening his tie.

"It's not too late to change your plans and join us."

"I'm good. Nick's dying to try out a new sports bar downtown. Cade assured him it'*s the bomb*." He drops his keys on the shelf by the door to the garage.

"Erin going?"

"Not tonight. Brothers only."

"Probably just as well. She doesn't like basketball."

Dad makes a face. "I know, what's up with that?"

"No one's perfect."

"You are," Dad loyally supplies, swiping a piece of mango from my salad with a grin.

I smile sweetly at him. "I meant, *besides me*." And pause in my stirring. "Justin dropped off a bunch of tile for the pool house. You're supposed to take a look at the grout you ordered. He thinks it's too brown."

"It's not too brown."

"Hey. Me: messenger."

He leans against the island. "So, how did things go with Kirstie this morning?"

Dad was surprisingly nonplussed last night when I broke the news to him that I wanted to end my modeling career and go to Brown this fall and major in Philosophy in pursuit of a law degree. *Show me your plan* was his only response. He didn't even say he'd miss me when he gave me a big hug.

"Still TBD. She needed time 'to process everything'. To be fair, Rosie warned me when I went in that Kirstie's schedule for the day was already crazy. If it hadn't been for the Tropically Kissed contract renewal deadline I would've waited for a better time to tell her."

"And we're telling Drew tonight?"

"*We* most likely, depending on how dinner goes and how it seems Drew is feeling, are geared up to at least give it a try," I say.

"Bryce mentioned Drew was thinking about majoring in Architectural Engineering."

"He is."

"He wants to take him on this summer, give him some experience."

"He should. Drew's a hard worker."

"What about his music?"

I sigh. "I don't know, Dad. I guess he just wants to make sure he has a way to pay his bills. Things were tough for them growing up. Drew's a dreamer but he's also got his feet firmly planted on solid ground."

"One of the many things I admire about him."

"I know. You love him. Charlie loves him. The whole family loves him. I am, coincidentally, also crazy about the guy. I'm really trying not to screw this up."

Dad's suddenly serious. "Just remember Kel, inevitably, part of loving someone is learning how to let go."

Maybe, but not tonight.

"Are we celebrating something?" Drew asks, slightly alarmed when he sees the candle light dinner for two I've laid out, the fresh flowers on the table, and Mom's silver, china, and crystal stemware. Norah Jones is playing softly in the background.

I pull off the apron I've been wearing to protect my dress. It's nothing fancy but I'm a hot mess when I cook. "Us. We're celebrating us."

"Oh, good. I love us."

I kiss him. "Me too."

Two summers ago, Mom had this mad itch to go on a cross-country road trip as a family. She mapped out all the quirky little towns we *had* to see; unearthed anything passing as action along the way and, with my assistance, made a compelling case in the form of a multimedia presentation to help convince my father, who, because of his long legs, hates to be cooped up in a car. Popcorn was involved. But first there was an amazing meal. She called it "improving your odds." An immediate, but thankfully private, serving of *dessert* might've also occurred when Dad reluctantly agreed – I try not to think too much about my parent's love life. The point is, and I do have one, it's important to set the mood.

I wait until Drew has had his fill of pot roast and new potatoes before finding a tenuous smile. "I have something to tell you. Three somethings actually." I pull him to his feet. "Dance with me?"

He takes me in his arms. He's in my neck and hair as we sway to the music. "Mmm, you smell incredible tonight."

I laugh. "I'm pretty sure that's the pot roast talking."

He smiles his half-smile. "You wear it well."

"Thank you." My hands slide into his hair, my forehead touches his. *This boy.* I know, I tell my heart. *I know.* I clear my throat. "So, the first something: I'm giving up modeling."

Drew looks momentarily stunned but then he pulls me closer and quietly says, "If that's what you want. It's your choice to make, Kel."

And without him saying another word I know that he knows what I'm about to say next. Maybe not the particulars, Brown could be one of any number of universities far away from Austin and him and us but leaving is still gone. "I'm sorry Drew. I want to be a lawyer. A good one. To do that I have to get the very best education I can get my hands on from the very best schools I can get into."

"Where?"

"Brown."

I can't see his face. He's tucked his chin on top of my head and his hand is holding me close. Incidentally, he too smells pretty amazing. Finally he speaks and his voice sounds so far away, "What's the third something?"

"I love you, Drew Jarrod. I don't know if you find your forever when you're only eighteen but you're all I can see right now."

We cling to each other, not moving at all. "Me too, Chicago. Me too."

Kirstie is sitting at her desk, perusing contracts when Rosie lets me in. We've both had a couple of days to sit with the news, I even told Aunt Shae. I think she took it harder than Kirstie did. "Still feeling the same way?" Kirstie says when I've slipped into the seat across from her, just as I have so many times before.

I square my shoulders. "Yes."

"Okay then. Well, your early read on your contractual obligations lined up with our lawyer's. I guess that's a good sign for your future chosen career." She looks up at me and takes her glasses off and pushes them wearily onto the paperwork, shaking her head. "You worked *so* hard, Kel. It felt like you were just really taking off."

"I think you did everything you could to make it happen, you're really good at your job, and I don't want you to think for one minute that I didn't appreciate it. You've taught me a lot." I force myself to not look at the ground but ahead, at her. *Tell me you're someone worth looking at, Kel.* "I just want something else. I hope you can understand."

She sighs. "I don't. But you know I only want what's best for you. And if you think becoming a lawyer is it, well, then, more power to you."

"Thanks, Kirstie."

"But a *lawyer*? Seriously?" She wrinkles her nose as if some unpleasant odor has just filled her nasal passages.

I smile at her. "With really good posture and well hydrated skin."

Drew formed a band with four other guys once his basketball season ended; they call themselves *Everested* because it passed the "imagine we get a Grammy nomination and someone's reading our name off a list" test. I'm president of their nonexistent fan club and first official groupie. Dave, the bass player, who looks like an unmade bed and shuffles everywhere, sometimes brings his girlfriend, Martha, to rehearsals. But she rarely looks up from her phone and frequently wanders off for a cigarette, which is definitely way more rock and roll. I'm usually doing homework. One of my main jobs is making early morning Saturday beverage runs for the guys. No judgment but their sound is fueled by surprisingly chichi drinks.

"Angel, your espresso macchiato. I've got a cappuccino with extra foam here for Dave. A flat white for Hardy, careful it spilled a bit on the ride over, you'll want a napkin. Todd, your blonde roast. And Drew, your pineapple coconut water." I give his to him with a kiss.

"It says *George* on my cup," Todd frowns, taking off his guitar.

I smile apologetically at him. "Apparently, to some people, Todd and George sound the same. It's yours. I checked."

He looks at Angel's cup. "How do they get his name right and screw up mine?"

"Thank you," Hardy says softly.

"Anytime." I wound my hair up straight out of the shower after my run this morning – an instant beach wave trick I shared with my Texas Tall followers. I release it so it can finish air drying. "So, how's it going?"

Drew glances at his phone. "We probably have another hour before I have to leave for work." He takes a healthy swig of his water, picks up his guitar, and makes a face. "We need it."

"Ah." I open my messenger bag. "I've got some sketches to finish for class. I'll just sit over here out of the way; the light's better."

Hardy's Uncle Bob builds custom motorhomes, like the one Pops and Gran own. He's letting the band use the back of his workshop for rehearsals before he opens for business for the day and after hours. It's not air-conditioned but it's free and clean and away from any grumpy neighbors. Before I take a seat on the folding chair Drew set out for me, I've learned to check for scary bugs. Not to brag or anything but we have a *lot* in Texas. And Uncle Bob's shop is practically teeming with them.

When I dropped choir back in January I needed a senior year humanities elective to graduate – because at Barton we're *well-rounded* snobs, thank you very much. Sketching might seem like an obvious choice; I'm no artist but you'd be surprised how far you can get with just an understanding of angles and proportion and the value of light. The hard truth is sketching was something I'd always done to spend more time with Mom in her studio. We'd work side-by-side. She'd capture a moment, lay bare a soul, and breathe life into two dimensions. Even under her patient tutelage, the best I could manage was a fair job laying out a portrait linearly. My artwork was framed and displayed everywhere in our home rather than her own, far superior pieces. It told me, then and now, our time together meant something to her. I wasn't sure I was ready to step back into that intimate space; avoidance has worked well for Dad and me. But I've found her again in the constant rhythm of building, softening, subtracting, and rebuilding and it's been surprisingly sweet.

The mechanical whirr of the massive shop door opening signals the end of our rehearsal time. The band stops playing; Uncle Bob saunters in still sleepily rubbing his eyes. "Hey boys, Kel. Sorry to cut you short. I've got a customer coming in first thing this morning." Because he's meeting a client, Uncle Bob is wearing one of his better Rolling Stones T-shirts today, or at least cleaner, and his mullet has been combed down with a heavy application of water. He's looking spiffy.

"Not a problem. I had to leave in a few minutes for work anyway," Drew says, taking off his guitar so he can shake Uncle Bob's hand. "Thanks. We really appreciate this. We'll load up and be out of here in five." Angel is already covering his drums; Uncle Bob very generously lets us keep them there since they're too hard to move. I think he likes to feel he's doing his bit to help out the next generation of rockers.

"See *you* tonight," Drew smiles, leaning in to kiss me as he holds open the door of the Mini for me. It's the end of an era; this is his last day at Strings. Uncle Bryce just hired him to work at McCoy Construction, full-time once school is out, until then, Saturdays while he learns the ropes. Most of my cousins worked for Uncle Bryce at some point – even Jake; it's like a McCoy rite of passage. To mark the occasion I got Drew a tool belt, which was an absolute beast to wrap in case you were wondering. Cade and Landry are taking the boat out tonight to celebrate Drew's last night of freedom.

Landry brings a girl. Not unusual, he often does. For as long as I can remember Landry's never lacked for female companionship, he's a close second to Jake in the looks department and effortlessly charming. He doesn't necessarily have a type but *good times, no commitment* is definitely a common thread. So it's striking to note that Kendra's got that boy on a short leash. Even more strangely, for a footloose, confirmed bachelor he seems over the moon to be there.

"So, those two," Sam looks at Cade. Landry is driving the boat and occasionally watching where he's going, mostly he's utterly besotted with Kendra. I'm not sure they even remember we're here.

"Yeah. I know." Cade shakes his head. Sarah, Cade's girlfriend, is out on the wakeboard and his attention is focused on her. "He's got it bad. Should've made it work with Liesel when you had the chance. You're on your own now, Sammy boy."

"He backed out of our diving trip." Sam looks disgusted. "He's going to New Zealand for *two weeks* with Kendra instead."

"She does look better in a swimsuit," I state the obvious.

Sam ignores me. "Drew?"

"Sorry Sam." Drew's arm is draped around the back of my shoulders. "I don't have the time or the money. Ask your brother. He might go. When he was here for Thanksgiving he mentioned how much he missed your trips."

"Ben?" Sam scoffs. "He doesn't do spontaneous. If it's not on his calendar for at least six months he can't fit it in."

"That's Ben. Slow it up, bro. Looks like Sarah's done." Cade hops to his feet to help her in as Landry cuts back and circles the boat around. "Who's next?"

Sam stands up and grabs a lifejacket, still grumbling. "Everything's changing."

I rest my head against the solidness of Drew and he pulls me close. Maybe it is. But that doesn't necessarily mean it's a bad thing. I'm counting on it.

16

"I keep on thinking that it's not goodbye,
keep on thinking it's a time to fly"
Vitamin C

"To Berkley scoring Barton's finest." I raise Aunt Shae's pink water bottle in a celebratory toast.

Becca taps her mostly kale smoothie against it with a metal clank and makes a face. "To Alicia Florrick surviving the hallowed halls of Brown. Yay. Go us." Sarcasm is her love language.

Next week AP testing starts in earnest, graduation is just around the corner. Campus is buzzing with summer and stress and clumps of students half clinging to the familiarity of friends but already with one foot out the door. "I actually think I'm going to miss this place," I say as Blake and Giulia wander by, hand in hand, on their way to his car.

"Why? You were never here."

I offer her a baby carrot stick. "Well, I'm going to miss you."

She pops it into her mouth and rummages around in her backpack. "Here. You might need this. I hear Rhode

Island can get lonely sometimes." It's my troll pencil topper. Once upon a particularly boring chem class, Becca christened him Melvin and it stuck.

I smile as I take him from her. Melvin's electric pink hair stretches out longer than his round little body and his face is eternally sunny. Must be carbs. I touch his bare belly fondly. "You better keep him, Bec. He's not really dressed for an east coast winter."

She shakes her head firmly and crosses her arms. "How about shared custody?" Like everything with Becca it comes out breezy but there's always a bit of an emotionally fraught edge. Melvin will keep us connected in a way Instagram will not.

I hug her. She lets me do that occasionally. "Okay. I'll send him to you in the fall. Otherwise, I might have to knit him a sweater. And no one wants that."

"Nooo. How's Drew's dad doing?"

"Not good," I sigh. In fact he's about as not good as it gets. He's dying of cancer. Apparently it ignited in his pancreas and spread like wildfire through the rest of his organs, raging unnoticed until it was too late; his life expectancy is now being measured in a handful of months. Drew and I went to visit him together in his sparse, cheerless apartment. Drew clung tightly to my hand the whole time. I've never felt so young and yet so old all at once. "Drew's moving in with him to help take care of him as soon as school's out."

"He's what?" Becca stops cleaning up the remains of her lunch. "I thought he hated his dad?"

"It's complicated. *They're* complicated. But Mr. Jarrod has no one else and at the end of the day Drew's still Drew." And you can depend on Drew Jarrod to do the right thing no matter how messy and landmine filled it gets.

She slowly nods. "Found an internship yet?"

I've had to do some serious schedule juggling around the last of my modeling obligations. My classmates have had theirs lined up for weeks, some months now. Mine have been very last minute. I just got notice I've been green lighted for my second this morning.

"I've got two: Habitat for Humanity because I'm a McCoy and everyone assumes I must know my way around a hammer – I don't – and I'm tutoring summer school. You all packed for Peru?" Becca is volunteering with the Peace Corps this summer. Becca's idea of camping is Club Med.

"I got everything we ordered."

Landry and Sam, who, for many summers, lived out of backpacks while they tromped through jungles or kayaked or climbed or surfed or soared or biked, helped us formulate a list of everything she would need. Well, not *everything.* "She's on her own with the girl stuff," Sam said gruffly, turning two shades of red and making Cade hoot with laughter.

I helped Becca track it all down online.

"And that's all going to fit in my pack?" Becca was skeptical. "And not weigh more than I do?"

I pushed a plate of cookies at her. "I think you want the floppy hat. It has this adjustable chin strap so you won't lose it if the wind kicks up."

She squinted at my monitor. "I wouldn't mind losing it. That's hideous."

"Since when do you care about – oh no. Bec, you didn't?" I stared at her in disbelief. "Are you seriously doing this because of some guy you've met?"

She was instantly defensive. "No. Maybe. What if I have?"

"You committed to *three* months."

"I know."

"In *Peru*."

"I know."

"Who is he?"

"Jon? He's the recruiter."

"Are you sure he's even going to Peru?"

"He said he was."

I grinned and shook my head. "Well you definitely are. And so is this hat. You need protection."

"Not if I'm wearing that hat," Becca grumped.

"So, did you manage to fit it all in?" I ask her now.

"Everything but my PlayStation."

I throw my arm loosely around her shoulder. "Yeah. Good luck with that, babe."

After school I stop by Pops and Gran's to give them their tickets for my graduation. Per decree by Barton's administration, each graduate is allotted eight. I need sixteen. Becca gave me five of hers, which still left me three short.

"Are you using all your tickets for graduation?" I'd asked Blake earlier that day. He moved his locker next to mine second semester. *You're on to something good, Grace Kelly. No one ever comes here.* And by "no one" he meant "no one who runs in his crowd." The band geeks and choir students – my people – might take exception to that. But he did have a point; it is off the beaten path. And when you like to make out during school hours as much as he does that's definitely an advantage. For him. And Giulia. *Mostly.* That boy is still a player.

"Why?" Blake wanted to know.

"I need three more."

"I thought you were an only child?"

"I am. But I'm also a McCoy. We're herd animals."

"Sorry." He shook his head. "I already gave my leftovers to Giulia. She's Italian. She's got family pouring in from both sides."

My mother's parents died in a freak, small engine plane crash when I was only four. Her older brother, James Kingston, is an archeologist who is always out digging around in some exotic location. We've sort of lost track of him over the years. Despite Dad's considerable efforts to let him know about Mom's accident, he didn't come to the funeral; he just sent flowers. I can't even remember what he looks like.

I shrugged. "That's okay. I'll keep looking."

Blake grabbed my arm before I could get away. "You and Drew breaking up?"

"What?"

"You're going to Rhode Island. He's not. You do the math."

"Why do you care?"

He smiled his trademark Blake Michaels' smile, which is equal parts snake oil and charm. "Who says I do, Grace Kelly?"

I turned and faced him. "I do. But for the life of me I can't figure out why. I have a boyfriend. You have a girlfriend. And Whitney. Let's not forget about her. Why do you even care if Drew and I are still together or not?"

"I like you."

It was so baldly honest that we both looked a little surprised and taken back. "You *like* me? Or you just want to play tonsil hockey with me?"

Blake grinned. "Both?"

"I don't know what to do with that."

He placed an arm against the locker behind me and started to lean in. "I do."

I quickly wiggled away. "Sorry, Michaels. Not happening."

"Come on, you're not going to give me anything to remember you by?"

"I'll sign your yearbook."

"You're killing me, Grace Kelly."

I just laughed and left to find Becca. But when I came back for lunch someone had tucked three more tickets to the graduation ceremony inside my locker.

Oddly, when I get to Pops and Gran's no one is home. Which is weird because they knew I was coming over this afternoon; I talked to Gran about it just this morning. She'd been excited to show me how her dahlias – which are tricky, but not impossible, for someone with her mad skills to grow in Austin – were doing. I'm just retrieving the spare key out from underneath the third rock in from the lavender pot at the back door when I get a text from Dad. They're at the hospital. Pops has had a heart attack. Hastily texting Drew I race back to the Mini, my heart slamming against my chest as I pray and drive. *Please let him be okay. Please.*

"Hey Squirt." Uncle Bryce enfolds me in his big arms the minute I walk into the waiting room. Dad is on the phone.

"How's Pops?" Everyone looks worried, Gran most of all.

"I told B he needed to watch his salt intake. And he eats far too much red meat." Gran is staring helplessly at her hands. Aunt Jill wraps a comforting arm around her shoulders as I bend to kiss Gran's wrinkled cheek.

Justin and Cade stand to hug me and then move over so there's more room on the bench. "We're still waiting to hear from his doctor. They haven't told us much of anything yet," Justin quietly says as Trey and Drew hurry in.

"How is he?" Drew asks.

"We don't really know," Dad replies, getting up to hug me and Drew. "I just got a hold of Chris. He's on standby and can be on the next flight out. I told him to wait until we had a better idea of what we're dealing with."

Gran nods.

"You okay?" Drew says quietly, taking me in his arms.

"A little scared." Maybe a lot.

"Me too. But Pops is strong; hold on to that."

Not twenty minutes later Landry and Kendra show up, hand in hand. Along with a look of concern on her beautiful face, Kendra is sporting a pretty big rock on her left ring finger. The entire family straightens noticeably and peripheral conversations stop. Landry McCoy is *engaged*?! Even his mother looks surprised.

"You couldn't wait?" Cade shakes his head at his little brother and smiles at Kendra as he reaches to hug her. "What? Did he just throw it at you when you got in the car? You must really love this guy. Welcome to the family."

"It was burning a hole in my pocket," Landry shrugs sheepishly, looking at Kendra like she's his whole world and kissing her hand. "How's Pops?"

"We're still waiting to hear," Uncle Nick says. "Congratulations son, Kendra."

Turns out that Landry being Landry and impulsively ditching his entire plan for a sweeping, romantic proposal that Aunt Jill had gone to considerable lengths to help him orchestrate for this weekend was a godsend. While none of us were under the illusion that Gran had stopped worrying about Pops, for a short while at least, it gave her something else to focus on.

Around 6:30 Dr. Stellenhauer, still in his surgical scrubs, finally steps into the waiting room to give us an update. The bypass surgery went well; Pops is in recovery resting. It will be a few more hours before he can have visitors and even then, probably only a few at a time. He says this last bit with a little smile as he takes in the McCoy mountain range instantly on their feet at his arrival.

"Drew and I will run home and take care of Charlie. Do you need anything from the house?" I ask Dad as the family starts to organize in shifts.

"Maybe a change of clothes?" He's still in his shirt and tie.

"How about something to eat?"

"Sounds like Trey is making a food run."

"Okay. Text me if you think of anything else."

We hug Gran and promise we won't be gone long. "He'll be back to golfing and dancing with his best girl in no time, you'll see," Drew says, leaning to kiss her on the cheek.

"Thanks for coming." Her hand is on his neck, stilling him before he can straighten. Gran's watery blue eyes are intent and serious as she looks earnestly into his. "Family is what gets us through the hard times, Drew." Then she blinks and slowly smiles at him. "But I know you already know that, don't you son? Because you're here."

"Yes, ma'am," Drew finally says. He's struggling with his emotions as Gran pulls him in for another hug. It's impossible to walk away from that woman and not know that you're loved.

We're packing Dad's running shoes, clean socks, some jeans, a T-shirt, deodorant and a toothbrush, toothpaste, mouthwash and dental floss into a duffel bag while Charlie tears around the backyard taking care of a long day's worth of holding it in, poor boy. "You hungry?" I ask Drew, opening the fridge and surveying our options.

"Always." He has the metabolism of an Ethiopian distance runner and the appetite of a Polynesian offensive lineman. I've never seen anyone who can eat as much as he does and I'm related to Landry. He places Dad's bag on the floor by the kitchen door to the garage and lets Charlie back into the house while I'm pulling out leftovers and placing them on the counter.

"Sniff test first," I advise. "That Thai's been in there awhile."

He's taking off lids but his mind is obviously elsewhere. "Drew? Seriously, I'm pretty sure that cashew chicken has gone off."

He dumps it on his plate and stabs at it with his fork. "I don't want you to go."

I slowly close the fridge door and lean against it.

"I mean, I don't want you to *not* go to Brown because it's obviously where you need to be right now and it's important to you. Just, for the record? Everything in me is screaming hold on to this girl. And at the end of the summer you'll be gone." He shakes his head and puts down his utensils. "Sorry Kel, that's a pretty lousy way of saying I'm going to miss you."

I thunk my forehead softly against the side of his head. "Me too. I'm kind of terrified that I'm making a huge mistake."

Drew sighs and wraps an arm around me. "You're not. Just don't forget about me, okay?"

"Impossible, babe." My hands are in his hair as I kiss him. "I'm your 5:15, remember?"

He slowly grins. "Yeah. You are."

And as we load up the car and head back to the hospital and my sometimes crazy, mostly awesome family, I realize *that*, more than anything, is my great miracle. I have people in my life who love me and I love them right back. Everything else? #frosting

ACKNOWLEDGEMENTS AND LETTER TO READERS

Hi everyone, Randi Rigby here!

Thanks so much for taking the time to read *Model Behavior*! I know there are a LOT of wonderful options out there for you to plunk down and commit yourself to so I'm incredibly grateful that you chose to invest in Kel's story.

Writing is a solitary madness that requires ignoring, for too long really, that you have a family, friends, and an aching neck and backside in the real world while you're busy creating a world of your own. So an eternal shout out to Brant, *my* Drew, for all your love and support. Lakin and Jordan – I finally did it!

Thank you to Cynthia Wright and Elaine Rigby for your invaluable feedback and work on editing. To my awesome beta readers: Paula Nielson, Kendall Dowden, Emma Eversole, Julie Balkman, Emma Christensen, and Alice Fuller – I greatly appreciated your feedback and enthusiasm. It gave me the courage to take that deep breath and publish.

The idea for this story came from a girl I saw in an airport. She was very tall, very pretty, and very shy. I couldn't get her out of my head. Like I often do (it's a problem), I started to imagine what her life might be like.

And I've turned it over to you. Let me know what you think? I'd love your feedback: write2randi@gmail.com

Keep reading. Keep dreaming. Keep searching for the magic in your life. It's there.

x
-r

20063561R00202

Made in the USA
San Bernardino, CA
26 December 2018